The Godsons Legacy

by

Paul Gait

Grosvenor House
Publishing Limited

All rights reserved
Copyright © Paul Gait, 2013

The right of Paul Gait to be identified as the author of this
work has been asserted by him in accordance with Section 78
of the Copyright, Designs and Patents Act 1988

The book cover picture is copyright to Paul Gait

This book is published by
Grosvenor House Publishing Ltd
28-30 High Street, Guildford, Surrey, GU1 3EL.
www.grosvenorhousepublishing.co.uk

This book is sold subject to the conditions that it shall not, by way of
trade or otherwise, be lent, resold, hired out or otherwise circulated
without the author's or publisher's prior consent in any form of binding or
cover other than that in which it is published and
without a similar condition including this condition being imposed
on the subsequent purchaser.

This novel is entirely a work of fiction. The names, characters and
incidents portrayed in it are the work of the author's imagination. Any
resemblance to actual persons, living or dead, events or localities
is entirely coincidental.

A CIP record for this book
is available from the British Library

ISBN 978-1-78148-218-6

Thanks

To my wife Helen, family and friends, for support, encouragement and allowing me to spend countless hours continuing to develop the Godsons story.

To Janet for again spending many hours proof reading my manuscript.

To the readers of the prequel, *Godsons-Counting Sunsets*, for wanting to know what happened to the characters, which encouraged me to indulge in writing this sequel.

Foreword

Geoffery Foster has left his three Godsons a legacy in his will.

But getting their hands on their inheritances isn't as straight forward as they'd hoped.

In life, Geoffery was a control 'freak' and consummate perfectionist.

He saw no reason to subvert those standards after he died.

For Geoffery still controls their lives from beyond the grave.

'The King is dead, Long live the King.'

'The Godsons Legacy' is the second book in the Godsons series. It follows the internationally acclaimed *'Godsons – Counting Sunsets.'*

PART ONE

Grief and Sorrow

CHAPTER ONE

15th December

Andy felt self-conscious driving the beautiful white Mercedes CL63 AMG into the estate. It was especially strange without Geoffery by his side. But now it was his car, just a few months old, almost brand new. The 'jumbo' coupe was a gift from his former hospice patient. The car was his extraordinary Christmas present and he was determined to enjoy it.

Surprised by his own easy acceptance of the present, Andy wasn't at all fazed by the ethical rights or wrongs of accepting it. On the contrary, he considered that he had earned it by undertaking all the 'special' extracurricular activities for Geoffery, which, although well rewarded, had taken its toll on him and his family.

Groups of hooded youths turned to watch the car's passage, as Andy steered the sleek motor through the potholed streets of the rundown housing development. This type of elegant car was out of place in this part of the city.

Over the years, Andy had become oblivious to the depressing gloom of the estate. However, tonight, the darkening winter sky and Christmas lights helped create a charade of ordinariness and the starkness retreated into the shadows.

He parked the car outside his home, a former council house, and released the passenger seat belt that had been holding the special bouquet upright on the front seat. Cradling the beautiful floral sculpture, as the florist had described it, in his arms he climbed out of his car.

Walking down the short flagstone path to the house he flicked the key fob to remotely lock the car, smiling to himself at the small childlike pleasure. Remote locking was a luxury he had never had before, all his previous old bangers required old fashioned key locking.

His festive spirits were further heightened by the string of Christmas lights which flashed colourful sequences from the house wall; a plastic Rudolf and a portly Snowman studded with small bulbs smiled at him from their festive positions stuck to the lounge window. Helen had obviously given way to his excited daughter and switched on the lights early, in spite of her previous concerns about mounting electricity bills.

'I guess we don't have to worry about that anymore,' Andy thought; for along with the present of the car, Andy's benefactor, Geoffery, had also given him a very generous cheque; a staggering two hundred and fifty thousand pounds, a mind-blowing quarter of a million.

The smell of Christmas greeted him as he opened the front door. He had only opened it a fraction before his four year old daughter, Amy, was at his feet, followed closely by his five year old niece, Rose.

'Hello darling, hello Rose,' he said, kneeling to hug the duo.

'Uncle Andy, did you know that it's only ten more sleeps until Father Christmas comes?'

'Yes I did. Isn't it great?' he said, smiling at the excited girls.

'YESSSS,' the two youngsters chorused, screaming with girly excitement.

'Are those flowers for Mummy?' Amy asked, spotting the bouquet.

'Yes Angel,' said Andy, putting his finger to his lips, suggesting it was a secret and she should be quiet.

'OK,' Amy whispered, conspiratorially. 'Have you brought anything for us?' she continued, in the same small voice.

'I might have, but first I'll give these to Mummy. So go and play and I'll be back in a minute.'

Andy hung his coat on the bottom stair post as the excited girls ran screaming back into the lounge.

Feeling pleased with himself by his thoughtful, if rare event, of buying her flowers, he walked into the kitchen hiding the bouquet behind his back. Helen had her back to him making up bottles for four month old Molly. He was dismayed to see she was still dressed in her pyjamas, an old shapeless jumper and sloppy grey jogging bottoms, her shoulder length hair looking limp and greasy.

'Hello, darling,' he said, kissing her neck.

'Hi,' she replied tiredly, continuing her task without turning around.

'I see the kids are excited.'

'You can say that again. They've been hyper all day. I'm exhausted.'

'I brought you these,' he said beaming, bringing the flowers from behind his back.

Helen turned and looked at the exotic bouquet, created with the flamboyant red Amaryllis, green 'Bells of Ireland' and white Camellia.

'Oh, they're lovely! Thank you. But you'll have to put them in a vase. I'm just so far behind at the moment.'

'You don't have to put them in a vase.'

'What do you mean? They'll die if you don't.'

'I thought of that,' he said, feeling pleased with himself. 'They come with their own water. Look!'

At the bottom of the bouquet was a large plastic bag full of water.

'See no problem, self-watering. Now I think that deserves a kiss don't you,' he said, putting the flowers on the worktop and embracing her.

'Look, it's not a good time,' she said, pulling back. 'I'm a bit behind with everything.'

'Come on, just a kiss. I'm not after anything else…but if it's on offer,' he said, hopefully.

'No Andy, I've told you. I'm not ready …for that yet.'

'Oh come on Helen, it's been nearly a year since we…'

Helen pulled away and turned her back to him, resuming her bottle making. 'I'm too tired. Ever since I had Molly, I don't seem to have a moment to myself. Just give me time. I thought we'd agreed about this… that you understood.'

'I do but…'

'Anyway, this isn't like you, buying me flowers. What's brought this on?'

'Well, it's nearly Christmas and I wanted to buy you something to brighten up your day and…we've been preparing Geoffery's room for somebody else.'

'Oh, I see.'

'I know I've said it before, but working at the hospice is a constant reminder of the fragility of life.'

'Yes, yes. Is this how you intended to brighten my day?'

Andy continued his doleful rhetoric, lost in his own thoughts. 'Death is no respecter of age. Even if you get over serious illnesses, there are procedures that might be lifesaving but they are also life changing.'

'Thanks for those cheery words.'

'I don't want to look back and regret missing out on opportunities, especially with you,' he said, hugging her from behind.

'You've got to understand I'm…tired, what with Christmas and the baby.'

'I thought with the new car and the cheque from Geoffery you might have been…you know, happier.'

'I am, but…please be patient with me Andy, just for a bit longer,' she pleaded.

CHAPTER TWO

15th December

'Daddy...Daddy, is Uncle Geoffery deaded?' Amy asked, running into the kitchen.

'Yes darling, I'm afraid so,' Andy replied, gently.

'Why couldn't you make him better?' she asked, with genuine concern.

'Well sometimes people get so poorly that they can't be mended.'

'Where do people go when they die?' she persisted.

'They go to heaven.'

'And on the telly too.' Rose volunteered, wisely.

'What do you mean?'

'Come and look. Uncle Geoffery is on the telly wearing a funny hat.'

Andy and Helen quickly followed the little girls into the lounge to see a picture of Geoffery lying in bed with a polythene bag over his head; his eyes bulging, the bag expanding and contracting with his faltering breath. By his bedside a woman, was firmly pinning his arms down against the bedclothes.

'Andy switch it off.' Helen shouted in a panic.

Andy jabbed a button on the remote control and immediately the screen went blank.

'Oh Daddy we were watching that. Uncle Geoffery looked funny didn't he?'

'Where did you get that DVD from?' Andy said, sharply.

Amy started to cry.

'It's alright Darling, Daddy isn't cross,' Helen coaxed. 'Where did you find the DVD sweetheart?'

'It was in Daddy's pocket,' Amy sobbed. 'Daddy said he got something for us.

'Andy!'

'It wasn't that which I got for them…Oh heavens, it must have been the disc the CCTV engineer gave me from Geoffery's room.'

'Why the hell did you leave it where the kids could get it?'

'I didn't.'

'Well you obviously did, if these two could find it and put it on.'

'I didn't know what was on it. I haven't seen it. I had no idea,' Andy pleaded, hurt at her allegation that he would deliberately expose them to such horror.

'Daddy, was that lady playing games with Uncle Geoffery?'

'Yes Darling. Now go and play in the garden, before it gets too dark…but put your coats on, it's cold out.'

'Careful of the Christmas tree,' Helen warned as the pair rushed by it.

'OK.' Amy shouted, as she disappeared into the hallway to get her coat.

'Bags I go on the swing first,' called Rose, running after Amy.

'How come you got that shocking recording? It's enough to give them nightmares.' Helen demanded.

'As I said, the CCTV technician gave it to me. I didn't know what was on it. I didn't even know there was a camera in his room. It must have been fitted when I was suspended.' Andy said, pleading mitigation.

'It looks like it recorded when that woman… what's her name?'

'Sue…the husband batterer.'

'When she tried to kill poor Geoffery,' Helen continued. 'We need to give it to the Police.'

'Yes you're right.'

'We ought to watch it first though.'

'Oh Christ, do we have to?'

'I think we ought to know what's on there, don't you?'

'OK, if you insist. But let's wait until the kids are in bed. She's already been remanded in custody for attempted murder and Geoffery's funeral is next week.'

Later that evening, after steeling themselves to watch the DVD images, they watched and listened as the whole drama unfolded.

It had been recorded from a camera which, it was obvious, neither participant knew of its existence.

The start of the DVD recorded the test shots when it was first installed by the technician. Geoffery's bed was empty. There followed a short period where the screen went blank. After a few minutes the screen sprang to life and Geoffery could be seen lying in bed reading. Shortly after, a woman arrived in the room.

That's Sue, the wife of Geoffery's Godson, Rupert,' Andy informed her.

'Yes, I know who she is.' Helen replied, testily.

After a short preamble they were astonished to hear Geoffery say.

'I want you to help me commit suicide.'

'My God, did you hear him say what I thought he said?' Andy said, in amazement.

'The sound is a bit distant and echoey. Re-run that bit again,' Helen directed.

Andy pushed the rewind button on the controller, increased the volume and re-ran it. They leaned forward to catch Geoffery's words.

'I want you to help me commit suicide,' Geoffery said.

'Oh my God,' Helen exclaimed, putting her hands to her face in disbelief.

'Listen! What does she say?' Andy hissed, urgently.

'You won't catch me like that,' they heard the woman say.

Andy and Helen listened in horrified silence to the rest of the DVD.

'What do you mean?' Geoffery asked. *'You hate me don't you?'*

'Aiding people to commit suicide is a criminal offence,' she said.

'I have written a suicide note.'

'That makes no difference.'

'It will, in this case.'

'Why do want to die like that? Just look at you! The cancer will kill you soon enough.'

'The pain is just unbearable. I can't take it anymore.'

'Well, you're asking the wrong person then, because I want to see you suffer. Just like you've made me suffer, taking my husband away from me.'

'There's money in it for you, if you do.'

'How much?'

'I have written to my Solicitor, instructing him to pay you two hundred and fifty thousand pounds after my death.'

'Why? What possible reason would you have for doing that? It's clear you hate me.'

'Just a dying man's wish to apologise for messing up your life.'

'But all I need to do is just wait for nature to take its course.'

'No, I'm afraid not. If you don't help me today, I shall telephone my Solicitor and tell him I wrote the letter while I was under the influence of drugs. And I'll ask him to destroy it.'

'Getting paid for having my revenge on you! It just sounds too good to be true.'

'That's the deal. Take it or leave it.'

'What happens if the nurse comes in?'

'Oh, he won't. Andy's replacement has got other patients to look after.'

'Your replacement?' Helen asked puzzled.

Andy paused the video.

'Yeah, remember when I was suspended because Geoffery gave Rupert some of his painkillers after the bitch had beaten him up. That Sue found the packaging that had the hospice name on it. She reported me for selling drugs.'

'Of course. God she's an evil piece of work.'

'Say that again.'

Andy pressed the play button and the recording continued.

'I've already written the suicide note.' Geoffery continued. 'The nurse will discover it later this evening, when you're long gone.'

'What...what do I have to do? I'm no good with blood.'

'Oh. It's nothing as barbaric as that. Suffocation is what I've chosen.'

'What? You mean putting a pillow over your face?'

'Oh no. The best way is a polythene bag over the head, and elastic bands around the neck.'

'Oh!'

'I will do that bit myself.'

'So what do I do?'

'Well it's human nature, that as I start to suffocate, my reaction will be to take the bag off.'

'And?'

'I just want you to hold my arms, to stop me pulling it off. That's all.'

'Just hold your arms?'

'Yes. That's all. I will kill myself and you'll be in the clear.'

'Finally Andy stopped the DVD.

'That awful woman IS innocent after all. Geoffery stitched her up,' Helen said, clearly shocked.

'What should we do?' Andy asked, depressed at the revelation of her innocence and fearful of the consequences on her husband of her release.

'Well we've got to go to the Police.'

'But that will mean she will be free to get to her husband again. He's already on the verge of a nervous breakdown.'

'Poor Rupert!'

'No we can't let that happen.'

'It's not down to us. We have evidence that could free an innocent person,' Helen said, shocked at his suggestion.

'Innocent of attempted murder, perhaps. But not for beating up her husband.'

'Andy, wake up. We can't suppress this information. What if the CCTV bloke goes to the Police and tells them he gave you the DVD?'

'He said he hadn't watched it. Didn't know what was on it. It was a trial. They were trying to sell a complete CCTV system to the Hospice, but reckons there was no funding available, so they took it out again.'

'But he will have a master,' she argued.

''I don't know. We shouldn't go rushing into making hasty decisions,' Andy persisted.

'Andy, it's not our call.'

'I wish the technician hadn't given it to me,' Andy said, forlornly. 'Obviously Geoffery didn't know it had been installed either.'

'No, but it was. Now we need to do the right thing. In spite of what we think about her abusing her husband, she's innocent of attempted murder.'

'Let me think about it.'

'What's to think about? You must go to the Police. Andy, listen to me.'

'I'm thinking. What would Geoffery do? After all, he did this to protect his nephew and we're going to undo all his planning.'

'Geoffery is gone. This is now our problem.'

CHAPTER THREE

23rd December

The roar of the Rolls Royce engines announced the arrival of the Gulfstream 500 as it descended over the roof tops of Churchup village on its final approach to touch down at Gloucestershire airport.

Aboard the small chartered business jet was Nadine, Geoffery's former girlfriend and eight casino dancers who had flown from Nice Cote d'Azur airport.

The small Staverton based airport, used mainly by air freight businesses, is located midway between the Roman city of Gloucester and the Regency town of Cheltenham and made commuting to the funeral easy.

After taxiing around the perimeter of the airfield finally the jet came to a halt and the small group disembarked and walked through the single story Main Terminal building.

The girls, Geoffery's 'long legged lovelies, had been flown in to re-enact their role as his pallbearers, which they had done a few months previously during his mock wake in Monaco.

Geoffery had laid on the extravagant mock wake, before his health finally deteriorated, for he knew it would be his final party. The event had been themed on the Rocky Horror show and he had spared no expense, so that as well as his costumed guests, he too, would enjoy the celebration of his own life.

With a heavy heart he realised that the organisation of the huge party in Monaco would be the last of many projects which he had accomplished in the principality before making his final journey, home to the Cotswolds, to die.

On his return to the Cotswolds, although gravely ill, Geoffery had continued his consummate professionalism by providing meticulous instructions for orchestrating every aspect of his funeral.

The group left the airport in two, sleek, six door Volvo 960s sent by the Funeral Director and were driven straight to a five star hotel on the outskirts of Gloucester.

Geoffery had chosen the luxurious 16th Century Elizabethan Manor House hotel, at the foot of the rolling Cotswold escarpment, because of its relative proximity to the Church on the Hill, where he was to be buried.

As the Volvos rolled up the drive, Nadine, used to staying at high class hotels, was immediately enamoured by the ancient building, its Cotswold stone exterior almost hidden by a living wallpaper of ivy. The thick canopy of evergreen leaves cloaking the hotel, camouflaging it into its rural surroundings.

The visitors were duly 'booked in' and went to their rooms to change for the funeral.

Andy and Helen were the first of the other mourners to arrive. Spotting them in the stylish entrance hall, the Funeral Director, a large portly figure wearing a calm sympathetic smile, greeted them warmly and handed Andy a letter.

'What have you got there?' Helen asked, as Andy apprehensively opened the envelope.

'I'll tell you in a second,' he said, scanning the brief note. 'It's instructions from Geoffery. I'm to introduce the Godsons to each other.'

'Why you?'

'I guess I must be the only one who knows them all.'

Andy positioned himself by the door into the oak panelled conference room, which had been reserved for them, to welcome the mourners as they arrived.

Geoffery had specified that the funeral was to be a celebration of his life and therefore he didn't want people to wear black. He had stopped short of suggesting that they wore fancy dress, as they had done for the mock funeral in Monaco.

Rupert and Joanne were the next to arrive hand in hand, wearing conservative coloured clothes. Rupert was very self-conscious as this was the first public appearance of his year-long affair with his work colleague.

Ben, one of Andy's scouts and friend of Geoffery, was next with his mother Beth. She looked very attractive, always meticulous with her appearance, in spite of the addiction problems for which she was being treated.

James arrived wearing an open neck shirt and the same clothes that Geoffery had bought him when he first arrived in Cheltenham, having been rescued from the streets of London, 'in the nick of time'.

Last to arrive was Tim, with girlfriend Carrie and Tim's mother, Kay. Kay had been one of Geoffery's early, pre-millionaire, lovers.

Andy gathered the mourners together and introduced the Godsons to each other, as instructed in Geoffery's note.

'Tim, this is Rupert and James,' he said, as Tim joined the group. 'My name is Andy Spider. As some of you already know, I was your Godfather's Nurse at the Hospice and his 'gofer' to help track you all down.

'This is James,' he said, gesturing in his direction. 'James and I met in London in very different circumstances.'

James thrust out his hand and delivered a firm handshake to the others. 'Hello, pleased to meet you,' he said in turn. 'Yes, at the time I was living on the streets, when the old boy decided to track me down and save me from myself,' James volunteered. 'I knew Geoffery many years ago when, like him, I, too, had a few 'mill' in the bank.'

'Thank you James.'

Andy turned his attention to Rupert. 'Rupert is, sorry, was... also Geoffery's nephew,' he corrected himself. 'He has literally had a bit of a rough time recently, matrimonially speaking.'

Rupert put his hand self-consciously to his bruised face and looked at the floor, clearly uncomfortable at Andy's explanation.

'What! Your wife did that to you?' Tim said, looking at Rupert's battered face. 'Christ...and are you still married to her? He asked, pointedly looking at Joanne.

'Oh, this isn't her,' Rupert said, defensively. 'This is my girlfriend Joanne,' he added, looking affectionately at her. 'No, I'm separated from my wife. She a...my wife's in prison,' Rupert volunteered, awkwardly.

Now it was Andy's turn to feel uncomfortable, for he knew that Sue, Rupert's wife, was no longer in custody and was wondering how best to break the news to him.

'I should think so too.' Tim added.

Andy interjected quickly to change the subject. 'And Tim here is…'

'Still knackered.' Tim said, interrupting. 'Do you know, that old bastard even got me running up 'effing' mountains. Even though I've got two artificial legs,' he added, tapping his prosthetic thighs. 'I brought my Mum and girlfriend Carrie. They both had a lot to do with the old man as well.'

Suddenly, a noise at the doorway stopped the small talk. All eyes turned to look at the bevy of beauty that entered, as Nadine led the eight giggling girls into the room.

Nadine was immaculate in a bright orange three quarter length coat over a pretty floral blouse, her long legs hidden by a pair of tightly cut black trousers; at her wrist a chunky gold bracelet.

The girls were wearing their 'special' funeral clothes that Geoffery had specified. A tantalising flash of long fishnet stockinged legs from under their long winter coats causing the mourners to do a 'double take'.

'Hello Nadine, pleased you could make it,' said Andy, walking towards her, his hand outstretched. To his obvious embarrassment, she ignored the hand and gave him a hug and planted kisses on both cheeks.

'Allo Andee. I 'ad to bring zee girls. I could not let Geoffery down. It was 'iz wish.'

Seeing that everybody had arrived the Funeral Director, resplendent in long black tailcoat and waistcoat addressed the group.

'Ladies and Gentlemen, I'd like to invite you to take your places in the cars outside; the hearse is on its way and will be here shortly,' he announced theatrically.

The group were directed into three, six door Volvos, two of which had brought Nadine and the girls from the airport earlier.

With impressive, split second timing, just as the last mourner's car door closed, the hearse arrived and drove to the head of the waiting convoy.

Ben swallowed hard as he saw the beautiful floral tribute that spelled out Geoffery's name in white flowers on top of the coffin.

The solemn procession set off down the long hotel drive. The Funeral Director walking slowly, top hat in hand, a short distance in front of the hearse. After a hundred yards he climbed in and the convoy drove at a respectful pace for the short journey to the Church on the Hill, crossing the busy A46 and slowing the traffic briefly as it drove through the village of Badgeworth.

After twenty minutes the cortege drove unhurriedly through the village of Churchup, seasonally dressed for Christmas, past the Bat and Ball pub bedecked with strings of flashing lights, past the Church of St Andrew, a sister church to their destination and eventually turned into a narrow lane. The cars slowed to manoeuvre some sharp ninety degree bends, the lane now barely single vehicle width.

Geoffery's meticulous planning, to ensure the smooth running of his funeral, included positioning marshals at the top and bottom of the narrow lane to provide traffic control. In addition, on the advice of the Funeral Director, even to hiring a gritting lorry and snow plough, to maintain access up the steep lane, in case of ice or snow.

CHAPTER FOUR

23rd December

The bright winter sun hung low in a cloudless blue sky, casting long shadows across the hill, as the funeral cortège pulled up outside the 12th century Church on the Hill.

The mourners sat silently in the cars while the Funeral Director went into the Church to make final arrangements. Satisfied that the preparations were in place, he invited them to disembark into the cold afternoon sunshine.

Geoffery's mahogany coffin was gently taken out of the back of the gleaming black hearse and lifted on to the shoulders of the Funeral Director's pallbearers, two of whom, Andy was surprised to see, were women.

It was arranged that Geoffery's 'long legged lovely' pallbearer duties would only commence once inside the church. The slope up to the doorway, through the old graveyard, was too steep for the inexperienced.

Geoffery, himself, had experienced the steepness of the ascent only three months previously, when he'd struggled to join Andy's christening party.

The Funeral Director's team carried the heavy coffin up to the low narrow church door; the Funeral Director himself walking behind to prevent the casket from sliding backwards. The procession of mourners lined up behind the eight girls who took their places behind the Funeral Director and walked silently up to the church.

As they arrived at the early English period south door, the coffin was carefully lowered to prevent the wreath being swept off by the low ancient arch and gently placed onto a shining stainless steel casket trolley.

Ben was surprised that the ancient parish Church was deceptively bigger inside than it appeared from the outside. As he stood just inside, he looked at the line of stone pillars which supported the large 13th century annex, increasing the nave capacity for bygone congregations, introducing a second, south aisle.

The walls were whitewashed, complementing the large black beams that spanned the roof. Flagstones led the faithful down the original narrow aisle between ordered lines of oak pews to the chancel, which was set back through a large stone archway. Beautiful stained glass east windows providing back lighting of the crucifix on the renovated Jacobean altar.

Just inside the threshold, the eight girls slipped off their warm winter coats to reveal their figure hugging black lacy basques decorated with delicate red ribbons. Their long, seemingly endless, legs were encased in fishnet stockings; the 'special' funeral clothes that Geoffery had specified.

Nadine gathered their coats together and enlisted Ben's help to carry the large bundle of delightfully perfume impregnated coats.

The combination of the cold December temperature and thin Basque material created an adolescent boy's delight, as the semi naked girls prepared themselves for their solemn duties. Ben gazed open mouthed at the voluptuous display of cleavage on top of the sea of fishnet clad legs.

Beth, who in spite of her addiction problems prided herself on looking good and had a shapely figure, now looked dowdy against the eight dancers.

The vicar, a jolly faced lady in her sixties, greeted the procession just inside the church. Although having been previously warned about the strange escort, she was distracted by the beautiful cortege of scantily clad pallbearers. 'Well,' she thought. 'Now I've seen it all!'

Conscious of the Vicar's distraction, the Funeral Director signalled to the sound technician and music filled the church.

Geoffery had chosen Frank Sinatra singing '*My Way*' for the procession of the coffin to the altar.

The eight girls took their places, four each side of the coffin and followed the smiling vicar down the aisle; each one of the octet placing a manicured hand on the cold wood and gently propelling the coffin on its trolley towards the altar.

'*I am the resurrection and the life,*' *says the Lord. 'Those who believe in me, even though they die, will live, and everyone who lives and believes in me will never die.*'…

Meanwhile the other mourners took their places either side of the aisle, leaving the front pews empty for the lovely pallbearers.

Andy was pleased to see that some of his hospice colleagues, who had also nursed Geoffery, as well as the hospice administrator Anne Place, were already there. Some of Andy's Scouts were there too, beneficiaries of Geoffery's generosity in providing the brand new Scout HQ.

As the coffin arrived near the altar, the Funeral Director put the brake on the trolley and his grey haired assistants ushered the scantily clad girls into the cold pews.

The church heating was unsuccessfully battling the cold December chill and many of the girls were starting to visibly shiver. It was only a few hours earlier that they had been in the warmer climes of the south of France.

However, thoughtfully, Nadine had already started draping the girl's coats over the back of the pews, Ben reluctantly handing over the warm, sensual bundle to her. The girls wasted no time in hastily putting them on.

Andy's mind wandered back to the day Geoffery had collapsed in the very same church during Molly's christening at the beautiful 14th century font.

The incident was caused when Geoffery's pain pump had delivered too much morphine and he had received an overdose, causing him to pass out. That was the same day that Geoffery decided to take on the bizarre quest to track down his Godsons and to help them sort their lives out. So much had happened in the last few months.

The Vicar addressed the congregation from the pulpit, still smiling from the experience of the strange escort.

'As you have already seen, today's funeral is a unique occasion; the like of which I have never seen in all my years in the ministry. I guess it epitomises the lifestyle of the man whose life we celebrate today. As you would expect from such a flamboyant person as Geoffery, he has yet another surprise for you. He has recorded his own brief eulogy. So prepare yourselves to hear his voice once again.'

The Vicar gave the sound man a cue and music from the musical *Starlight Express* filled the church, followed by Geoffery's voice.

'Hello everybody, thanks for coming today to see me off. I have made this eulogy myself because I didn't want to put anybody else under pressure trying to find words, kind or otherwise, to say about me.

I have enjoyed my time here with you all and now I'm off to organise myself in the next life.

One piece of advice I will give you all, and that is to enjoy life. Remember, it's not a rehearsal. As many of you know, there are many decision points in life. Always look for opportunities to expand your horizons. Remember, it's never too late to be who you could have been. Thanks for sharing your life with me.'

The music of *Starlight express* swelled again…

Only you have the power within you.
Just believe in yourself -
The sea will part before you,
Stop the rain, turn the tide.
If only you use the power within you
Needn't beg the world
To turn around and help you
If you draw on what you have within you
Somewhere deep inside.'

Joanne squeezed Rupert's hand as she watched a single tear run down his cheek.

'OK?' She whispered.

'Yes,' he said, his voice telling a different tale. 'The words of that song are so poignant, I just wish I could live up to them.'

'You can Rupert, I'll help you.' She said, pressing his hand.

At the end of the ceremony, the girls again removed their coats leaving them on the pews and, dressed only in their basques, once more braved the cold. The pretty procession lined up and gently pushed the coffin back through the line of pews and out towards the ancient doorway, where Norman chevrons and sculptured heads still adorned the inner face of the archway.

Suddenly the strains of '*Always look on the bright side of life*' resonated through the church. The Monty Python theme tune from the film 'Life of Brian' brought smiles all round and helped to lift the gloom even further.

Andy laughed and felt the pinprick of tears at Geoffery's whimsical choice. He swallowed hard to maintain his composure. Geoffery had a sense of humour after all.

As the girls passed by on their solemn duty, all the male mourners said a quiet 'thank you' to Geoffery for giving them a moment's voyeuristic pleasure.

On arriving at the Church door, the undertaker's team took over again. Meanwhile, Ben and Nadine had retrieved the girl's coats from the pews and had given them back to the girls, who gratefully slipped them back on for the short journey to the graveside, Geoffery's final resting place.

Gently lifting the coffin off the casket trolley the Funeral Directors team carried it carefully through the door and down the sloping pathway.

The Funeral Director, now with his hand on the front of the coffin, walked backwards down the slope. The same method that Carrie had seen the bodies of many of her former army colleagues repatriated, down the ramps of Hercules transport planes.

The procession crunched its way through the frozen grass of the old graveyard. Carefully avoiding the icy, meandering tarmac path, they entered into an adjoining burial ground, managed by the Parish Council.

Although, officially, Geoffery did not meet the strict criteria for being interred in the burial ground, several significant donations to the Parish Council and Church helped secure his final resting place.

The young people of the Parish had benefitted from Geoffery's generosity, with the purchase of a complex of recreational equipment, skate ramps, BMX track and various other facilities.

The Church had benefitted from a major tree clearance project. Removing the Austrian firs, planted in the 19th century; which had been causing subsidence to the ancient building.

The local population benefitted from the avenues of view to the Church, that it had opened up. The beautiful Church on the Hill was now visible from miles away. It was sight many had never seen before.

Geoffery's grave had been 'generously' excavated. Appropriate financial arrangements had been made to pay the Gravedigger a bonus to ensure that sufficient earth had been removed so his coffin didn't get stuck whilst being lowered.

He likened it to the executioners of old who were given money by their victims to make sure it was a quick, professional kill.

The vicar was visibly shivering as she hurriedly made her address, her cheeks marbled by the icy wind in spite of wearing a long black flowing cloak over her robes.

As the coffin was gently lowered into the frost edged grave she said. '*We commend unto thy hands of mercy, most merciful Father, the soul of this our brother departed, and we commit his body to the ground, earth to earth, ashes to ashes, dust to dust...*'

Once the coffin was in place, the Vicar completed the commitment. She then offered the mourners a small wooden box containing dirt and invited them to take some and sprinkle it over the coffin.

Nadine tensely took up the offer and sprinkled a small handful onto the casket. At the sound of the dirt hitting the wood, Nadine started to cry. Her tears painting tramlines of mascara down her cheeks.

Geoffery's nightmares about Nadine throwing dirt over him in his grave had been a premonition after all, except now, he knew nothing about it.

'She's got a nerve coming over here, especially after she left him,' Kay said, quietly.

'Pardon?' Carrie said. 'Who do you mean, like?'

'That French tart. The one throwing dirt on his coffin. She was Geoffery's partner and left him when he started his cancer treatment; just when he was at his most vulnerable. When he needed her the most.'

'Perhaps she's after his money, now he's gone,' Carrie added.

'Well she ain't having none of mine,' said Tim, belligerently. 'I earned mine going up those bloody mountains he made me climb.'

'It did you good though son,' Kay said, proudly.

'That's a matter of opinion. It nearly killed me.'

'You should be grateful. He did a lot for you. He introduced you to Carrie as well, didn't he?'

'Yeah, I suppose he did at least one good thing,' Tim reluctantly agreed, squeezing Carrie's hand.

Suddenly the air reverberated as a large double rotor helicopter flew overhead. Carrie immediately let go of Tim's hand and knelt on the ground in an awkward crouching position and put her arm up as if holding a rifle.

'Stop messing about Carrie,' Tim berated her.

'What are you doing? You're at a funeral, for heaven sake. Have some respect,' added Kay uncomfortably.

Carrie was moving from the waist, swivelling her arms as she was apparently scanning the area around her.

'Carrie stop. It… It's not funny, Stand up! This is England, not effing Afghanistan.'

'Sector 'A' clear Sir,' she said, in a controlled voice, ignoring the rebuttal.

'Carrie, stand up. Everybody's looking at you.'

'Is she alright?' asked Andy coming over.

'Carrie! Carrie! Stand up you prat.' Tim shook her.

'Waiting for medevac clearance. Sector 'A' still clear.'

'Stop it now, this isn't funny.'

'Just leave her.' Andy instructed, looking into her staring eyes. 'She might be having a seizure. Is she epileptic?

'Not that I'm aware of. No.'

'I think she's in a trance.'

'A what?'

'Is she in the forces?'

'No. Well, yes she was. But not now though.'

'I think she's experiencing some sort of flashback.'

'Flashback?'

'Yes. I've read about it in the medical press, but never seen it before. Lots of service personnel are coming back with PTSD.'

'PTSD?'

'Yes, Post Traumatic Stress Disorder. It comes and goes. Usually something triggers it off. Has she been injured?'

'Yeah, lost both legs in an explosion.'

'That'll probably be it then. That helicopter, a Chinook, wasn't it? Probably took her mind back to being on duty. It was used for Medical Evacuations.'

Suddenly a yellow Sea King helicopter flew over on a similar flight path as the Chinook.

'Medivac over! Roger. Standing by.' Carrie continued.

Immediately Carrie came out of her trance. 'What am I doing down here?' she asked puzzled, looking at Tim.

'You tell me. You made a right prat of yourself,' he said, lifting her up.

'Look at your dress, it's all dirty now,' Kay pointed out.

'You OK?' Andy said, looking into her eyes.

'Yeah, why what happened? Carrie asked, mystified.

'Nothing, you must have slipped over,' said Andy, looking to Tim to support his story.

'Umm…yeah…You must have.'

CHAPTER FIVE

23rd December

With the interment over, people started drifting away leaving Andy and Nadine watching Ben planting a simple wooden cross at the head of the grave which had yet to be filled in.

'He made it from some charred timbers from the old Scout hut.' Andy informed her. 'Geoffery paid for a replacement after it was burnt down.' Ben really liked the old man. He's even carved Geoffery's name on it, too.'

'Zank you for what you did for ma Geofferie. I wish I 'ad been here sooner. When he was still...still alive,' she said, filling up. 'It was a lovely service. He would have approved.'

'Yes, I agree. He left strict instructions for the Funeral Director as to what should happen.'

'E always knew what 'e wanted,' Nadine reflected, 'Monsieur Perfection.'

'Yes, in more ways than one,' Andy added, thinking about Geoffery's manipulative powers ensuring that things were done his way.

'The sun is going down, it will be dark shortly. We should be going, no?' Nadine said looking around.

'I gather this was his favourite part of the day, watching the sun set. On the last day when he...he died...I took him up to the Cotswolds to see...the...his last one.' Andy's thoughts flashed back to Geoffery's final outing to Cleeve Common.

'Mais oui, that was when I arrived at the hospice, remember?'

'Oh, of course.'

'Ad he not chosen to go there...I would have seen 'im...alive, perhaps. But I saw the sunset down at the hospice. We watched the same sunset at the same time, even if we weren't together.'

'I can take you to see the sunset today if you like,' Andy said, awkwardly. 'You get a great view from the top of the hill here. I have to add that I don't always proposition strangers like this,' he joked. For this was the first in-depth conversation he'd had with Nadine.

'But of course. It will be right to see a sunset today. 'Iz final sunset,' Nadine said, looking at the cotton wool clouds now tinged pink. 'But what about ze others?' she asked, concerned. 'Shouldn't we be joining zem?'

'It's just a few hundred yards; the others won't even know that we are missing for a few minutes.'

'Oui. Let us go and see Geofferee's final sunset,' Nadine agreed.

Andy led her away from the group of mourners who were standing chatting in the car park.

They walked a short distance along a narrow tarmac road, funnelled in both sides by chain link fences. On the other side of the fences were large grass covered mounds hiding subterranean reservoirs.

'Is zat the red light we saw when landing at the airport?' She asked, gazing at the light on top of a tall radio pylon.

'Yes, there are two red ones. There's another one on the aerial over there. I assume that they act as a warning to the planes using the airport about the height of the hill,' he suggested.

'I seem to remember a white light too,' she added.

'Yes, that will be the light shining on the crucifix above the Church. Look, there!' Andy said, turning her around and pointing back at the church.

'Now I see it. How beautiful,' she said, gazing at the Cross.

'You can see all three lights from miles away. It's like a homing beacon for the locals.'

'Mais oui.'

'Apparently the cross was first illuminated in 1953 to mark the Queen's Coronation and now it's a personal memorial to somebody or other,' he added, relaying some history that he'd read in the local magazine.

As they approached the end of the tarmac section suddenly they were startled by a loud 'HOOOOOOOONNNNNK' as a noisy chorus from several geese announced their presence. The feathered burglar alarm fortunately was the other side of the fence.

Nadine grabbed Andy's arm, frightened by the sudden noise.

'Noisy creatures aren't they?' Andy said, loudly, over the continued honking.

'Oh zey made me jump. Oh excusez,' she said, letting go of his arm.

'That's OK,' Andy said, flattered by her embrace. 'They make good guards don't they? I guess you need some form of alarm living up here. It's the only house on the hill.'

'Where to go now? She asked, peering around, keen to move away from the feathered noise machines. 'The road it 'as stopped.'

'It's opposite that low level building, the one with the large satellite dishes on the roof.' He pointed.

'Mais oui, I see it. I 'ope it's not muddy. These eels aren't zee best for scrabbling up footpaths.'

'No, I think you'll be alright. The ground is frozen, although it might be a bit slippery. Would you like to hold my hand while we go up this short slope to the top?'

'Merci,' she said, proffering her gloved hand demurely.

Her fingers felt childlike in his big hand. 'This must be like shaking hands with royalty,' he thought bizarrely, trying not to scrunch them as he led her up the track.

'Mind that bit,' he cautioned. 'The sun obviously doesn't reach there; it's still got frost on it.'

After climbing ten yards up the frozen rutted track; the pair emerged from tree cover to arrive at the top of the hill with an unrestricted view of the surrounding hills and valleys.

Marking the summit of the five hundred and ten foot hill was a large waist high Cotswold stone plinth, on top of which was a stainless steel topograph, erected to commemorate the Millennium. Close by, two small benches had been provided for tired sight-seers.

At their feet, the hill fell sharply away. Winter naked trees and bushes cloaked the slopes either side of a flight of muddy wooden steps that descended to another small hillock. Beyond, they could see frost covered fields which lay in jumbled disorder, like discarded bed sheets. A small landscaped lake, frozen by nature's cold breath, sat by the side of a busy bypass.

All around them, they could see a panorama of darkening hills and valleys, a necklace of orange lights shining brightly from an artificial ski slope on the side of a large hill, a few miles distant.

There were headlights of cars circumnavigating the winding roads of the Cotswold escarpment, sending semaphore signals, as the vehicles plunged up and down into hidden valleys.

'We're in time. Look! The sun is just going down.' Andy said, satisfied that their trip was going to be fruitful. 'Can you see that lighter patch, to the right of the hill?'

'Where?' she said, following his gaze.

'Over there in the distance, Andy said, pointing. 'It's the River Severn as it meanders its way to the sea.'

'What is that over there? Nadine said, shifting her gaze further round. 'The hill is rounded, like a ladies… how you say? Bosom…why it even has a nipple.' She giggled nervously, embarrassed at her own observation.

'I've never thought of it like that, but now you come to say, I agree with your description,' he chuckled. That's May Hill. What you refer to as the nipple, is in fact a small cluster of a hundred trees crowning the top. Legend has it, that nature kills off any attempt to plant anymore.'

'Incroyable!'

'Look the sun is setting,' he said, turning their focus back to their mission.

The sun was starting to dip behind the grey erratic line of the distant Forest of Dean hills. The red disc already missing a large section at its base, the sky suffused with myriad hues of blazing orange.

'Geoffery would have loved it. C'est manifique,' she said. 'Just like when he and I used to…used to…stand on the balcony of his penthouse and watch it.'

Andy could see a rivulet on her cheek, as tears escaped. Her mostly dry eyed composure, at last, penetrated by nostalgic memories.

'I just came too late for 'im didn't I?' she said, reaching for a tissue from her handbag. 'If only I'd…'

Unable to contain her grief and guilt any longer she dissolved into tears. Her stoic resolve crumbling as the emotional flood gates opened. She buried her face in her gloved hands, creating a mournful noise, her whole body shaking in her distress.

Andy instinctively put his arms around her and drew her gently to his chest, as he would, for any grieving relative at the hospice.

'It's OK. Let it all out,' he instructed to the crown of her beautifully coiffured head. 'You'll feel better after you've had a cry.'

'I am zorry,' she sobbed. 'You must think terrible things of me for leaving 'im when he was so ill.'

'Not at all,' he said, holding her. 'We are different, we all have different sensitivities.'

'I just couldn't get my head around ze changes that occurred in 'im when he was having 'is treatment.'

'I know, I know,' soothed Andy, having heard the same confession from countless partners of patients.

'E was not the same man I fell in love with,' she continued.

'Look, the sun is disappearing now,' Andy interrupted her confessions. 'Say goodbye to him and all your regrets. There's nothing to be achieved by hanging on to what might have been. Remember the good times you had with him and cherish those special memories.'

Nadine turned around to watch the sun's final rays, the sky now leached of colour.

'Would you 'old me, like he used to?' she sobbed. And without waiting for a reply, she put her back into his chest and crossing her hands across her stomach, took Andy's hands in hers.

Andy felt embarrassed. The sympathetic hug was part of his armoury of consoling the bereaved, but this was something else. Cuddling a beautiful woman he had only just met, in what he'd describe as a lovers clinch was surreal. But he had to admit that it was erotically exciting too. Desperately trying to rationalise what was going on, he tried to calm his rising ardour by reminding himself, that it was just the French way of expressing emotions.

They stood like this for several minutes gazing at the disappearing orb, when a woman's voice interrupted their vigil.

'Andy, what the hell do you think you're doing?' Helen barked, angrily.

Startled, Andy shook himself free of Nadine and addressed his wife.

'Nothing…um. Nadine wanted to watch the sunset to say goodbye to Geoffery, that's all.'

'Yes and I suppose you were just holding her to stop her from falling down the hill. Well you'd both better get your arses back to the cars. People are waiting to go to the hotel for the wake.' Helen said, angrily turning on her heel and almost slipping on the frozen mud.

CHAPTER SIX

23rd December

Sue was making short work of the climb up the steep track that led from the road to the Church on the Hill; her vitriol fuelling her fast ascent to the top, hoping to be in time for the funeral.

Hearing the sound of several engines below her, she turned to see the headlights of the convoy of funeral cars moving along the road, past the track entrance that she'd just left.

'Damn, I've missed them,' she cursed. Flummoxed for a moment, she wondered what to do, her plans of disrupting things thwarted by getting there too late. 'Bugger it. Well I might have missed them but I can still spit on his grave,' she said, venomously.

Breathing heavily, beads of perspiration running down her face, she strode purposefully uphill on the frozen track, stepping carefully on the crude, unevenly spaced, wooden steps; the legacy of a local conservation project.

She reached a narrow wooden kissing gate and squeezed through to emerge on stone steps by an old graveyard. The coffins of its residents having been carried up the same steep path on the shoulders of two teams of six pallbearers. The names of those interred long since eroded from the leaning gravestones by centuries of weather and pollution.

Although the winter sky was darkening quickly, a cemetery at night held no fear for her, especially with her vindictive focus on getting to his grave.

Her time in the Police cells had given her plenty of opportunity to plan her revenge on Geoffery for setting her up on the 'trumped up' attempted murder charge. She kicked herself for being outsmarted by the old man and livid that the Grim Reaper had beaten her to him.

She had also planned to resume her dominant regime over her pathetic husband Rupert, who she knew would be at the funeral too. But the sound of the cars leaving meant that her plans had failed in its entirety.

'Damn, Damn,' she muttered, angrily.

The track at last levelled out and meandered around the side of the hill. Throwing caution to the wind she strode out quickly only to slip on a patch of ice.

Instinctively grabbing hold of some undergrowth to save herself from falling, she felt the barbs of a barbed wire fence piercing her finger.

'Shit,' she said, regaining her footing, 'that hurt,' and sucking her finger, she tasted blood.

Quickly she wrapped a tissue over the bloody finger which was throbbing painfully.

This was the final straw that flipped her; for having missed the funeral and the opportunity to berate her pathetic husband. Exhausted, hot and sweaty from the climb, she became angry, uncontrollably red hot angry. Woe betide anybody who came across her now.

She entered the cemetery by a black metal kissing gate, angrily slamming it against its stop once inside, the metallic reverberations disturbing the birds and polluting the tranquillity of the cemetery. She gazed into the gathering gloom hoping to see the signs of a recent funeral.

'There's bound to be piles of wreaths,' she thought. 'Now where is it?'

She wandered along the tarmac pathways subdividing the plots, walking between the orchestrated rows of gravestones and wooden crosses until she found what she was looking for – a mound of freshly dug soil with bouquets and a large wreath bearing the word '*Geoffery* 'spelt out in white carnations. She knelt down and read the card attached to it.

Geoffery,

Forgive me.

Nadine XXX

She read the other cards, getting angrier and angrier at the sentiments expressed to '*a lovely person*'; the red mist of hatred boiling in her head. She finally flipped when she read a card with the handwriting she recognised. It was from her husband.

Uncle,

Thank you for giving me a new start.

Love Rupert and Joanne.

Her anger erupted seeing the name Joanne associated with HER Rupert. She went berserk.

'You bastard,' she said, kicking out wildly at the wreaths and bunches of flowers. 'You have destroyed my life. How dare you die before I could kill you myself.'

Carefully crafted bunches of flowers flew apart as she viciously kicked out at them, scattering them over nearby graves.

'I might have missed you in life, but I'll see you in hell,' she screamed, 'and look at me. I'm the one left to dance on your grave,' she yelled, manically leaping up and down on the fresh mound of soil, oblivious to the mud that was caking her shoes.

She angrily yanked out the simple wooden cross that Ben had emotionally planted earlier.

'Think you can out smart me, eh?' she yelled at the cross. 'Well think again.'

She was about to throw it across the cemetery, when the Gravedigger, who was just getting into his car, heard the shouting and came running back towards the source of the noise.

'What the hell you think you do?' he shouted angrily, his question heavily accented by his Polish mother tongue.

Sue was so wrapped up in her St Vitus dance on Geoffery's grave that she didn't hear him at first.

'I said, what the hell you think you do?' the thickset Gravedigger demanded again. 'I'm going call Police.'

At this, Sue stopped her gyrations and fixed the Gravedigger with an evil stare.

'Police! You're going to call the Police? So what? I'm not scared of them and you'd better bugger off before you regret it.'

'Ha, you think? I bigger than you. You little...little jerk,' he shouted reaching in his trouser pocket for his phone. 'You no scare me.'

'Don't I? Well perhaps a whack on the head with this will help to persuade you,' Sue said, menacingly advancing towards him, waving the wooden cross threateningly.

The Gravedigger stood firm and as she swung at him, he grabbed her arm, clamping his huge hand around her wrist.

'You want get physical lady? I can do physical too,' he shouted. 'Nobody messes my graves. You come with me.'

'Oh no I'm not,' she screamed, and kicked him between the legs.

The kick connected with the man's testicles, indescribable pain exploding in his stomach. Immediately he let go of her arm, his attempt to restrain the woman now forgotten.

He bellowed like a wounded bull, bent double, clutching himself. As he did so she hit him on the crown of his head with the wooden cross. He dropped to his knees, holding head and groin.

'Bitch, now you're for it,' he shrieked, stumbling to his feet.

But instead of backing off, Sue advanced towards him, lifting the wooden cross again. The Gravedigger fended off the blow with his forearm, but got the message and started to back off, taking his mobile out as he did so.

Sue raised the cross again, at the same time trying to kick the mobile out of his hand.

Suddenly a flash lit up the area as he took a photo of her. Temporarily blinded by the light, she mistimed her kick and pirouetted, nearly falling.

'You stupid bastard. Give me that phone,' she said, recovering.

'You a bloody maniac,' he shouted breathlessly, running back towards his car. 'It's lucky for you, I don't hit women. Police will get you from photo'

'Well it's unlucky for you that I have no problems hitting an arsehole like you,' she said, chasing after him, now fully pumped up with blind rage.

Frantically he ran towards the gate, shocked by her aggressive attack, weaving in and out of the gravestones like a rugby player avoiding tackles, the pain in his groin and head temporarily anaesthetised by fear.

Sue followed in hot pursuit, shouting obscenities at him. He could hear her angry breath close behind, like a tiger hunting down its prey.

Fear had given him a turn of speed that he thought his drinking lifestyle had deprived him of years before. Slowly he was increasing the gap between them and felt confident enough to turn around and see how far behind she was.

Unfortunately as he turned to look, he ran straight into a small bench, one of four surrounding a tree; a feature in the centre of the burial ground.

As his shins hit the top of the seat he pitched forward and glanced his forehead on the tree trunk.

He put his hands down to save himself, grazing his palms on the granite chippings as he did so.

He landed heavily, shocked, winded and disoriented by the collision with the tree.

Still on his hands and knees attempting to stand, Sue caught up with him. She had lost all control of herself and still clutching Geoffery's wooden cross, she rained blows on his head, hitting him again and again until he collapsed, unconscious.

Now manically 'pumped up' she viciously kicked the unconscious figure

'Not so cocky now are we?' she said, breathlessly. 'Don't ever talk to me like that again,' she said, gazing at his motionless form whilst pacing up and down like a caged lion.

Satisfied he wasn't going to give her any more trouble, she threw her weapon; Geoffery's wooden cross, like a boomerang into the night.

Irrationally she strode back to Geoffery's grave breathing heavily from her exertions, a full moon showing the devastation that she had wreaked. Satisfied that she had achieved what she set out to do, she walked back to the prostrate Gravedigger who was still unconscious.

The red mist was clearing from her angry mind. Cunning, scheming rational thinking was required. She needed to plan her way out of the incident.

She recalled he had used his phone to take a photo of her. She needed to find that phone.

She lifted his hands They were huge. She realised how fortunate she had been to get the first blow in, otherwise he would have taken her head off. He was a big man with a big frame. It was lucky for her that the Gravediggers courage didn't match his size. Both hands were empty.

Frantically she searched the area around the benches, frightened that the Goliath she had taken on would soon regain consciousness. Reassured by his regular, albeit, laboured breathing she widened the area of her search around him, dropping down on to her knees, her hands methodically sweeping the area in front of her.

Still nothing.

Now that her anger had subsided she was starting to feel cold, the winter chill making her shiver uncontrollably.

She continued her search going further and further away from the prostrate figure, until she was so cold that she could no longer feel her fingers.

'Damn, damn, damn,' she said, angrily. Then she spotted the drain cover. 'Perhaps it's gone down there,' she muttered, cursing her luck.

Reluctantly she made her way out of the cemetery without the mobile, but stopped at the sound of a car engine and voices.

Fearful that it might be the police, she quickly knelt down by the car park gate and tried to identify the source of the noise. She strained her ears listening to the conversation. 'Was it a Police radio?'

Suddenly the voices were replaced by music. It was a car radio.

'Perhaps somebody's out for a passionate session under the stars,' she thought, 'rather than the constabulary.'

She opened the gate quietly and slowly crept forward until she could see.

It was a black VW Polo with the driver's door open. The courtesy light was on inside. It was empty. The engine was just ticking over; a mist from the exhaust carpeted the tarmac around it, like a ghostly ectoplasm.

'Of course,' she thought. It's the Gravedigger's car. If I take it, that will further delay him getting to the police. I might get away with it yet.'

She ran to the car and quickly climbed in. She was again reminded of the size of the man she had taken on by needing to slide the driver's seat forward so that her short legs could reach the pedals.

Fortunately the demister had kept the windscreen frost free and the car was marginally warmer than the outside air.

She accelerated down the steep single track road, the rear of the car sliding sideways as she cornered, a reminder that the cold night would mean icy roads.

'Steady girl' she said to herself, 'we don't want to blow it now by going off the road.'

Things hadn't gone to plan. She needed to think quickly. The mobile phone might yet be her downfall.

CHAPTER SEVEN

23rd December

The procession of funeral limousines arrived solemnly back at the hotel. There had been little conversation during the short journey from the interment at the Church on the Hill. Each lost in their own thoughts.

As the mourners alighted from the sleek cars, they were directed back to the large oak panelled conference room where an impressive buffet awaited. Uniformed bar staff stood ready to take orders and serve drinks.

At the far end of the room several rows of chairs had been arranged facing a large, conference sized, flat screen monitor.

The eight 'long legged lovelies' quickly disappeared to their rooms to get changed from their revealing basques into 'something more comfortable'.

Eventually the girls re-appeared looking headturningly stunning, wearing a variety of fashionable Dior dresses. With their solemn duties behind them and having warmed up in a hot shower, they were giggling and talking non-stop.

Once the girls had got their drinks, the perceptive Funeral Director asked everybody to be seated, directing the three Godsons to specific chairs in front of the big screen. Ensuring that everybody was comfortable, he dimmed the lights and music filled the room.

Nadine instantly recognised the Billy Joel tune, '*Uptown Girl*'. It was one of Geoffery's favourites. He told her that its lyrics truly reflected their relationship. She reached for a tissue.

The screen lightened to show a glorious sunset, the foreground of which Nadine also recognised as the camera zoomed back. It was the same penthouse balcony that they had shared together many times, and watched the Mediterranean ablaze with the dying day.

She swallowed hard to fight back the tears and was winning until Geoffery's face appeared in shot. The wave of emotion overwhelmed her and she sobbed uncontrollably.

People around her shifted uncomfortably in their seats at her upset. Andy, as vigilant as ever, spotted her distress and was about to put his arm around her shoulder, but, Helen clearing her throat loudly, stopped him mid move.

Having already been 'caught out' in a compromising situation on the hill, he reluctantly withdrew from his mercy mission, placing his hands in between his thighs to show Helen he had understood the message. He knew Helen was too polite to create a scene at the hotel, but he was mentally preparing for a 'domestic' when they returned home.

'*Hello,*' the face on the screen said. '*I hope I haven't shocked you too much by seeing me after you've just buried me; for the only reason you'd be watching this video is because I am six foot under.*'

Several people gasped and jiggled in their seats at his bluntness. '*Don't worry, I won't expose you to my spectre for too long. But it would be bad mannered of me not to introduce you to each other – assuming that those I expect to be watching this are there and those that shouldn't be are still incarcerated.'*

At this comment Joanne grabbed Rupert's hand.

'Don't worry Rupert,' Geoffery continued, uncannily looking where he was seated. *'If your wife has managed to evade incarnation, the hotel security people have her photograph and will prevent her arriving here.'*

Rupert wasn't appeased by Geoffery's video assurance, especially as he was convinced he had seen her on the track, as they drove away from the Church.

Geoffery continued, *'Hopefully my good friend and Nurse Andy, has already introduced my Godsons to each other.'*

Geoffery's gaunt face was replaced by a photograph of Rupert.

'This is my Godson Rupert,' the voice informed them.

Heads at the gathering turned to look at him.

Rupert stared at the screen, wanting to avoid any eye contact with anybody.

'He is… sorry I must remember to use the past tense now I'm on the 'other side'. I was his uncle. Rupert has experienced some marital upheaval recently but I won't elaborate as I don't want to embarrass him. But hopefully the future looks brighter for him.'

Joanne again squeezed Rupert's hand and looked at him concerned.

'It's OK Jo,' he said, squeezing her hand back. 'I'm OK.' She could detect the fear in his voice at his unconvincing reply.

Rupert's photograph was replaced by one showing Tim walking on a mountain carrying a rucksack.

'Don't be fooled by this photo, Tim, another Godson, is a childhood amputee. Under those trousers he has two prosthetic legs – but as you can see, it hasn't stopped him getting on with life…that is, eventually.'

Carrie recognised the photo as one she had taken on one of their many training hikes for Geoffery's challenge for Tim of completing the Three peaks race.

In spite of the considerable difficulties involved, Tim had done it. So say, to spite Geoffery, not because he liked him.

She recalled Tim's vitriolic remarks when he'd heard about Geoffery's death; 'I reckon me climbing all three mountains finished him off. He realises now I'm eligible for getting some of his money after all.'

She let go of Tim's hand as he stood up and exhibited himself to everybody,' hand in the air, smiling, like a gold winning athlete.

'Quite the exhibitionist now,' thought Andy. 'Not like the self-centred, games playing, computer geek, that Geoffery used to tell me about.'

Tim's photo was replaced by a smart looking James.

'James hasn't always looked like this,' Geoffery intoned. *'Until recently James looked like this.'*

The picture of the smart looking James was replaced by the surveillance photo of a tramp sat on a London park bench clutching a bottle.

'So he has changed too.'

A ripple of amazement went around the room. Heads swivelling to see where James was sitting. James put his hand up to his face and looked down, seeking obscurity.

'James was helped by my young friend Ben.'

The tramps picture was replaced by one of Ben on his mountain bike.

Ben 'filled up' at being identified publicly as one of Geoffery's friends. His association with Geoffery had started only after a mysterious fire had destroyed their Scout Hut, in which Ben was sleeping at the time.

Geoffery had paid for a bigger and better hut and made sure any suspicions that Ben had caused it were categorically refuted by presenting evidence of an electrical fault, that was supposed to have caused it.

Geoffery had also been funding Ben's Mother's treatment at an addiction clinic; her problems if left untreated could have seen Ben being taken into care.

Ben was upset at seeing and hearing Geoffery. James saw his distress and sought to reassure him.

'Bit of a shock seeing him isn't it?' But, the old boy is in a better place now,' he whispered.

Ben nodded, still gazing at the screen through misty eyes.

Geoffery's on screen persona continued, *'Ben has had lots of challenges in his short life, but he has not allowed things to get on top of him. Indeed, he saved James's life and has desperately tried to help his Mother get off the alcoholic bandwagon.'*

But Beth was not watching the screen. She was distracted by the attentive waiters constantly circulating, offering drinks from silver trays. She was therefore totally oblivious to anything else. The temptation of free alcohol was torture for her.

At the start of the wake her resolve had been strong, but she felt herself weakening. 'Just one to toast the old man,' she thought, 'wouldn't harm.'

Ben's picture was replaced by an unflattering photograph of Beth obviously drunk. Her reputation for meticulous attention to hair and makeup all but destroyed.

Suddenly spotting herself on the screen, she felt it was necessary to defend her image. 'It's not easy being a mother,' Beth muttered, embarrassed by the exposé.

'Having now met my Godsons, you also need to meet the man who has helped me to get some quality out of my last remaining days. This is my hospice nurse and friend Andy Spider.'

Andy's picture appeared on the screen in his Scout uniform.

'For as well as being a good nurse, he is also a good Scout Leader. Andy runs a Scout Troop in a deprived area and he gives respect to his young people who respond likewise. He provides something positive in their lives, so they can grow their self-worth and confidence.'

Andy unused to public praise coloured up, fortunately unseen in the gloom.

'Right, so you've met each other. It's time for me to get back in the box, so to speak.'

The screen showed Geoffery in his coffin at his mock funeral in Monaco.

'Oh it would be remiss of me not to thank my beautiful 'Long Legged Lovelies'. It was a pleasure I wish I'd had again.'

The girls all giggled at the photo of them posing by his coffin.

'Until we meet again. Yes, you'll be seeing me again at the reading of my will. Just because I'm dead, you can't get rid of me that easily.'

The screen went black and the lights came on. The shocked silence collapsed into a buzz of astonished conversation.

Nadine felt slightly hurt that she wasn't mentioned in the video, but her mood changed when the Funeral Director handed her a note.

Nadine recognised Geoffery's handwriting. She went to a quiet corner of the huge conference room clutching it to her heart. She looked at it for several minutes, unsure whether to open it or not.

'What would he have written? Did he hate her even now? Should she live with the delusion that he forgave her?'

Unable to contain her curiosity any longer, she tore open the envelope, her polished finger nails slicing apart the gummed flap. Inside was a single sheet of paper. Immediately she smelt her special perfume, the essence especially commissioned by him, for her, all those years ago. The delicate scent had stained the paper like tear drops in the ink. She gazed at the few words that he had written. It took a few minutes for the mistiness of tears to clear to allow her to focus on the content. Her heart stopped as she read.'

My dearest darling Nadine,

I have always loved you. He had crossed out. ~~I have loved you until my dying day~~. *I will love you for eternity, even in heaven.*

Geoff. XXXX

Her loud sob instantly stopped the conversation in the room.

CHAPTER EIGHT

23rd December

As soon as the video had finished, Andy went to find Rupert. He was sitting in a corner with Joanne wondering when he could leave; embarrassed by being in the company of strangers and now fearful because of Geoffery's reminder about Sue.

Andy cleared his throat, wondering how he was going to be received.

'Rupert, Joanne, Hi. Umm...I wonder if I could have a word with you Rupert?'

'Yes?' Rupert said, nervously scanning the other's eyes for any hint of the topic.

'Alone, if that's OK,' Andy said, looking at Joanne.

'No, that's OK. Jo knows what's been going on. We have no secrets,' Rupert said, squeezing her hand and looking at her for confirmation.

'Yes, that's OK,' she replied, quietly.

Andy drew up a chair, turned it around and straddled it facing them, the chair-back against his chest, a psychological defence to deflect the expected angst.

'Mmm...I'm not sure where to start, but...mmm, I think...Well, I'm sorry to have to tell you that Sue has been released from custody.'

'What!' Rupert gulped, standing nervously, scanning the room.

'Yes, I'm sorry…but…'

'How? Why? Oh God this is terrible. Terrible.'

Joanne stood too and put her arm around Rupert who was now visibly shaking.

'It appears that in his efforts to help you to remove Sue from your life, Geoffery stitched her up.'

'Stitched her up, what do you mean?'

'He encouraged her to help him commit suicide and then accused her of trying to murder him.'

'Suicide! I don't understand.'

'What, I mean…how do you know all this?' Joanne asked, anxiously.

'From a CCTV recording.'

'Surely the evidence was…'

'All cleverly devised to get her committed.' Andy said completing her sentence. 'It's difficult for me to say this but I…went to the Police with new evidence that cleared her.'

'Why? What did you do that for? You knew she was torturing me! Why the hell would you set her free?' Rupert demanded, hysterically. 'Oh God. I can't go through all that again. We need to go,' he said, grabbing Jo's hand.

'No, please let me explain.'

Rupert wasn't listening. His mind was overwhelmed by fear. He needed to run and hide before she tracked him down again.

'No time. Come on Jo, we need to hurry.'

'Rupert, please listen. I need to explain,' insisted Andy.

'I've heard enough. She's out. Oh God, Oh God!'

Rupert was struggling to put on his winter coat as he walked rapidly to the door, followed by a frantic Joanne, trying to keep up with Rupert's half walk, half run exit.

Andy chased after the departing couple.

'Please let me explain, please,' he pleaded.

'There's no point. She's out there somewhere. She'll be waiting.'

His words were prophetic, for Sue was in the car park. She had found out where the Wake was being held by telephoning the Funeral Director's office, where a sympathetic receptionist was only too happy to 'redirect the lost mourner'.

Sue couldn't believe her luck as she watched Rupert and a woman hurriedly exit the front of the hotel and get into his car.

Instinctively she ducked as their car drove past her out of the car park and shot off down the drive.

Andy had followed them out still trying to explain what had happened and saw the black Polo tear out of the car park just after them, but thought nothing of it.

'Damn,' he said, angry with himself, for letting Helen talk him into handing in the recording. 'Shit, I knew it wasn't going to be easy.'

Andy was making his way back into the Wake just as Nadine came out.

'Ah, Andee,' she said, her franglais accent much more pronounced with the volume of champagne that she had consumed.

'I 'ave to zank you zo much for looking after my Geofferee, Merci.'

'It's OK, he said. 'It was my job and well…we became sort of friends.'

'I see zee lights on zee Church where 'e is sleeping now…but he will nevver awaken again,' she said, looking into the distance.

She broke into alcoholically exaggerated tears and stumbled towards him to bury her face in his chest. Initially he hesitated to comfort her, fearing a repeat of the incident when Helen found them previously at the top of the hill. However his compassionate nature overcame his reluctance and just as he enfolded her petite sobbing frame in his arms, Helen arrived at the hotel entrance. His heart sank.

'This is getting to be a bit of a habit, isn't it?' she said, angrily.

'I can explain,' he shouted as she disappeared back into the hotel.

'I am zorry for getting you into trouble ma Cherie,' Nadine said, planting a kiss on his lips. The kiss lasted marginally longer than it needed to, until he, reluctantly, pulled away.

'I need to go, I'm sorry.' Andy said, moving towards the door.

'But of course. You must explain to your wife. I will stay and talk to ma Geofferee,' she said, wiping her tears with the heel of her hand.

CHAPTER NINE

23rd December

Rupert and Joanne had joined the M5 at junction 11a heading south towards Bristol. The motorway, a black ribbon between the frost coated fields, was busy with Christmas holiday traffic.

Rupert was now paranoid that Sue might be following them and kept constantly checking his rear view mirror. He had spotted the headlights of a car following them from the hotel but was relieved to see, when they went through lit road sections that it was a black VW Polo and not Sue's blue Peugeot.

'I'm sorry about your uncle,' Joanne said, sympathetically.

'I didn't know him too well, but I guess he came along at the right time. I couldn't have broken away from Sue without his help.' Rupert said, his eyes fixed on the road ahead.

'Let's not talk about her. The day has been depressing enough.' Joanne said, firmly. 'What about us?'

'Well as soon as the divorce comes through, I was going to ask you to marry me Jo.'

'Marry you? Oh!'

'Don't you love me?'

'Yes, of course…it's just that…'

'Just, what?'

'I'm not sure marriage is for me anymore. You know I've been married before…twice and it didn't work out either time.'

'What! I thought every woman likes the security of marriage.'

'Yes, I'm sure you're right, but not for me any longer. Did I tell you I got married in a boiler suit over a river bungee jump in New Zealand. It was exciting at the time, but it didn't work out.'

'But presumably you loved him then?'

'Yes, but as soon as we got married things suddenly fell apart. It's as though we didn't try anymore. I don't want that to happen to us. I'm sorry.'

'OK, I just thought…I need you, don't want to lose you. It's just…I love you Jo,' Rupert croaked.

'Are you OK to drive?' Joanne asked him, anxiously.

'Yes I'm fine,' Rupert said, unconvincingly.

In the flashes of approaching car headlights she could see that he was crying. A tear ran down his bruised cheek, his face still bearing the results of Sue's anger. He was blinking furiously to clear his misty vision. He bit his lip to control his chattering teeth. His knuckles were white as he tightly gripped the steering wheel.

The car behind them followed at a discreet distance. Sue was wondering how to exact her revenge on her 'disrespectful' husband.

'Pull over Rupert, please,' Joanne said, anxiously.

'I can't. It's too dangerous to stop on the hard shoulder,' he replied, his voice choked with emotion.

'It will be more dangerous if you crash into something,' she said, putting a gentle hand on the back of his neck. 'Please pull over,' she repeated softly.

After a few seconds, she saw his fingers move on the steering column and heard the clicking of the indicator as he steered the car on to the 'hard shoulder'.

As soon as they stopped, she immediately pressed the red triangle on the dash to activate the hazard lights.

I'm sorry Jo,' he said, turning to her and dissolving into her arms.

'The funeral and now this, about her being free…It's all too much, I'm sorry,' he blurted.

'Ssssh, it's OK,' she whispered.' You've been through such a lot recently. Don't worry. We'll get through this together. Come on, let's change places and we'll stop at Michael Wood Services and have a coffee. OK?'

'OK.'

'Now be careful opening your door. You know what motorway drivers are like.'

As if to emphasise her concern, the car rocked on its suspension as a large Downton forty tonner sped past, heading back to its base in Hardwicke.

Sue had been taken aback by Rupert's manoeuvre onto the hard shoulder, but had quickly mirrored his actions a few hundred yards back; switching off her lights, so as not to alert them to her presence.

Looking in his rear view mirror, Rupert spotted a gap in the traffic and quickly they swapped places and belted back in again.

Joanne switched off the hazard lights and started to accelerate along the hard shoulder, indicating to pull back on to the carriageway.

On seeing the car moving again, Sue started her own manoeuvre to continue shadowing them.

Desperate to 'stay in touch'; instead of getting up to speed on the hard shoulder, she pulled out directly on to the carriageway, fully expecting that the approaching Discovery, would move to the middle lane and overtake her. However, in her haste, she had forgotten to turn her lights back on.

Because her car was unlit, the driver of the approaching 4 x 4 spotted her only at the last second and instinctively took avoiding action, unfortunately swerving into the path of a Qashqai already in the middle lane.

This set off a catastrophic chain of events. For the Qashqai driver instinctively swerved out into the third lane, his car colliding with the rear wing of a BMW which was overtaking him, travelling at 100 mph. The impact of their collision caused the BMW to slew around and smash into the central reservation.

Joanne had just checked her rear view mirror to pull back onto the motorway when she saw the collisions occurring behind her.

'What's up,' Rupert said, catching her open mouthed, transfixed by the mayhem displayed in the mirror. The sound of a car skidding answered his question.

The BMW bounced off the central barrier and was sent pirouetting across all three lanes, smoke billowing from its protesting tyres.

In a frightening explosion of noise, it collided with Rupert's car, impacting just behind the driver's pillar. The force of the collision pushing his car sideways from the edge of the hard shoulder, its tyres squealing as it was forced across the tarmac.

It stayed upright until it hit the kerb edge and then was sent spiralling sideways several times, coming to rest on its roof.

The BMW crashed down on top of Rupert's car, its wheels resting on the exposed floor tray, its ruptured petrol tank draining into the upturned car beneath.

Soon other vehicles were involved in the carnage. A cacophony of disaster filled the night air with the 'gut retching' noise as cars and lorries collided with each other, metal scraping on tarmac, bodywork and glass erupting over North and Southbound carriageways.

Strings of red brake lights illuminated the night as drivers sought to avoid the mayhem.

Sue's stolen Polo was hit in the rear and collided with other cars caught up in the road traffic collision.

As all the southbound cars eventually skidded to a halt, there was a split second of absolute silence – and then the screaming started.

Fortuitously, a Highways Agency Traffic Officer patrol was on that section of the motorway and had arrived at the scene within a few minutes. Their call to their control meant there was little delay before the specialist fire and rescue unit were despatched.

Both Rupert and Joanne had been knocked unconscious by the impact. They hung upside down, restrained by their seat belts.

Meanwhile, Sue had staggered out of the Gravediggers wrecked car, suffering from a sore neck from a subsequent rear end collision. She also suffered mild facial burns and a split lip when the airbag inflated as she was shunted into the wreckage in front.

Shocked at the sudden turn of events, she crunched her way through broken glass that littered the road like hailstones.

Ignoring the panicky advice of other shocked motorists and good Samaritans, who tried to stop her, she forced her way to Rupert's upturned car and peered in, the strong smell of petrol making her eyes water.

She smiled at the still bodies, dangling from their seatbelts.

'That'll teach you to mess with me, won't it?' she shouted at the unconscious figures.

Pleased to see that Rupert and girlfriend were injured, possibly dead, she decided to leave the scene quickly. Not wishing to be involved in the police inquiry that would follow.

As she turned to leave, she trod awkwardly on some debris and her ankle twisted under her, she felt something snap; with great relief she realised it was only the heel of her shoe.

Slowly she hobbled south along the now deserted southbound carriageway away from the mayhem, the broken heel giving her a strange gait as she made her retreat.

Behind she could hear the increasing crescendo of wailing sirens from a fleet of emergency vehicles all heading towards the motorway carnage. Stroboscopic blue lights signalling the urgency of their hectic dash in their rescue mission.

Having got to the first road bridge crossing the motorway, she walked up the grass embankment and carefully hopped over the fence onto the road.

Behind her a fireball lit up the night sky, coupled with a large explosion that echoed across the winter white fields. She smiled evilly. 'Goodbye and good riddance Rupert.'

A sudden thought came to her. 'As your grieving widow, I will inherit your estate, which will include some of Uncle Geoffery's millions! My God, I couldn't have expected more, even if I'd planned it myself,' she said, excitedly.

In spite of the inevitable mobile network congestion, she was eventually able to call a local taxi firm and was taken home. The roads gridlocked as traffic diverted away from the now closed motorway.

The taxi driver was unable to get any form of conversation from her as she re-ran the sequence of events in her mind.

In spite of the shock from the accident and her minor injuries, she felt elated with her day's work, for she had danced on Geoffery's grave and seen her pathetic husband and girlfriend killed. And to top it all, she had become a millionairess.

CHAPTER TEN

23rd December

Andy spotted that Ben had left the wake in a 'strop'. He followed him out into the corridor where he found the teenager leaning against the wall, clearly upset.

'What's the matter Ben?'

'Nothing!'

'Come on, I've known you long enough now to spot when something's bothering you.'

'I said there's nothing,' Ben repeated, moving away from Andy.

'Oh, OK, don't get angry about it.'

'I'm not. It's just that – Oh you wouldn't understand.' Ben said, shifting his gaze to the ceiling, barely hiding the tears.

'No you're probably right,' said Andy. 'I'll get back to the party then.'

'Yeah, well, how come you adults can even think about having a party and laughing and stuff when you've just been to…to his funeral?'

'Are you upset about his wake?'

'No. I mean yes. It's just disrespectful. You're all spongers! Happy cos you're going to get his money. You don't care he's dead.' Ben said, distraught.

'Oh is that what you're upset about?' People laughing?'

'No...well it's not right.'

'Let me explain something to you.'

'No. I don't want to hear. You'll only come up with some 'cock and bull 'story. I don't want one of your lectures.'

'Hear me out. I appreciate you might have difficulties understanding what's going on here, with all this apparent joviality. Is this your first funeral?'

'Yeah, I didn't go to my Gran's funeral last year. Anyway what's that got to do with it? People should be sad that he's dead. He was a nice man and...'

'Yes...I agree, and we are all sad that he's no longer with us.'

'You could have fooled me.'

A hysterical giggle from one of the long legged lovelies rang out.

'See what I mean?' Ben said, dismayed.

'Look Ben...how can I explain it?' Andy said, struggling to find the right words. 'We all know that death is inevitable for all of us.'

'Yeah, so!'

'So when we go to a funeral we are all sad. You saw that earlier, right?'

'Yeah but...'

'Let me continue...'

'Go on, but you can't convince me that it's right.'

'What we are doing now at the wake is celebrating his life. We are reliving some of the happy times we had with him. Not, as you think, disrespecting him.'

'Well, those 'dolly birds' that walked by the side of his coffin didn't know him...and why were they dressed like that...half naked.'

'They were following his wishes.'
'What do you mean?'
'Before Geoffery left Monaco, he held a mock funeral.'
'Mock funeral?'
'Yes he had a big party for his friends and the girls dressed and performed as they did today…he mentioned it in the video earlier. He went to his own wake.'
'That's weird!'
'Yes but it showed that he had a sense of humour about his own mortality.'
'What do you mean?'
'He had come to terms with his illness and decided to enjoy life to the full, while he could. That's why he didn't want people wearing black, the traditional colour for mourners to wear at funerals.'
'Oh!'
'A wake is the start of the healing process for friends and family when somebody dies. It helps people get over the grief of losing their loved one.'
'Well I suppose you're right. But it still doesn't seem the right thing to do.'
'You'll understand, eventually. The more funerals you go to, the tougher the veneer on your emotions.'
'What?'
'It doesn't hurt so much. Come on, let's see if there are any cakes left.'

Putting his arm around Ben's shoulders, he steered him back into the hall where the 'long legged lovelies were doing a lively floor show, their normal occupation.

CHAPTER ELEVEN

23rd December

The wake party was still in full swing as Andy and Helen left. The 'long legged lovelies' were dancing to loud music and enjoying entertaining anybody interested in watching.

Helen had followed Andy around as he said his goodbyes. Nadine as expected gave them both a hug and kisses on the cheek.

'Andee, when you come to Monaco, please call me.' Nadine called as Helen virtually dragged him through the doorway.

'You stink of that woman's perfume!' Helen said, angrily.

'Oh, I quite like it, I was going to buy you a bottle,' he continued.

'Dream on! That is an exclusive perfume. It's probably about five thousand quid a bottle.'

'So ! Anyway, you're worth every penny of it,' he said, getting into the Merc.

'Yeah, right!'

'A special Christmas present for a special lady,' he said, giving her thigh a squeeze.

'You can pack that up for a start,' she said, pushing his hand away.

'Helen,' he said, in an endearing voice.

'No chance, after what you've been up to with that woman,' she said, sternly, crossing her legs and turning away from him. Angrily she looked out of the passenger window into the dark night.

As he drove down the long hotel drive, he noticed the car park was full with top end cars. The hotels rich clientele had arrived in a variety of expensive motors including Bentleys, Jags, Ferraris and Rollers. For the first time in his life he didn't feel inferior in his car, all thanks to Geoffery.

At the bottom of the drive they were forced to stop as the main road was jammed solid with static traffic. The queue stretched as far as Andy could see, there was little movement.

'Blimey look at this traffic.'

'Don't change the subject. What were you up to with that woman?'

'What do you mean?'

'Don't come the innocent with me!'

'I was comforting her, she was upset.'

'Twice!'

'Well it was quite a distressing day for her.'

'Yes we were all sad. But we didn't all come sobbing to you.'

'Come on. These foreign types wear their hearts on their sleeve. They're all kissy, kissy. But it means nothing.'

'She was flirting with you.'

'Nonsense, she was distraught.'

'Had a guilty conscience I should think.'

'About?'

'Leaving Geoffery, when he was ill.'

'Are you jealous?'

'No, of course not.'

'You ARE jealous aren't you? Don't worry she is so far out of my league to be on the moon.'

'Sometimes they're after 'a bit of rough'.'

'You've called me many things in the past, but a rich woman's 'bit of rough' is something new!'

They had been stationary at the end of the drive for some time, unable to join the main road because the traffic was not moving.

'Where's all this traffic come from?'

'I thought I heard the receptionist saying that the motorway was closed.'

'Oh, that'll be the reason then.'

'I'll ring mother and let her know we're going to be late picking the girls up.'

'Good idea, this is gridlock.'

Eventually they managed to cut across the traffic and find their way through the back lanes, avoiding the congestion and picked the children up.

'There's lots of stars out tonight Daddy,' said four year old Amy as they drove home.

'Yes Santa will be busy packing his sleigh, ready to start flying around the world tomorrow. I expect he'll be pleased that it's such a lovely evening.'

'Look, there's a very shiny star. Is that the Christmas star that shone down on baby Jesus crib?'

'It could be, yes.'

'You know you said, people go to heaven when they die?

'Yes.'

'Do they become stars? Because there's hundreds and hundreds and hundreds of stars.

'Yes, I'm sure some special people do.'

'Is Uncle Geoffery a star?'

'Yes darling, he's a star,' Andy said, moved by her poignant observation.

'Right here we are,' said Helen, as they pulled up outside their house.

Inside the Christmas tree lights blinked on and off to welcome them home. 'And it's straight to bed for you missy.'

'How many more sleeps before Santa comes?' Amy said, getting out of her car seat.'

'Only two now.'

'Two. Oh goody,' she said, running excitedly into the house.

Having put the sleeping baby into her cot and the excited Amy to bed, Andy and Helen watched television for a few hours before going to bed, a thick atmosphere of mistrust between them.

Andy decided to go for a shower before turning in but couldn't resist the temptation to pose in front of the mirror.

Holding his stomach in and puffing his chest out, he vainly admired his physique. 'Not bad,' he said, striking a pose, 'not bad at all.'

His ablutions over, he was disappointed when he got to the bedroom to find that Helen was already asleep. His passionate ambitions dashed. As he lay in bed he reflected on his two close encounters with Nadine.

'Bit of rough,' he whispered, savouring the words from their earlier conversation.

His observation wasn't quiet enough, as the dig in his ribs indicated that Helen wasn't deeply asleep.

CHAPTER TWELVE

24th December

Ben had left the wake still unhappy; for in spite of Andy's explanation, the experience of going to his first funeral and wake had upset him. He couldn't understand the irreverence and apparent lack of grieving by the adults. Worse still was seeing and hearing Geoffery again, in the video.

Consequently the whole episode went round and round in his head and his sleep was plagued by nightmares.

He dreamt that Geoffery had been buried alive and had eventually dug himself out of his grave. As he crawled away from it, all his friends were laughing at him. The eight girls turned into 'she devils' and they kept throwing him back and reburying him. Ben had been powerless to help Geoffery, his legs frozen to the spot.

Having lain in bed tossing and turning all night he decided to get up early and go to see Geoffery's grave, just to check. He hoped to sort his head out too; for although he considered himself tough and worldly, Geoffery's passing had, uncharacteristically, hit him hard.

Getting dressed, he crept quietly downstairs. Collecting his, expensive, high spec mountain bike from the hall he wheeled it outside. Geoffery had bought him the bike as a reward, for helping him to find and bring back his Godson James from London.

Ben had been staying in Churchup with his Grandad Harold while his Mother was undergoing 'drying out' at an addictions clinic.

In spite of all her failings, Ben was very fond of his Mother and had looked forward to her return from the treatment regime. It was especially important for him over the Christmas and New Year.

He hoped that this year she wouldn't spoil it by being 'out of her head' all the time; for like any child he craved a 'normal', happy family Christmas and was envious of his mates who told him of all the good family fun they had at this festive time.

There had been a heavy frost overnight; the roof tiles on the houses opposite were white; so before venturing out he wrapped up warmly

Within minutes of clipping into his pedals, the cold air chilled him, penetrating the scarf that he'd wrapped around his face, making his nose tingle.

As he cycled through the village a vapour trail of his exertions marked his route in the still morning air.

The few people he saw were all cocooned against the cold in thick layers of clothing.

Rather than taking an easy, but 'boring' road route, up the steep hill, he chose instead a challenging one. He wanted to test out the performance of the expensive bike with its twenty seven gears and active full frame suspension.

His chosen route to get to the cemetery at the top of the hill took him over frost covered fields and up through the steep slopes of a small wood.

Although the field grass was stiffened white by Jack Frost's visit, many of the slopes under the trees were still very muddy and slippery; for in spite of Ben's comprehensive mountain biking expertise, the patches of mud took him by surprise and he crashed several times as the bike went from under him.

By the time he arrived at the top of the hill his black tights, gloves and Sidi clip-in shoes were thick with mud.

The uphill track that Ben followed took him to a different gate that Sue had entered the previous afternoon, but immediately he saw the devastation on Geoffery's grave.

His heart stopped as he took in the carnage. 'Oh my God,' he gasped. 'It's true! Geoffery was still alive.'

Mesmerised by it, he dropped his bike, slowly approaching the mess of scattered wreaths and damaged flowers.

He was relieved to find the mound of soil in place, not like in his dream. However, he struggled to understand what had happened. Was this an animal or a human that had caused it?

Surely no human would do this irreligious demolition of somebodies grave? This was a heinous crime. The devastation incensed him. He realised he was shaking, a tear beaded his eye and ran down his cheek. He picked up part of a wreath with the letters GEO still intact.

'Oh my God, where's the cross I made him?' he said, looking around. Desperately he searched, but without success. 'I must tell Andy.'

Distraught, he dropped the remains of the wreath and leapt on his bike, deciding to take the faster road route back down the hill to get to a telephone.

Unusually, he was the only one in his class who didn't have a mobile phone, not that he particularly wanted one, but his mother kept stealing his savings to feed her addictions.

As he cycled through the burial ground he failed to see the frost covered body of the Gravedigger still in the centre of the burial ground, hidden behind the benches, where Sue had mercilessly beaten him to the ground.

However he did see the Gravedigger's mobile on the path. It was several yards away from the search area which Sue had scoured in her desperate night quest.

Ben skidded to a halt, sliding the back wheel around 180 degrees and picked up the rime covered phone.

'Somebodies dropped their phone! I wonder if it'll work?' he said, wiping the frost off and pressing a button on the top. Immediately it sprang to life, a raft of apps and options presenting themselves to him.

'How do I make a call?' he wondered, quickly flicking through the screens. 'Ah, here we are.'

Although he didn't have a mobile himself, he had memorised Andy's telephone number and was relieved to hear it ringing out. After only a few rings the familiar voice answered.

Not recognising the calling number identity, Andy greeted him formally. 'Andy Spider, who's calling?'

'Andy, it's me. Ben. You've got to come, quick,' he said, urgently. 'Something terrible has happened.'

'I'm just getting ready for work Ben. Will it wait?'

'No...It's... It's Geoffery's grave. Somebody's vandalised it. And they have taken the cross I made for him too.'

'Are you there now?'

'Yes.'

'What the hell are you doing there at this time of the morning?'

'I couldn't sleep....I...can you come please?'

'Ok, but I can't spend a lot of time there, otherwise I shall be late for work.'

'Hurry, please.'

'OK, I'll be on my way shortly.'

Ben put the mobile into his pocket and made his way back to Geoffery's grave. He was distraught, as he started picking up some of the floral debris.

Focussed on his task, he failed to hear an early morning dog walker approaching, the animal panting, straining at the leash.

'Here, what the hell are you doing?' the dog walker, a thickset man, called.

'I...somebody's done this. It's my friend's grave.'

'A likely story,' the other said, coming over to him. 'Look at this mess. This place is always being vandalised. I think you have some questions to answer. I'm going to call the police.'

'It wasn't me, honest,' Ben pleaded.

'No? Then why are you covered in mud?'

'I fell off my bike.'

'Yes? Tell me another,' the man said, sarcastically.

He immediately pulled out his mobile and started peering at it to do as he'd threatened.

'I've only just arrived myself,' Ben added.

Ben was gutted that anybody could even think of accusing him of damaging his friend's grave and irrationally picked up his bike.

'Don't even think about it. You're going to stay here until the Police arrive. I'll set the dog on you if you try and run off.'

Ben needed to escape, he couldn't think. The hurtful accusation was crushing his rational thinking. But Andy would vouch for him. What if Andy went to work instead? Surely his police record would go against him.

His irrational conclusion was therefore to run. Assessing the fat pooch's ability to attack him, he decided to risk it. Quickly turning his bike around, he ran back towards the black metal kissing gate, while the man was still fumbling with his phone.

Deftly he manoeuvred his bike over the top of the gate and leaping on to it, he hurtled off down the same steep track that Sue had puffed her way up the previous afternoon.

The track would take him to the road, where he could intercept Andy on his way up to the burial ground and warn him about the dog walker's allegations.

Behind him he could hear the dog walker shouting.

'Come back you little sod. I know who you are, you won't get far. The Police are on their way.'

His hectic flight from the burial ground took him past the ancient church, down a flight of narrow stone steps. He dismounted to go through the small wooden 'kissing gate' and waited for a few, seemingly endless, minutes until he could hear the distinctive throaty roar of Andy's approaching Mercedes.

Hopping on to his bike again, he descended the steep muddy path, weaving left and right, avoiding the wooden steps that Sue had struggled up. Rapidly, he slipped and slithered his way down towards the road. He needed to get there first to flag Andy down.

He heard the car slow for the first sharp bend in the narrow lane and split seconds later the second. There was only one more corner before he would be on the straight. Time was running out.

As he manoeuvred the final bend on the track, Ben spotted a problem. He had forgotten the line of stout wooden posts erected across the junction with the road; cut down telephone poles had been installed to prevent motorbikes using the track. The gaps between them were only wide enough to allow pedestrian access. But he was going too fast to stop. He made a rapid decision to carry on his downward flight rather than deliberately falling off to try to halt his hectic descent.

Quickly he identified a marginally wider gap between two posts and aimed his bike there. As he sped towards it he suddenly realised that even this gap was too narrow for his handlebars to go through. He was about to smash his hands into the posts, which would somersault him into the road, straight in front of Andy's accelerating car.

But it was too late to stop, he was committed now. In a desperate gamble he pulled a high speed 'wheelie' to lift the handle bars over the top of the posts.

Balanced on his rear wheel, he hurtled through the gap, his gloved hands just brushing the tops of the posts, one pedal scraping against the bottom of the post.

Relieved to have survived the stunt, he realised the danger was not over yet, for in his peripheral vision he could see Andy accelerating towards him. Instantly he dropped the front of the bike back down and in a split second slewed the back wheel around into the width of a narrow 'pull in' place edging the road.

He hoped he'd got his timing right, otherwise he would emerge directly at the point where Andy's car was going be.

As his front wheel touched the tarmac, he frantically leant the bike over and turned right, uphill, the same way that Andy was going.

He hoped the car was going to be on the far side of the narrow single track road in order to miss him.

Unfortunately, he hadn't taken into account the icy road conditions and as his rear wheel dropped onto the frost covered tarmac, it skidded out from beneath him.

Ben managed to unclip his right foot and planted it down which saved him from falling off, a trick he had mastered during many mountain bike races.

But now the Merc was at the same point on the road.

Andy's reaction was like lightning. Yanking the steering wheel over to the left he avoided colliding with Ben's errant rear wheel by fractions, instinctively flooring the brake and allowing the sophisticated traction control to bring the car to a slithering halt.

Had Andy not slowed down for the third ninety degree bend the outcome would have been very different.

'You stupid idiot! 'Andy shouted, as he opened the car door, 'I could have killed you. What the hell were you thinking of?'

'Sorry, I wanted to see you before you got up to the burial ground.'

'You nearly gave me a heart attack.'

'There's a bloke up there who thinks I've done it,' Ben shouted, interrupting. 'He's called the Police. Sorry, I panicked.'

'Well we'd better get up there and sort this out then. I haven't got much time or I shall be late for work, especially as the roads are so busy this morning.'

'I'll go up the track, by the side of the stables, and meet you at the top by the church car park.'

'Right, well be careful for crying out loud.'

'I will, don't worry' said Ben, clipping back into his pedals and pushing off.

Andy drove up the steep winding road, his tyres leaving black tramlines over the frost covered road. As he pulled into the car park, the dog walker and his overweight Labrador waddled over to him.

'Here, have you seen a kid on a bike?' the other enquired. 'I caught the little bugger vandalising a grave. He had kicked all the flowers all over the place.'

'I'm sorry, but I think you've got that wrong.'

'What do you mean I got it wrong? What do you know about it?' the other replied angrily. 'You weren't here to see him.'

'I know the kid. He wouldn't do that. The person in the grave is a friend of his.'

At this point Ben arrived at the top of the track and seeing the discussion between Andy and the dog walker, he stopped and listened, keeping out of sight.

'Oh, so you know all about it do you? I supposed he lied to you as well.'

'No, that's not....'

'These kids are all the same. Bloody troublemakers,' the dog walker continued, not listening. 'They ought to bring back National Service, that would soon sort the little buggers out.'

Andy listened patiently to the much overworked belief that army discipline was the answer to all the ills of miscreant youth.

'I can assure you that this young man isn't a trouble maker.' Andy said, firmly.

'What do you know about him? Are you his father?'

'No, I'm his Scout Leader.'

'Oh yes,' the dog walker said, knowingly. 'You're one of them eh?'

'If by that, you mean I'm a volunteer, I give a lot of my time to help young people become better citizens, then you're right. I am one of them.'

'Volunteer! You Scouts are all part of a government con, I reckon.'

'A government con? Well, that's new one on me. You're obviously involved helping as a community volunteer yourself then, are you?' Andy said, getting uncharacteristically angry.

'No.'

'I thought not. It's the old story. Those that can, do; those that can't, talk about it.'

'What are you on about?' the other said, confused.

Ben could hear the raised voices and not wishing to be embroiled in the argument decided to stay where he was.

As the heated discussion between Andy and the dog walker continued, Ben heard a car approaching in the lane. Shortly after, it drove into the car park. The Police had arrived.

Two Police officers emerged from the patrol car. Ben could see they were cocooned in thick black stab-proof vests, which were festooned with various paraphernalia of the job; radio, handcuffs, pepper spray canister and collapsible truncheon.

As he watched, they walked over to Andy and the dog walker.

'Coo, you were quick,' the dog walker said, at their approach.

'Yes we're only stationed a few miles away, just off the motorway by the A40. We can't take too long, last night's smash and subsequent closure of the Motorway mean's we're a bit busy. Somebody report a case of vandalism?'

'Yes,' said the dog walker. 'It was me.'

'Ok would you mind showing us the damage please?' the female Police officer asked.

The dog walker led the small group to Geoffery's desecrated grave. Ben could no longer see or hear what was going on, but decided to stay where he was; for the Police force and he had a 'strained' relationship.

'Here it is,' said the dog walker, gesturing at the messed up grave. 'I caught a kid doing it.'

'No you didn't,' Andy said, quickly.

'Sorry sir, but who are you?' asked the Policeman, mildly annoyed at Andy's intervention.

'I'm the young man's Scout leader. He called me when he found the mess.'

'I saw him doing it,' argued the dog walker. 'He was holding some flowers in his hand and he was covered in mud. It was obvious he'd done it. Typical of young kids today, no respect. They ought to bring back flogging. That would sort them out.

'You might have seen him with something in his hand, but I can assure you officer, the young man wouldn't have done it. He was a very good friend of the man buried here only yesterday and he'd come to pay his respects.'

While Andy and the dog walker were arguing over whether Ben had been the culprit or not, the female Police officer had left the group and was looking around for any possible clues. Returning after a few minutes, she called to her colleague.

'Jeff, we got more than vandalism here. We need to call in the troops. We've a body over there.'

'You sure?'

'Yes. It looks like he's been dead for some time. He's covered in frost.'

'Oh my god,' said the shocked dog walker. 'So the kid not only vandalised the grave, but he killed somebody as well. See I told you he should be locked up.'

'Don't be so stupid. The person has obviously been dead for a long time, if he's covered in frost.' Andy said. 'Would you like me to have a look? I'm a nurse.'

'I'm afraid this poor fellow is gone past needing your skills. But thanks for offering. We also need to preserve the possible crime scene, too.'

'I bet it was the kid.' the dog walker added, maliciously.

'Ok you two, that will be enough. Right, while my colleague calls this in, let's have some names. Let's start with this young man shall we?' The Policeman said, getting his notebook out.

'OK, if you insist. His name is Ben Bird, he is fourteen,' volunteered Andy.

'Ben Bird…Ben Bird, I know that name from somewhere,' said the Policeman, frowning. 'I've got it. He was the one that went missing after assaulting an old man wasn't he?'

'See I told you,' said the dog walker, smugly. 'A troublemaker, through and through.'

'It wasn't like that,' Andy replied, defensively.

'Well, we'll certainly want to see him to eliminate him from our enquiries anyway.'

CHAPTER THIRTEEN

24th December

As the group walked back to the Police car, the dog walker spotted Ben waiting by the Church gate.

'There he is. That's the vandal over there, look,' he said, pointing.

The Policeman followed the dog walker's indication and started walking towards Ben.

'Excuse me young man. I'd like a word please.'

Ben hesitated for a moment, unsure what to do and then turned his bike around and bounced off down the track, as fast as he could go.

'Bugger,' said the Policeman, reaching for his radio.

'Let me sort this,' Andy said, running towards the Policeman. 'Ben,' he shouted at the departing figure, 'Ben. It's OK. Ben, come back.' Turning to the Policeman, he said. 'Don't worry, I'll get him and bring him back. I know where he's staying.'

'What did you say his name was?' the Policewoman quizzed.

'Ben…Ben Bird.'

'Oh, he's the one we had the helicopter up for a few months ago,' she revealed. 'Oh yes, that's him. The runner.'

'See, I told you, it was him that did the grave,' the dog walker, smirked.

'No he didn't, I tell you. The helicopter thing was all an overreaction to a minor incident,' Andy said, quickly. 'The boy bumped into somebody whilst riding on the pavement that's all.'

'Not the way I heard it,' said the Policeman. 'Ok. We'll leave it to you to take him to the Police Station in Gloucester or Cheltenham. Say, by five o'clock this afternoon or he'll be on our wanted list, again. Right, let's have some details from you two.'

Meanwhile, Ben had 'flown' down the steep muddy track, fearing any moment to hear the Police car chasing after him down the road.

He took short cuts down all the alleyways and quickly got to his Grandad's house. Kicking off his muddy shoes he raced inside, hastily packing things into a bag.

He was just putting his shoes on again and on his way out through the front door with the bag when James arrived.

'Hello Ben, old chap. Going somewhere?' James asked, smiling.

'Yes I'm…I'm having a sleep-over at my friend's house. Can't stop,' Ben said, climbing on to his bike, looking furtively.

'So long as you're not running away,' James said, jokingly.

Ben was looking in the direction of an approaching car. 'Sorry I've got to go.'

'Hang on a second. I've brought you a Christmas present.'

'Thanks. Drop it in the hall. I've got to go,' he repeated.

'Are you in trouble?' James asked, suspiciously.

'No, no…I just promised that I'd be at his house, now.'

'What's up Ben?' James said, 'We might have known each other for a short time, but I know when you're lying.'

'No I'm not, honest. I'm sorry you've had a wasted journey. I need to go.'

James put his hand on Ben's handlebars. 'I recognise a lie when I see one,' he said, firmly. 'What is it?'

'It…it's the Police, they're after me,' Ben confessed, 'Now can I go?'

'What have you done?'

'Nothing. Look can we go somewhere and I'll tell you. The Police will be here any minute.'

'OK, you know this place better than I.'

'Have you got a car?'

'Yes, it's a hire car. Tell me where you want to go.'

Ben returned his bike into the house and quickly got into the hire car. As they drove away, they could see Andy's distinctive white Mercedes approaching them.

'Look, it's Andy, shall I stop?'

'No, no keep going. They might be following him.'

'OK, duck down,' James instructed. 'He won't be looking for my car.'

Andy drove past them heading towards Ben's Grandad's house without recognising James.

'There's nobody following him. Let's go and see Andy to find out what this is all about.' James said, slowing the car.

'No, the Police might be here soon.' Ben said, despondently.

'So you still haven't told me what her majesties constabulary is chasing you for.' James said, watching his rear view mirror as Andy turned into the road they had just left. 'We'll wait until Andy comes back and flag him down.'

'Somebody has vandalised Geoffery's grave and this bloke called the Police and told them it was me,' Ben said, in an avalanche of words.

'What!'

'I called Andy and he was talking to the Police, but I bottled it when they wanted to speak to me.'

'Well if you've done nothing wrong, you've got nothing to hide.'

'Yes, I know but…'

'By running away they'll automatically assume you're guilty.'

'But I haven't done anything wrong. Why won't anybody believe me?' Ben said, desperately. 'I only went to look at his grave…the cross I made for him, is gone as well. Who would do that to Geoffery's grave, James?'

'Could be local vandals, somebody with a grudge. I gather he bought his way into the cemetery, so it might be somebody with an axe to grind about that.'

'Yes I suppose.'

'Could it have been an animal, do you think?' James suggested.

'No, the flowers were scattered all over the place, his…his name spelled out in flowers was broken…And the cross I made for him was missing too.'

'Shall we go and have a look?'

'What if the Police are still there?'

'I shouldn't think they would hang around for a case of vandalism, and anyway, Andy has obviously left them, so….

'Yeah, I suppose.'

'No I reckon they'll be long gone. They got more important things to sort out, especially with the motorway still closed.'

'Why's that?' Ben said, half-heartedly.'

'Didn't you hear about the big accident on the M5 last night?'

'No. I think Andy said something about heavy traffic today.'

'It was pretty bad by all accounts. It was a multivehicle collision. That's why there was traffic chaos when we left the hotel last night. Everybody was diverting off.'

'Oh.'

'Yeah, the whole lot caught fire too.

'Yes, I thought I heard sirens.'

'That's probably what it was.'

'Well it looks like Andy has gone the other way, otherwise he should have been back here by now,' said James, studying his rear view mirror.

'He's probably gone to work then. He said he was in a bit of a rush when I rang him.'

Andy had, indeed, gone to the hospice and rang the Police from there. He reiterated his earlier belief that Ben wouldn't have done anything to the grave, because of his close bond with Geoffery. Quite the contrary, he explained, that Ben was genuinely distraught at the desecration.

However, at their insistence, he made an appointment to take Ben to Cheltenham Police HQ to discuss things in the New Year.

The desk Sergeant was quite happy with the arrangement because of the already busy seasonal workload, exacerbated by the M5 crash and the body in the cemetery.

'Ok we'll carry on up to the Church to see what you're talking about.' James said.

'If you go left up here,' Ben directed, 'we can get up to the lane from this direction.'

James steered the car around a mini roundabout and up a short lane. However, as they crested a rise they saw a Police car with its blue lights flashing parked across the road, blocking the lane leading to the Church.

It was too late to turn around and make a dash for it. Ben's heart stopped as James drew the car to a halt at the Policeman's direction.

'Where were you hoping to go, Sir?' the Policeman asked, leaning into the car. Ben turned away to hide his face, but could see in the reflection of the window, that it was not the same one who wanted to speak to him earlier.

'The Church.' James said, tensely, hoping he hadn't inadvertently handed Ben into the 'arms of the law.'

'Sorry Sir. The Church and top of the hill have been sealed off to members of the public, while they undertake forensic analysis of the area.'

Ben's heart skipped a beat. They were treating this seriously after all.

'Forensic tests,' repeated James. 'Something nasty happen then?'

'Yes. A body has been found.'

'Oh dear,' James said, looking quickly at Ben, who paled at the mention of a body. 'OK, I'll just turn around then. Any idea when it will be open again?'

'No. Depends upon the Forensic people really. Try tomorrow.'

'OK, thanks very much.'

James executed a nervous three point turn by the green and drove back down the way they'd come.

'Is there something you're not telling me Ben,' James said, sternly.

'I swear to God, I never knew anything about a body. Oh my God, you'll have to take me somewhere where they won't find me.'

'There's a hell of a difference between vandalism and dead bodies. What's going on Ben?'

CHAPTER FOURTEEN

24th December

Coincidentally, the Vicar and the Parish Clerk were in the church preparing for the Christmas services, when they heard the Police activity outside.

In the car park there were several Police cars and a white transit van with the word SOCO signwritten on it. 'Excuse me,' said the Vicar, addressing a man wearing a blue coloured disposable overall. 'What's going on?'

'We've found a body in the burial grounds, Madam.'

'Oh dear,' she said, shocked. 'Can we be of any help? It might be one of my parishioners. We obviously know a lot of people who use the hill.'

'The burial ground is my responsibility,' said the Clerk.

'Well, that would be most helpful if you could.'

'It's not a messy one is it?' the Vicar asked quickly, hoping she hadn't inadvertently, let herself in for a traumatic viewing.

'No, the guy appears to have frozen to death. Although there is some head trauma.'

After looking at the body, they quickly retired back through the frost coated metal gate that separated the car park from the burial ground.

They confirmed it was the Gravedigger, Jan Criscroski.

'Poor Jan,' the Vicar said, shocked, looking at the Clerk.

'He was a hard worker,' the Clerk said. 'We'll have a job to find somebody who was so hard working.'

'Look, I'm not going to keep you long in these freezing temperatures,' the Murder squad detective said, his breath a halo of mist in the still cold winter air. 'Tell me what you know about him.'

'We believe he is Polish, but not sure,' the Vicar said, clearly shocked by the event. For although, in her working life she had seen many dead people and comforted the bereaved, to get involved with a suspected murder in the churchyard where she often worked alone, was disconcerting.

'But where's his car? I didn't notice it in the car park,' the Parish Clerk said, looking around.

'Car?' repeated the Detective Constable.

'Yes, he drove it up here yesterday,' the Vicar confirmed.

'What type of car is it?'

'It's a VW Polo. Its black,' the Clerk volunteered.

'Have you got the registration?' the DC quizzed, about to write the details in his notebook.

'No. I'm afraid not. But he used it as his mobile home. He kept all his personal stuff in it.'

'Well, it's not here now. Somebody must have taken it. Mmm, intriguing,' the DC added, thinking aloud. 'Did he have a mobile phone?'

'Yes, have you found it?' the Clerk enquired.

'No, not yet. Have you tried ringing it?'

'Yes, I tried calling him earlier. But it's switched off. No reply.'

'No reply!' the DC repeated.

'Well obviously not, if he's...dead,' the Clerk said, laughing nervously.

'You'd be surprised what sometimes happens when mobiles go missing. Can you give me his number, please? We'll get his mobile provider to track it down when, or if it's switched on again.'

'Yes I've got it,' volunteered the Parish Clerk and passed on the details.

'Thanks,' said the DC, writing down the number. 'Do you know where he was living?'

'In his car, I believe. When I wanted him, I called him on his phone. He always answered almost straight away. I thought there must be something wrong when he didn't reply this morning.'

'How was he paid?'

'Always cash in hand.'

'Was he mugged? Did they rob him?'

'No, his wallet was still in his pocket with money in it.'

'Do you know how he died yet?' the Vicar asked, compassionately.

It looks like some sort of trauma to the head and face. Possibly somebody hit him with a blunt 'instrument'. We reckon he probably died of hypothermia though. The Post mortem will obviously identify the cause.'

'He was a big bloke. You'd have thought he'd have put up a fight.'

'It looks like he didn't get a chance to fight back; no sign of bruising on his knuckles.'

'What! A big guy like that? It must have been a giant to have done that to him,' observed the Parish Clerk.

CHAPTER FIFTEEN

24th December

'You want to tell me about it?' James asked, gently, as they drove away.

Ben had become morose, staring blankly through the windscreen, his mind overwhelmed by a crushing plethora of emotions.

'A body...Oh my God, it's come true!'

'What? What are you talking about? What's come true?'

'I dreamt that they buried Geoffery alive...that he wasn't dead. But I went and checked. Perhaps I didn't look properly. Do you think it could be him?' Ben said, looking haunted.

'No, of course not. Poor Geoffery was...trust me, the body isn't his.'

'What if a grave robber had dug his body up and... and...was disturbed?'

'Whoa, where did that come from?'

'We did it in history. Years ago they sold the bodies to the surgeons and...'

'You're letting your imagination run away with you. People leave their bodies to medical research these days. There's no market in digging up dead bodies.'

'What about that weird artist who pickles bodies and puts them on display?'

'Even he gets his bodies from people who want to be immortalised in his art work. No, put the thought out of your head. It's not Geoffery. I mean it could be anybody. Anybody can walk through there, hikers, people visiting the church, dog walkers, anybody.'

'It was a dog walker that started all this… he accused me of wrecking Geoffery's grave.'

'Why?'

'I was stood by it, holding part of the wreath and he came along and accused me of doing it. Honest James. It wasn't me. Somebody had already done it.' Ben uncharacteristically began to cry. 'Why don't they believe me?' he sobbed. 'And now a body…they'll be accusing me of killing somebody next. I've got to go,' he sobbed. 'Drop me off here.'

'Go! Go where?'

Ben was now looking around wild eyed, desperately trying to think of a plan to escape.

'London, Birmingham, France…anywhere.'

'Come on Ben. You've already seen what it's like running away. I told you about the Gangs who kidnap runaways and force them into prostitution or drug running.'

'Yeah. But I know all about that now. I can avoid that sort of thing.'

'You know nothing, believe me.'

'I'll go to Bristol then…no that's too near…Scotland. That's it, I'll go to Scotland. Nobody will find me there.'

'Come on Ben, it'll be the same anywhere you go. There are bad people out there, who will use you, hurt you.'

'But the Police...won't listen to me. It's my word against that old bloke. Who are they going to believe?'

'They'll listen to you. They'll know this bloke has got it wrong. Andy will stick up for you too.'

'As soon as I found the mess, I rang him and he came up straight away. He was talking to the old bloke and the Police while I was hiding, but the dog walker saw me and told the Police. So I ran away,' Ben said, absentmindedly repeating, the sequence of events.

'Look, Andy's bound to be concerned where you've gone? He's obviously looking for you.'

'He'll tell me to hand myself into the Police...I know he will.'

'Isn't that the best thing to do though. Clear this up and get it sorted? You don't want this hanging over your head during Christmas do you? Sometimes the anticipation of punishment is worse than the actual event.'

'I don't want to spend Christmas day in prison.'

'Oh Ben. They won't lock you up just for doing something to a grave.'

'Now even you don't believe that I didn't do it,' Ben said, despondently.

'No Ben, that is not what I meant. Now you're twisting my words. I was not saying you did it.'

'Let me out. Stop the car,' Ben demanded, reaching for the door handle.

James ignored Ben's request and continued driving. 'You can't keep running away every time somebody falsely accuses you of doing something. You need to stand your corner and prove them wrong.'

'Take me back to my Grandad's house please.'

'Not if you're going to run away again.'

'No…I…promise. I just want to sort a few things out,' he lied.

'Your Mum and Grandad will be devastated if you do.'

'Look, I've already said…'

'Sorry. OK. You have to understand that I am only trying to help you, as a friend. It's not for me to tell you what to do.'

'OK. It's just…what with the funeral and now his grave being… you know…messed up. I mean, how could anybody even think of doing that anyway?'

James decided to change the subject. 'Are you and your Mum having Christmas with your Grandad?'

'Yes. I just hope she stays off the booze that's all.'

'Well as they told both of us, now is going to be the hardest time. The lure of easy booze at Christmas is so great. Many people weaken and undo all the months of treatment. Here we are,' James said, pulling the car to a halt.

'Oh no!'

'What is it Ben?'

'Mum. Look! She's sat on the doorstep. She looks like she's been at it again,' Ben said, despondently.

At the sight of the car, Beth struggled unsteadily to her feet and staggered her way down the path towards them.

'Hello Bengie my little boy,' she slurred, putting her arms up to hug him.

Ben dodged the swaying hug. 'Mum have you been drinking again?'

'Well… I bumped into some of my school friends… Well… I couldn't refuse a drink with them could I?...it is Christmas after all.'

'You could have had a non-alcoholic drink,' Ben said, pointedly. 'See James, this is what I'm up against.'

'Beth how could you? Especially after the Clinic people had told us about the seasonal temptations.'

'Oh it's you. Hello James,' she said, wobbling over to him. 'I just had a few for old times' sake. I can resume my drying out… after Christmas. It's a test.'

'A test! What sort of test?' James demanded.

'It's a test to show them… I can give it up any… anytime I like.'

'That's the whole point of staying dry all the time. That you keep off it ALL the time. You've wasted weeks of treatment, thrown it all away. All that hard work!' James sighed, at her stupidity. 'You'll have to go back to square one again. Remember the cravings, the stomach pains, the DTs, the endless longing for a drink? Now you've got to go all through that again. You stupid woman.'

While James was berating Beth, Ben had left the two and opened his Grandad's front door turning around he shouted. 'Thanks for spoiling another Christmas Mum,' and slammed the door behind him.

'What's he saying? I was only having a Christmas drink, with my friends. Wos wrong with that?' she said, grabbing James's arm to steady herself.

'Come on,' James said, locking the car remotely. 'I think you need to sober up.'

'Wos the matter with my little boy? What have you been doing to him? I just remembered you're gay aren't you?'

'Come on Beth, we've been through this discussion before, Gay not Paedo.'

James grabbed her arm and steered her into the house. 'Let's get some coffee down you before your Dad gets back. You don't want him to see you in this state again, do you Beth?'

'My boy Bengie loves his Grandad. Why doesn't he love me anymore?' she wailed, drunkenly.

'I think this is one of the reasons,' James said, lifting a small bottle of Vodka out of her bag. 'He does, but you keep letting him and yourself down. Time to face facts Beth, you either kick the booze for good; no more little tests, or you lose Ben forever. He's stood by you time and time again. It's now time for you to become his mother, not his burden.'

James could hear Ben upstairs opening and closing draws, and sobbing.

CHAPTER SIXTEEN

24th December

Sue hadn't escaped unscathed from the M5 incident. She'd had a sleepless night as the pain in her neck and shoulders from the whiplash increased. The minor burns to her face and thick lip were more annoying than painful. Had she been vain about her appearance, she might have thought otherwise.

Consequently she had remained in bed all day, dozing fitfully until the newspaper boy disturbed her, whilst delivering the Christmas eve edition of the local paper.

She lay there for a while, wondering what the papers were reporting about the crash. Eventually her curiosity got the better of her and she made her way painfully downstairs.

The short journey to the front door took five, agonising minutes. She paused on each step, gripping the banister tightly to recover from the spasms that threatened to cause her to blackout, each footstep, jarring her neck and sending searing pain up her spine.

At last she arrived in the hallway, her pyjamas wet with the perspiration of her determination. To her dismay, the newspaper had not lodged in the letterbox but had fallen on the floor.

'Damn the kid. The only time I need it to be left in the letterbox flap, he pushes it all the way through.'

The irony of the situation hadn't escaped her, for she was constantly berating the paper boy for not pushing the newspaper all the way through; sometimes even 'staking out' his arrival and chasing him up the drive if he failed to do as he'd been told.

It took her some time to figure out how to pick up the newspaper off the hall floor. She tried several abortive, frustrating ways, until eventually deciding the only way was to put her hands against the wall and slide frontwards down on to her knees.

Having now picked up the newspaper, she had to figure out how to stand back up again. Eventually putting it in her mouth, she slowly reversed the operation to stand up. It went easier than she had anticipated.

Exhausted by her efforts she went and sat on the stairs and was pleased to see that her mission had been worthwhile. The front page headlines screamed *'Man dies in M5 Inferno.'* Quickly she read the article.

One man died and several people were injured, some with life threatening injuries in a crash on the M5 which happened last evening on the southbound carriageway near junction 12.

Police last night described the multivehicle collision on the motorway near Gloucester as a major incident.

Shortly after the initial collision fire broke out in the wreckage and quickly spread to all the vehicles caught up in the accident.

The inferno reduced vehicles to unrecognisable lumps of twisted metal and melted the tarmac road surface.

Witnesses talk of seeing a fireball as petrol tanks exploded with vehicles burning out of control.

Following the incident, Police mounted a search for a woman seen leaving the accident site, fearing she was injured. If anyone has any knowledge of the missing person they are advised to call Gloucestershire Constabulary.

There were chaotic scenes as Christmas shoppers and diverted traffic brought gridlock to the area.

The motorway is expected to remain closed for two days while resurfacing work is undertaken to repair the carriageway.

The article contained a picture showing a large number of burnt out, rusted, vehicles with numbers crudely painted on them. Sue thought that she recognised the remains of the Gravedigger's car and, on the edge of the photograph, Rupert's charred car underneath the burnt-out shell of a BMW.

'Goodbye and good riddance Rupert,' Sue said, spitefully. 'You wouldn't listen to me would you? You chose the wrong person to cross. I am now a widow, a very wealthy widow.' She smirked, uncharacteristically happy.

'Geoffery Foster, turn in your grave. That's two to me, nil points to you,' she said, in a mock French accent.

The sharp pain in her neck, reminded her that the 'fortunate' incident hadn't come without a cost. However, the thought of having a few million in the bank was a small consolation for a bit of neck pain.

'I suppose I ought to do something about my neck. Perhaps I should get a collar. I don't want to go to the hospital, just in case people tie me up with the missing woman report.

I wonder if I can get something off the internet,' she thought.

As she gazed at the picture of the carnage, she pondered if there was anything that could link her directly to the crash. 'My fingerprints would have been incinerated by the fire. Hopefully nobody there recognised me. Umm… are there any road traffic cameras in that section? Perhaps I ought to look at the internet.

What about the Taxi driver? He was too talkative for my liking. I wonder if he had one of these in-car cameras?

I might need to think about an alibi, just in case.'

With all these thoughts flooding through her head, she slowly and painfully returned to her bed and plugged in her laptop.

CHAPTER SEVENTEEN

25th December

Amidst all the family festivities, Geoffery's beneficiaries, with the unfortunate exception of Rupert, spent time variously reflecting on their changing fortunes and forthcoming inheritances. Each reassessing how their lives had changed unexpectedly for the better in such a relatively short time. Father Christmas had brought a new helper with him this year, his name, Geoffery Foster.

Tim and Carrie joined Kay at her home for a traditional, 'with all the trimmings', Christmas dinner, that she'd cooked for them.

'This might be the last time you have to do this Mum,' Tim said, his mouth full of turkey, 'because this time next year we will be holidaying in the sunshine on a beach, rather than freezing our wotsits off in a miserable British winter.'

'I'll drink to that,' Carrie said, chinking her glass against Tim's.

Kay smiled, but said nothing. She recognised that she would be unwise to assume she would be included in that arrangement.

Although she had been pleasantly staggered by the changes in her formerly self-centred son, he might yet surprise her.

Tim had, at last, become uncharacteristically concerned about somebody else other than himself. Carrie had transformed him.

Carrie had become his 'rock', and her 'episode' at the funeral had brought out a caring side of Tim's nature that Kay had never seen before.She had even influenced his Christmas present list too. For the first time in many years, Tim had no games for his Xbox. She had banned all war games.

'These are an insult to real soldiers who put their lives on the line,' she'd said, intensely scrutinising his collection. It's despicable that people actually think that war is a cosy affair. War is hell. There is no glamour in killing. Most people would shit themselves and run scared if they were shot at.

Every day while you're serving, you wonder if it's going to be your last. The worst thing is losing a mate, somebody with whom you have come through the good and bad times together. They become family. You share everything with them. I know it must be difficult for you to understand, but no more war games, OK?'

Tim had agreed. Kay was amazed. Carrie was definitely in charge.

James was slowly getting his head around being in the rat race again. This would be the first Christmas for many years when he was going to be sober and he wasn't sure about coping with the emotional baggage.

Certainly it was the first time, since he was a kid, that he shared a meal in the bosom of a family, albeit a slightly tense one.

Ben's Grandad had invited him to share an alcohol free Christmas meal with him, together with Ben and Beth at his house.

Although he was pleased that he'd been able to talk Ben out of running away, at least until after Christmas, he empathised with the mounting pressures that the boy was experiencing.

The death of a friend, accusations of desecrating his grave, the body in the burial ground, the forthcoming Police interview, the 'found' mobile phone and his mother's seemingly incurable addictions, were terrible emotional burdens.

'If you could choose absolutely anything for Christmas,' James had asked Ben, 'what would it be?'

'Anything?'

'Yes, anything.'

Ben thought for a few minutes and said, 'I want a Dad and a normal family life.'

Uncharacteristically, James swore 'Shit! You don't want much do you, old man?'

But Ben's naïve desire rekindled James' own childhood dreams of having a normal family life.

Orphaned at an early age, he had spent most of his childhood in 'Public' schools and felt deprived of the love and joy he assumed all children received at home.

He 'choked' when he thought about the emotional gap in his own life that he shared with Ben.

Composing himself he said, 'I'm sorry, Ben. You and I both share that dream. On a practical level, what can I buy you for Christmas?'

Ben had thought about it for a moment, 'Would it be possible to have a rucsac.'

So James had bought him the rucsac. He just hoped that it wouldn't be used as an enabler to run away and escape from all the problems in which he appeared to be 'drowning'.

James wondered what he should do with his inheritance. Did he want to go back to his former social set or not. If he did, he would have to forget the past and start again by finding some real friends, rather than those superficial parasites that helped him spend his money and then deserted him when he needed help following Sebastian's death. He wasn't sure.

He wasn't sure about a lot of things, including the future of his own health. Would his body allow him to enjoy the legacy, after abusing it for so many years? Would he be strong enough to stay alcohol free?

In spite of all the angst, Ben had a bonus year for Christmas presents- Geoffery's early present of a couple of bikes, the rucsac from James and a light weight tent from his Grandad. His Mum tried to make up for her relapse and 'fall from grace' by buying him a sleeping bag. Materially, he was fortunate. Emotionally he was less fortunate.

Beth kept herself busy doing the household domestics; food preparation, table laying, washing up, all the while trying to keep her demons away, still fighting the craving for a drink.

Andy had a traditional family Christmas with the excited Amy getting more fun out of pulling the paper off the presents than the presents themselves. Molly slept through the excitement in spite of being dressed in a Christmas baby-grow. Helen had a bottle of Eau de Toilette in a posh box. Andy got the cold shoulder.

Sue spent a lonely and miserable time dosing herself up on painkillers to relieve the agony of her whiplash injuries. She managed to struggle to the kitchen and made herself some soup, which she duly spilt down herself carrying the tray to her chair.

Rupert and Joanne missed Christmas altogether.

CHAPTER EIGHTEEN

26th December

Sue heard the Boxing Day edition of the local newspaper being delivered and was anxious to read of any updates about the Crash.

She slowly eased herself out of bed and carefully, putting on her white towelling dressing gown, painfully shuffled, stiff shouldered, downstairs to the front door.

She was relieved to see that the newspaper boy had ignored her instructions this time and the paper was stuck by the flap of the letterbox, so she didn't have to go through the convoluted procedure of the previous occasion.

She slowly hobbled her way into the kitchen and taking her time, sat down carefully at the kitchen table. She decided to spread the newspaper over the table to read it, hoping this method wouldn't strain her still painful neck.

Unfortunately, as she did so, she knocked over an empty champagne flute that she had been using to celebrate her newly acquired millionaire status. Although she'd struggled to open the bottle, she had been determined to celebrate whilst jubilantly fantasizing about her new life as a rich widow.

'Bugger,' she said, as it rolled off the table and shattered on the ceramic kitchen floor tiles. 'I hope that's not an omen.'

The front page headlines caught her eye '*Body found in Hill Cemetery*'; with concern she quickly read the article.

Police cordoned off Churchup Hill on Christmas Eve following the discovery of a man's body. The man, who has not been formally identified, is believed to be that of a Gravedigger who had been working in the Parish burial grounds. Police are treating the death as suspicious until the results of a post-mortem examination are known. Night time temperatures in the area were reported to have plunged to minus six degrees and there is speculation that the man could have died of hypothermia.

'So the Gravedigger died! Oh dear what a pity,' she said, callously. 'Well, I only hit him on the head. He was alive when I left him.' Sue reassured herself. 'I didn't kill him. Well every cloud has a silver lining. At least he can't identify me now,' she added, coldheartedly.

A sudden thought came to her, 'Drat, what about that photo he took on his mobile though? Perhaps it didn't come out or perhaps his phone went down the drain after all. Damn, that's an irritation I could do without. Well, what's done is done. As soon as I get Rupert's money I intend to leave the country anyway.'

Further down the page she discovered a small article entitled '*Vandalised Grave.*'

Police are appealing for witnesses to help identify vandals who desecrated a grave in the Churchup Hill Parish burial ground. A teenager is currently helping

Police with their enquiries. A representative of the Parish Council was not available for comment.

'Well, well. This is my lucky Christmas.'

She was buzzing with excitement. She couldn't believe her luck. She had not been linked to either the death of the Gravedigger or the vandalism.

'I guess sometime soon I should go to the Police and report Rupert missing,' she mused.

However her mood soon changed as she turned to page two and read the headlines *'Christmas Crash victim identified.'*

*Police today said the man killed in the pre-Christmas M5 crash was a married 35 year old Salesman from Stoke on Trent. His name has not been released until his family have been notified…..*she threw the paper down angrily without reading anything more, her dreams of inheriting her husband's legacy all but disappearing.

'If Rupert's not dead, where the hell is he? Why hasn't anybody contacted me?' she fumed. 'Even if he was injured, somebody should have called me as I'm his next of kin? Unless of course he isn't badly injured and then they wouldn't need to call me,' she mused. 'Damn it!'

She chided herself for celebrating too soon.

'I'll have to ring some hospitals to see if I can track him down,' she said, standing up.

As she did so, she stood on a shard of glass from the flute which cut the sole of her foot.

'Shit!' she said, quickly sitting down again and pulled the glass out of her foot, the hem of her white dressing gown now stained red.

Carefully avoiding any more glass, she hobbled across the kitchen leaving a series of bloody footprints.

After wrapping a tea towel around her bleeding foot, she set up her laptop and logged on to the internet, quickly searching online phone directories for the telephone numbers of nearby hospitals in Gloucester, Cheltenham, Stroud and the specialist hospital dealing with head injuries and burns, Frenchay in Bristol.

CHAPTER NINETEEN

28th December

Because of the severity of their injuries, Rupert and Joanne had been taken from the crash site to hospital by Air ambulance.

Rupert had been put in a controlled coma because of his head injuries which had caused swelling and a small bleed to his brain. In addition to multiple bruising, he also sustained a fractured collar bone, where he had been suspended upside down by his seatbelt. However, after a few days when the brain swelling had reduced he was brought out of the coma.

'Where am I?' What happened?'

'You were in a crash. Don't try to talk,' the nurse instructed.

'Crash...crash! We...we were going home. Where's Joanne?' he asked, frantically. 'Where is she? Is she alright?'

'She's being cared for in a separate room. You can see her shortly, but first you need to rest. You were badly hurt yourself.'

'No, I'm alright.' Rupert tried to sit up and immediately passed out from the pain.

The following day, he eventually convinced the medical team, that he was strong enough to go and see Joanne. Carefully transferring to a wheelchair he was wheeled into the intensive care ward to see her.

Joanne was lying in bed, unconscious. She was very pale and had a rash of small cuts across her face.

She was connected by tubes and wires to all manner of medical paraphernalia; drips and drains dangling from assorted stainless steel hangers.

There were sensors attached all over her body relaying her vital signs to a monitor above her bed. The display showed lots of different coloured wiggly lines that meant nothing to Rupert.

As they arrived in the room she was being attended to by a Doctor and Nurse.

'Oh my God! Jo,' he said, devastated. His mind numbed by the shock of seeing her lifeless figure. 'Is she…is she going to be alright?'

'She's in a serious, but stable condition. We've put her in an induced coma and as you can see she's on a life support machine,' the Doctor said. 'I'm pleased to see you up and about though. I'm Doctor McFady, trauma specialist. How do you feel now?'

'I'm a bit sore, bruised all over. But what about Jo?'

'Joanne appears to have received significant impact injuries. I'm afraid as well as significant head trauma there are crush injuries to her back and pelvis,' the Consultant explained.

Rupert manoeuvred his wheelchair to the side of her bed and gently touched her hand, gazing forlornly at Joanne's unconscious figure.

'I understand she was initially trapped, pinned between the seat and the steering wheel. Is that correct?' the doctor quizzed.

'I don't know, I was knocked out. I didn't know anything about it until I came around in the ward yesterday. What day it is?'

'Well I'm sorry, but you missed Christmas this year. It's a couple of days after boxing day, it's December the 28th.'

'God, have I been out that long?' Rupert asked, trying to comprehend the lost days.

'Your…young lady? Your wife?'

'Girlfriend.'

'Your girlfriend and you are lucky to be alive. The Highways Agency people were first on the scene and pulled you out, just before the whole lot caught fire and exploded. Somebody up there was looking after you.'

The hairs on Rupert's neck stood up at the thought that Geoffery could still be looking after him, from beyond the grave. He shook his head to clear the thought.

'You mentioned something about her back. Oh my God. Is she going to be…will she be able to walk?' Rupert asked, frightened of hearing the prognosis.

'We don't know at this stage. There is too much swelling in that area to be able to assess the damage properly.'

'Oh God!'

'We aren't sure about the baby yet either.'

'Baby! What baby?'

'Didn't you know? She is about four months pregnant.'

'No I didn't. She hadn't told me. I knew she'd put on weight but…,' Rupert continued, completely flummoxed by the news. 'What happens while she's in a coma? Will the baby be OK?'

'We'll monitor the baby as best we can. As you can see she's connected to a lot of monitors.' It's up to her now to fight for herself and the baby. We just have to watch and wait I'm afraid.'

'It's all my fault,' Rupert said, welling up. 'If I hadn't stopped, none of this would have happened.'

'Don't get blaming yourself. From what I gather you just got caught up in somebody else's accident.'

'Yes but…'

'She needs you to be strong for her now.'

'But she's the strong one. She's my 'rock.'

'Now it's your turn to be her 'rock'. She will need your support.'

'How long will she be like this?'

'It's difficult to tell with head injuries. It's likely to be some time. We'll manage her coma and see how it goes.'

'Is there anything I can do?'

'Not really, unless you're a religious man and you might like to say a prayer for her and the baby.'

CHAPTER TWENTY

28th December

Rupert had spent an hour at Joanne's bedside holding her hand, talking gently to her, telling her how much he loved her; when he felt his wheelchair move and assumed a nurse had come to take him back to his ward.

But the voice from behind him made his heart miss a beat; his worst nightmare had just stepped back into his life.

'Hello Rupert, you survived the crash then?' Sue said, 'I bet you're pleased to see me?'

Rupert froze, the icy hand of fear clutching his heart.

Sue had battled through layers of unhelpful NHS bureaucracy but eventually tracked Rupert and Joanne down to Frenchay Hospital.

'Nasty little crash wasn't it?'

'What are you doing here?' he struggled to say, his mouth dry with fear.

'I've come to visit my sick husband of course,' she said, with false concern. 'It was a terrible accident. Unfortunately you're lucky to be alive.'

'Was it…was it you…that that caused it? he stammered.'

'Oh you flatter me too much,' she said, feigning false modesty. 'I can't take credit for planning that mayhem,' she said, spinning his wheelchair around to face her and fixing him with a medusa stare.

Rupert looked away, avoiding her malevolent eyes.

'I couldn't orchestrate something as dramatic as that, as much as I would have liked to. That is, I don't think I did. But, then again, I was at the scene and pleased to see that you were both hurt,' she said, maliciously.

'What a pity you survived, I felt sure you'd died in the fire.'

'The Highways Agency guys got us out,' he replied, irrationally feeling he had to justify the miracle of their survival.

'Shame,' she said. 'I quite liked the idea of being a rich widow. Still, we are married, so how is my husband? Will you mend?'

'I'd prefer not to talk to you, if you don't mind,' he said, bizarrely. Years of her bullying conditioned him to still be respectful of her.

'Mind! Of course I mind,' she said, leaning down and shouting angrily in his face.' I've come all this way to see you and you try to shun me. Well, think again.'

Rupert's planned stance to be Joanne's rock and to be strong against the stresses and strains of the world evaporated. Instead he resorted to type and sat meekly by, wondering what to do.

'I see you went to HIS funeral,' she said, regaining her composure.

'Yes, of course. He was my Uncle.'

'And you sent him some flowers.'

Rupert sat subdued, wondering what she was getting at.

'What did you say on your card? Oh yes, I remember. *Thank you for giving me a new start,* wasn't it?'

'How did you know that?'

'Wouldn't you like to know? So, is this the new start you had in mind? In hospital, visiting an unconscious girlfriend?' Sue laughed wickedly.

Rupert grabbed Joanne's hand again, hoping to draw some strength from her mere presence.

'Well I suppose his funeral was another good thing that happened this Christmas.' Sue continued.

'That's a horrible thing to say.'

'Not if you were falsely blamed for attempted murder,' she said, furiously. 'Your dear Uncle wasn't so clever after all, was he? Even his wet nurse couldn't support his lies. He turned queen's evidence against him. Now what are you going to do without Uncle Geoffery to protect you? Eh?' she said, inches away from his face.

At the sound of Sue's raised voice Sister King came into the room.

'Is everything OK?' she asked, looking at Rupert for confirmation.

Rupert felt Sue's nails digging into his shoulder. 'Yes,' he said, unconvincingly.

'Well you certainly don't look it. I'm sorry but Mr Screen is still very weak. I think you'd better go. He was seriously injured and has only just regained consciousness. Mrs…?'

'Mrs Williams-Screen, I'm his wife.'

'Estranged wife,' Rupert added, bravely shrugging off Sue's hand.

'I see…I think in that case you'd better leave Mrs Screen, before I call security.'

'It's Williams Screen, if you don't mind,' she said, indignantly, turning on her heel. 'I'll see you again Rupert. Be sure of that.'

'Not if I see you first,' the Sister whispered, as she ushered her out of the room.

CHAPTER TWENTY ONE

31st December

A fine rain was starting to fall as the group of Taxi drivers huddled together, outside Gloucester Train station, waiting for the next train to discharge its passengers.

'Well at least, this rain ought to help us get a few fares at last.'

'Yes, hopefully. I need to pay off the credit card bill from me holiday.'

'Ere, you were a lucky sod getting time off over Christmas.' Chris said, enviously, pulling his collar up against the biting wind.

'Yeah, lovely hot Tenerife sunshine.' Ian replied, rolling his sleeve up and showing off his tanned forearm.

'How was it over there?'

'Bloody hotter than here,' he said, stamping his feet. 'All inclusive; didn't get me wallet out once.'

'Always were a stingy sod,' the other joked. 'I tell you what though, you were in the right place. It was bloody chaos back here with the motorway being closed.'

'Oh yeah, I forgot about that. What was the final death toll in the end?'

'Fortunately it was only one poor sod. It could have been a lot worse,' the other replied reflectively. 'Here, that reminds me. Did you pick up a fare from down by the M5 just shortly after it happened?'

'Yeah, miserable cow. No tip and face like thunder. Had muddy shoes too, messed up my carpet. I had to clean it before my next fare.'

'Huh! Typical.'

'She was whinging about difficulties getting a signal on her phone and having to wait for a long time.'

'Well what did she expect? It was gridlock. Stupid woman,' the other replied, supportively.

'Oh and she moaned about being very cold. The bitch even ordered me, didn't ask, but ordered me to put the heater full on. I was tempted to sling her out.'

'Too true. I would have.'

'Why do you ask?'

'The Police were trying to find her or somebody like her down there.'

'Don't surprise me. She was evil.'

'No. She wasn't on the run or anything. They were concerned that she had been injured and might have collapsed somewhere.'

'No, she looked alright to me. Didn't say a lot apart from ordering me to turn the heater up and telling me where she wanted to go.'

'Perhaps you should give them a shout to let them know then.'

'What for?'

'Because you know we bin having a bit more help from them recently sorting out the late night drunks problem.'

'Yeah, I'll get control to call them. They'll have the address I took her to.'

Several days later the Taxi control rang the Police control via the non-urgent incident telephone number 101 and the details were recorded.

CHAPTER TWENTY TWO

3rd January

The apprehension of the forthcoming Police interview spoilt Ben's Christmas, in spite of Andy's reassurance that it would simply eliminate him from their enquiries.

But as the date drew nearer Ben became more and more anxious. To add to his worries his Mother's inability to conqueror her addiction problems meant that he could possibly be taken into care.

Finally, Ben could handle the pressure no longer, with the visit to the Police station scheduled for the following day, he decided to take a positive course of action.

Ben decided to run away.

He put James' dire warning of getting tangled up with evil people to the back of his mind. 'After all,' he argued, when he'd run away before, nothing happened to him then. No, this was the right course of action,' he concluded.

He chose his moment when his Grandad was out. His Mother was already back in the addiction clinic again.

He contemplated leaving a letter to reassure them that he would be alright and not to worry, but decided to telephone them instead, for he still had the phone he'd picked up from the burial ground and it appeared still to be working.

Carefully putting his Christmas present money in an old wallet that his Grandad and given him, Ben stuffed it into his back trouser pocket.

He filled his new Rucsac with his new sleeping bag and lightweight tent. Ben had naively planned to live in the tent, rather than run the risk of living in squats. Thus, he'd persuaded himself, he'd be addressing one of James' warnings about exposing himself to some weirdoes who occasionally inhabit squats.

With his clothes and some food finally packed, he shouldered his rucsac, caught a bus into Gloucester and walked over to the nearby rail station, hoping not to be seen by any of his friends.

On arriving at the station he was surprised by the number of uniformed British Transport Police on duty.

'Had somebody already alerted them to his intention to run away?' he wondered. He was even more apprehensive when one of them approached him.

'That Rucsac looks mighty heavy,' said PC Hall, in a kindly voice, showing genuine interest. 'Going hiking?'

'Um, yes,' Ben said, self-consciously.

'Duke of Edinburgh or Scout Hike?'

'A…Scouts,' Ben replied, apprehensively, expecting him to ask for his name next.

'How many miles?'

'Um…' Ben struggled to think of a sensible distance.

'Ten, twenty?' the Policeman suggested, aware that he was causing the boy some angst.

Ben recalled the Scouts Cotswold Marathon hike that he did the previous February and said, 'thirteen miles.'

'Thirteen miles! with a heavy rucsac like that. Better you than me. Anyway best of luck,' he said, walking away, suddenly responding to his radio.

Relieved, Ben moved quickly to the ticket office just inside the station entrance and got his one way ticket for the 1246 train to Paddington.

'In just under 2 hours I'll be in London away from all my problems,' he thought.

He bought some sweets and drinks from the café for the journey and moved away from the group of Policemen on to the long platform 2.

At nearly 2,000 feet in length, it was the second longest railway platform in Great Britain, he read. Slightly shorter than Colchester. Originally designed to handle two Inter-City 125 trains at the same time. Because of the track layout, trains have to reverse out to pick up the main line again.

Time seemed to drag as Ben waited for the train to arrive. Nervously he kept looking at the arrivals board, frightened that somebody would see him and thwart his plans.

Eventually the station speaker announced the arrival of the 1246 to London Paddington and the train glided alongside the long platform, its wheels squealing as if protesting at the interruption in its journey.

Along the whole length of the approaching train, people already had head and shoulders out of the windows, holding exterior door handles. Finally the train stopped and the doors burst open, haemorrhaging a noisy crowd of football supporters.

Ben stepped back against the corrugated wall to get out of the way of the jostling crowd. Out of the corner of his eye he could see the Police already starting to shepherd the group out of the station.

There were very few passengers boarding the train and Ben quickly found a seat with no-one around him.

He eased the heavy rucsac off his shoulder pushed it over to the window seat and sat next to it.

After a few minutes, he heard the multiple slamming of carriage doors and the train reversed its route out of the station, quickly building up speed.

Ben relaxed. He had done it. He had escaped. A new chapter beckoned.

The train rattled over Horton Road level crossing, past motorists and cyclists impatiently waiting for the barriers to rise, a frustration that he too had experienced here many times before.

The train threaded its way through the closely packed housing estates bordering the railway line, the meandering route, giving him tantalising glimpses into the inside of people's houses and gardens. Although it was the New Year, most houses still had their Christmas decorations up.

As they left the city, he caught sight of his own home and the alleyways along which he regularly cycled.

The roof of the new Scout Hut that Geoffery had bought and equipped, sped by, the sight of which reminded him of one of the reasons for making his escape.

Seeing it, was like a slap in the face. His eyes brimmed and he swallowed hard to get his emotions under control as the Ticket Inspector, a short rounded, bright faced woman demanded 'tickets please.'

'Is that your rucsac, son?'

'Yes,' he said, protectively putting his hand to it.

'Would you mind putting it in the luggage area please?' Noticing his moist eyes, she asked, concerned. 'Are you OK son?'

'Yes,' he said, unconvincingly.

'Is there anything wrong?'

'I...it's...my friend,' he muttered tearfully, 'he died recently,' he was surprised to hear himself divulging about Geoffery's death.

'Oh, I am sorry,' she said, with genuine sympathy.

Over the next ten minutes, he confided everything to the Ticket Inspector who had sat down on the opposite side of the small table and listened compassionately while he told her about his miserable Christmas and New Year.

'So are you running away?' she asked, bluntly.

'What else can I do?' Ben said, helplessly.

'It sounds like your Mum still needs you. And what about your Grandad? How old are you?'

'Fourteen.'

'Fourteen! You're at a difficult age. I'm sure that you find life is very confusing at the moment. Full of contradictions and adults with double standards.'

'Say that again.'

'I wish my son was still there for me. You might think I'm making it up, but I can assure you it's true. My son ran away, just like you. I was devastated; it was then that I discovered the real, painful, meaning of a broken heart. It was awful.'

'Oh! I'm sorry...' Ben said, empathising with her sadness.

'The next time I saw him, he was on a mortuary slab,' she continued, avoiding Ben's wide eyed gaze. 'He'd got in with the wrong crowd. He was only eighteen.' She turned her gaze back to Ben. 'Just think about those who love you son. Sometimes it might not feel like it, but you are loved, believe me. Give them a chance to show it.'

'I know but...I can't take any more of this hassle.'

Suddenly the public address system burst into life and a voice requested that the Ticket Inspector should return to the buffet car.

'Sorry son, I've got to go. But have a think about what I said. How will your actions affect other people too? Best of luck on whatever you decide.' She turned and left.

Ben was now even more confused and less confident that he was doing the right thing.

Shortly after, the train pulled into Stonehouse station and on impulse he grabbed his rucsac and got off.

Surprised at his own actions, he watched as the train pulled out, his carefully thought out plans now in tatters. He sat on a cold station bench for a while and reviewed what he was going to do. Eventually he decided to go back to face the music and cope with whatever else would happen. James and Andy would help him, he felt sure.

Having made the decision, he strode purposefully to the ticket office and asked for a ticket back to Gloucester, but as he reached into his back pocket to pay, he realised his wallet wasn't there. His back pocket was empty. His wallet and money had gone.

In frantic desperation, he looked around him on the floor and apologising to the ticket agent, raced back to where he'd sat on the bench. Nothing. On the station platform where he'd got off the train, again nothing.

His heart sank. 'It must have fallen out on the train or perhaps it was stolen,' he thought.

He remembered being jostled by some people in the crowd as he was waiting to board the train. Perhaps it had been stolen there.

Misery upon misery. Would nothing ever go right for him? He sat on the bench, head down, close to tears and wondered what to do.

'What would Andy suggest?' he asked himself. He knew if he rang him, he would come and pick him up, So too would his Grandad. James would have done it as well, but he was back in the clinic.

'No, I'll do this myself,' he said, determinedly. He knew that the Cotswold Way long distance footpath ran nearby and he calculated he had time to walk back home and nobody would be any wiser of his aborted plans to run away.

If he wanted, he could even set up camp on Churchup hill and pretend that's what he was going to do all along. He warmed to the idea, shouldered his heavy rucsac and left the small station in better spirits, heading for the nearby Doverow hill.

CHAPTER TWENTY THREE

3rd January

The office walls of the Traffic Team assigned to the M5 'Road Death Investigation' were covered in scores of photos and crash sequence drawings. Each one carefully annotated and referenced back to a master plan. Each one recording in photographic horror the terrible aftermath of the collision and inferno.

As the investigation continued, the two Policemen, Collision Investigator John Sparrow and Senior Investigating Officer, Sergeant Graham Fredericks were processing evidence in the busy headquarters building in Cheltenham.

'Damn,' said John, studying an email.

'What's up?' his colleague asked, looking away from his own screen.

'Just had an email from South Wales Police. You know that unclaimed, burnt out Polo, registered to an owner in Gwent?'

'You mean the one we identified by the Vehicle Identification Number?'

'Yes, that's the one. The owner claims to have sold it to a big Polish bloke he met in a Tesco's car park.'

'Did he get a name?'

'No name, but he showed them a receipt with a squiggle of a signature on it.'

'How do we know he's not lying and it was really him?'

'The guy was in hospital recovering from an appendix operation. South Wales checked it out… and it's right.'

'OK, so we're looking for somebody else then. You sure there was nobody in the wreckage of that Polo?'

'The Fire and Rescue team say not. There was only one poor sod caught up in the fire and it wasn't him. Miraculously everybody else was rescued before the whole lot went up.'

'Then if he wasn't killed, are we sure he wasn't injured and ran off somewhere?'

'No. The injured were all accounted for, with the exception of that one woman who wandered off. I guess we need to track her down…Otherwise I've got the list here which ties everybody else to a vehicle.'

'So nobody reports seeing a big guy at the scene?'

'No. I've checked all the witness statements again.'

'So, where is this big Polish bloke then?'

'Silly question, but what if he wasn't driving it?'

'OK, but how did his car get there? Did it just materialise?'

'Stolen, perhaps?'

'In that case, why hasn't he reported it?'

'Perhaps he's an 'illegal' and doesn't want to get involved with authority.'

'Let's get some 'eyes on the ground' with the patrol guys to see if they can spot a likely candidate.'

'But we don't even know that he came from this area do we?'

'No, but at least it's a start.'

Right. So what are we going to put on the bulletin to alert the troops?'

'Wanted in connection with enquiries into the RTC on the M5 on 23rd December an Eastern European, possibly Polish. Aged?'

'About 50.'

'Height?'

'The bloke reckoned over 6 foot 6.'

'Build?'

'Very big, reckons he was built like a brick...house.'

'OK. Any distinguishing features?'

'Not that we're aware of. So we're going to the press with this as well as the internal alert bulletin?'

'Yeah might as well. Somebody might know him and tie him up with the Polo.'

Together they had successfully solved many difficult cases by simply revisiting all aspects of an accident several times using the 'Caseboard technique'.

'Remind me again why we're looking for him?'

'One witness reckons it was the Polo pulling out from the hard shoulder with no lights on that triggered the pile up.'

'Let's put it up on the whiteboard then.'

'Right. So sequence 2, Polo pulls out, no lights,' he wrote on the board.

'Sequence 2? Surely you mean Sequence 1?'

'No. Sequence 1 is, when did the Polo pull on to the hard shoulder and switch its lights off?'

'Right, I see where you're coming from.'

'But did the Discovery driver, who avoided the Polo, see who was driving it?'

'No. He reckons he was too busy avoiding the collision to see who was driving.'

'Right. So avoiding rear-ending the Polo that's Sequence 3… Sequence 4 and onward are the multiple collisions,' which together they meticulously recorded.

CHAPTER TWENTY FOUR

3rd January

It was a beautiful winter afternoon, as, suitably attired in a windproof fleece, beanie hat and gloves, Ben started his walk back to Churchup. The clear blue sky and the warm sun helped lift his spirits.

Thanks to the brief chat with the Ticket Inspector, he was now in a more positive frame of mind and had clarified some of the confusion in his head.

Furthermore, he'd decided he was going to attend his appointment at the Police station after all, and would contact Andy later to reassure him of his intentions.

However, as he sweated his way up the steep slope from the train station to the top of Doverow Hill, he was having second thoughts about his ambitious plans. He wasn't sure walking back was a good idea after all. But at least he wasn't cold anymore.

Although he reckoned he was pretty fit, because of his competitive Mountain Bike riding, he had packed to camp, not to walk. The rucsac was far too heavy for his intended walk back home, which he estimated to be about 23 miles and over some very hilly terrain.

Stopping to 'catch his breath' he reassessed his options.- either to go back to the station and ring for a lift or carry on.

The easiest option, he decided, was not to get anyone else involved. So he tightened up his shoulder straps and carried on.

Trying to justify his decision to himself, he'd use it as a training hike, for the 18mile Silver route, on the Scouts Cotswold Marathon due to be held the following month.

He had no qualms about navigating his way back home without a map, because he knew he could follow well marked and established Long Distance footpaths. These were comprehensively waymarked by a series of painted Acorn symbols, one of the things Andy had repeatedly told them at Scouts.

'Acorns on the signposts, diamonds on the map,' was his training mantra.

Consequently, from the top of Doverow Hill he linked up with a section of the 104 mile Cotswold Way that would lead him to Crickley Hill Country Park, near Gloucester. Then he would join a short section of the Gloucestershire Way which would take him to his Grandad's house in Churchup.

From the frost coated Doverow Hill he walked through winter chilled Standish Woods, near the undulating BMX mud track, where he had ridden many times.

On the other side of the wood, he passed through a car park, and found the topograph he was looking for. Wiping the rime off the miniature brass dome with his gloved hand, he studied the detail on the circular plaque. The surrounding landscape had been mapped and recorded, directional arrows radiating from the centre of topograph indicating the names and distances of nearby hills and villages.

He crunched his way across the still frozen grass to the 'trig point' on Haresfield Beacon, leaving a trail of footprints in the frost coated fields. Here he took in the spectacular panorama of the Severn Vale, the wide sandbanks of the meandering River Severn at low tide, warmly lit by the low sun.

His route took him along a brief green lane and road section, through narrow lanes passing a memorial stone commemorating the siege of Gloucester in 1643 and then on through the long deserted Cotswold stone quarries of Scottsquar Hill near Edge common.

From there, the route took him down into a series of pretty valleys, which were closely associated with the ancient wool and cloth mills, although Ben was unaware of the historical significance of the buildings he passed.

The light had now gone from the clear January sky, as he entered the picturesque and historic village of Painswick.

He decided it was time to stop for a much needed break and he found a bench in the ancient fifteenth century St Mary's Churchyard facing the magnificent 174ft tall spire.

He slipped the heavy rucsac off his aching shoulders and immediately felt the chill on his back, his thick fleece damp with perspiration.

Digging into the side pockets of his new rucsac, he quickly found the chocolate bars and tetra pack drink he'd bought at the station.

As he ate his snack quickly, he took in his surroundings and couldn't help but notice the amazing conical shaped topiary, to which each of the churchyard yew trees had been treated.

As artistic and pretty as it was, he couldn't imagine why anybody would want to spend time on such a thankless task, trimming ninety nine trees to look all the same.

Having walked many hours through the tranquil countryside, he was very conscious of the busy rush hour traffic behind him, as it made its way through the narrow Bisley street. The ancient road, with several overhanging buildings, was ill-suited to modern day traffic where few drivers observed the 20 mph speed restriction.

Deciding to get back to the solitude of the countryside, he cut his rest short as the chill of the evening crept over him.

Lifting his heavy pack on to his sore shoulders, he strode off down the main street, using his head torch to help him find the 'acorns' leading him to Painswick Beacon.

His journey continued up a road and then, mercifully, cut away from the traffic and went across to the Painswick golf course.

Slowly he puffed his way up to the high point of the quarry scarred Painswick Beacon. He recalled somebody telling him that these quarries had provided the mellow Cotswold stone from which many of the town's beautiful buildings had been built.

Here he stopped in a fog of his exertions, as his breath clouded around him in the still air.

It was so quiet here. It was as if he was all alone in the world. Strangely, he wasn't scared. He felt totally relaxed, seduced by the beauty of it all. It was a scene straight off a Christmas card. The trees fringing the greens were white coated, as if it had snowed or someone had sprinkled icing sugar on them.

However, the freezing temperatures encouraged him not to tarry for too long and he was soon walking across the second part of the sprawling golf course, now bathed in moonlight.

He carried on across the frozen tracks through the woods to Prinknash Corner; near to the former retreat of the Benedictine Monks at Prinknash Abbey.

From there he found his way through the dark Brockworth woods and onto the top of Coopers Hill, known locally as the 'cheese roll'.

The hill is famous throughout the world for its annual Spring bank holiday Cheese Rolling competitions, where a Double Gloucester cheese is rolled down the very steep 'one in one' hill, pursued by competitors, who throw caution to the wind and, out of control, run after the bouncing cheese. Understandably there are usually casualties to this traditional 19th century event, the prize of which is a seven pound cheese and the glory of winning.

Ben had seen the 'cheese roll' many times, but had never been tempted to take up the 'crazy' challenge, in spite of riding down similar terrains on his mountain bike.

After descending by the side of Coopers Hill, Ben followed the undulating frozen forest tracks through Buckholt woods to Birdlip. Where, as he skirted the edge of the wood, just above Witcombe, he caught glimpses of the shimmering lights of Gloucester.

As the distance and terrain started taking its toll on his tired legs he stopped again on the rocky outcrop known as 'the Peak' to gaze down at the Witcombe reservoirs painted silver in the moonlight. The creeping cold again foreshortening his brief rest here.

He was exhausted as he dragged his weary feet through the car park at Barrow Wake viewpoint and crossed the busy A417 road near the Air Balloon public house.

His morale was starting to fail, as was his headtorch. He had been walking for eight, long, tiring hours and his resolve was crumbling. The temperature was continuing to drop, as he climbed yet another hill.

Carefully planting his feet, methodically, one in front of the other, on the icy, heavily rutted paths through a small Chestnut wood, he eventually emerged on to the chilly common at Crickley Hill country park.

He paused and took in the magnificent panorama at his feet, the lights of Brockworth and Hucclecote and in the distance Gloucester.

On the horizon to his right, he could see the distant spine of the Malvern Hills, bathed in moonlight, like some gigantic slumbering dinosaur.

Looking back along the wooded curve of the escarpment, where he had travelled, he acknowledged the reason for his tiredness, and at the same time feeling a great sense of achievement.

In front of him at last, almost within touching distance his gaol, the two red and one white light that marked Churchup Hill. But it was a further 7 miles away. Tonight however, for him, it was a hill too far.

'That's it,' he said, to himself, 'I've had enough. I'm camping here tonight.'

Glancing at his watch he noted that it was nine o'clock.

He decided to erect his new tent near a rocky outcrop called the Devil's Table where he could pick up the Gloucestershire Way in the morning. Being just off the usual tourist route, it would ensure he wouldn't be seen by late night dog walkers and courageous courting couples.

Plumbing the depths of his energy reserves, he erected his tent and crawled wearily into it, quickly 'shaking out' his new three seasons sleeping bag, to 'aerate' the compressed down. He wasted no time in sliding into its embracing warmth.

He couldn't be bothered to light his small gas stove, so he ate some of the cereal bars and as his water bottle was frozen, he drank another carton of squash.

Remembering that he needed to make some calls he got out the mobile he'd found and rang his Grandad and Andy.

'Hello Grandad.'

'Ben?'

'Yeah it's me.'

'Oh, I was just starting to get a bit concerned.'

'I'm OK. I'm ringing to tell you I've gone camping. I'll be back in the morning.'

'You haven't forgotten that you're going to the Police station in the morning have you?'

No, I haven't forgotten. I'll be back by then.'

'You make sure you are. Well, you've picked a right night for it, haven't you? It's flipping cold even indoors. Anyway have a nice camp and I'll see you in the morning.'

'Yeah, thanks Grandad. Goodnight.'

'Goodnight son, take care.'

Ben cleared the call and immediately punched in Andy's number. After a few rings Andy answered.

'Hello Andy, it's me, Ben. I'm camping with my new tent and sleeping bag tonight. But I'll be back in the morning to go to the Police station.'

'You haven't changed your mind then?' Andy asked, cautiously.

If only Andy knew how close he had come to breaking the appointment.

'No I haven't changed my mind.' Ben said, trying to sound enthusiastic.

'So I'll pick you up from your Grandad's house in the morning, OK?'

'Yes, I'll be there.'

'Whose phone are you using?'

'It's the phone that I found in the burial ground. Perhaps I should hand it in when we go tomorrow. What do you reckon?'

'I think it's a good idea. Goodnight then Ben.'

'Goodnight.'

Meanwhile, in the mobile phone company control room an alarm sounded, alerting technicians that a phone they had been hoping to trace had been used.

The Technician quickly informed the phone company Police liaison duty. 'Sorry, had a problem with the data. We couldn't get an accurate location, but it's definitely in the Gloucester area. However, we can tell you the numbers called if that's any use?'

'Yes please. At least that's a start.'

The technician gave him the information.

'I'm going home in a minute. I'll pass that on to Gloucestershire Constabulary in the morning. Thanks. If it comes on line again, see if you can get a better location.'

'Yeah, will do.'

As Ben was about to turn the phone off his curiosity got the better of him. He decided to have a look to see if there were any photos on it, that might help to identify the owner.

Choosing the 'camera roll' option, he was disappointed to see that there were very few photos on it. However the most recent one showed an out of focus picture of a person. It took him a few moments to see that it was the face of a woman.

Although it was slightly blurred, she was obviously not happy. The angry look in her blood red eyes, he assumed from the flash, made her look demonic.

'God, that's scary,' he said, peering at the small screen. 'Hang on! What's that in the corner of the picture? That's…that's the cross I made for Geoffery. When was this taken?'

Just as he went to check, the battery went flat, before he could study the timestamp against it.

'Oh my God! If that's what I think it is, it could be the person who attacked the Gravedigger. In which case this…is…his phone.'

Ben threw the phone down as if it was on fire.

'It's a dead man's phone,' he said, staring at it in horror.

CHAPTER TWENTY FIVE

4th January

Ben was awake early the following morning, for, in spite of the fatigue of the hike, he'd spent a restless night thinking about the picture on the phone and what to do with it.

As he opened his eyes he could see a fine frosty rime on the inside of the tent where his breath had frozen, but apart from having a cold nose, the new sleeping bag had kept him snug.

It was another cold morning as he emerged from his tent, the sun just lighting up the cloudless eastern sky.

The grass around him was stiff from Jack Frost's nocturnal visit and the tent guy lines were coated white.

Steeling himself for the final part of his journey, he quickly packed his camping gear and lifted the heavy rucsac on to his aching shoulders. He knew he'd walked a long way. The stiffness in his legs and sore feet were a reminder of his achievement.

Carefully, he started the steep frosty descent down from the escarpment, his legs protesting at each step. He was now following the 'Cathedral' signs for the Gloucestershire Way long distance footpath. His route took him via Greenfield Farm, where a circular horse training path added some geometric form to the landscape.

As he walked through Little Shurdington, Ben was pleased that, at last, the hills and valleys were behind him. He was back on to flat terrain.

Turning a corner, he spotted some buildings, which seemed familiar to him. It wasn't until he got closer that he realised it was the hotel where the wake had been held. The realisation was a shock.

Memories of seeing Geoffery in the video flooded back. He tried to shut out the images of the disrespectful behaviour of the adults. Worse still, the whole burial ground episode erupted in his head again.

The tranquillity he'd experienced during the walk was now cruelly displaced by the anxiety about facing the Police questioning. His spirits plummeted.

He crossed the busy A46, his mind in a whirl. Subconsciously he followed the waymarks, walking by a frozen stream and along footpaths where he had previously seen roe dear.

He didn't hear the high voltage cables crackling and spluttering in the damp winter air as he walked under them.

Mechanically, he climbed over a footbridge into a small, muddy field, populated by curious wild eyed bullocks.

He dragged his tired feet through on to the small green at Badgeworth. Here he rested briefly in the magnificently carved gateway of the 14th Century Holy Trinity Church, its lovely circular archway tempting worshippers to enter. But that didn't interrupt Ben's preoccupation with the forthcoming interview..

Checking his watch to make sure he was going to be on time, he continued along the Gloucestershire Way, becoming more and more agitated as he crossed a road bridge over the M5 motorway. With Churchup Hill nearly within touching distance, he walked back by the rear of the school buildings and returned tiredly to his Grandad's house.

His stomach knotted with anxiety, he was now having second thoughts about going to the Police and handing in the phone. He needed to talk it through with Andy.

Perhaps he should have gone to London after all.

CHAPTER TWENTY SIX

4th January

It was the Parish Clerk who spotted the Police request for assistance, in the local newspaper. He went to see the Vicar for advice on what he should do.

'Have you seen the paper?'

'Not today's. No.'

'The Police are looking for a Polish guy driving a Polo involved in the M5 crash. The description of the man sounds like Jan.'

'But surely the Police know that Jan is dead and his car is missing.'

'I don't know. Perhaps it's different departments dealing with everything. Maybe we'd better ring them anyway.'

The report from the Control, about the Taxi picking Sue up, had got lost in the system, for it was not until the following week that the report was spotted by a vigilant control room Sergeant.

He understood the relevance of the report and quickly passed the information on to the M5 Crash investigation team.

John Sparrow subsequently went and met the taxi driver, who gave him a description of his fare that night.

The policeman confirmed that it matched with the person for whom they were looking. Having now got the address from the Taxi control, he immediately went to Sue's address to interview her.

Firmly he knocked on her door.

Sue never had visitors and assumed that she would be confronted by a door to door salesman, who didn't know of her caustic reputation.

It was nearly two weeks since the accident and Sue's facial injuries had almost disappeared. Although her neck was still painful, she was no longer wearing her neck brace all the time.

Grumpily she opened the door.

'Good morning, madam. Are you the occupant?'

'Can't you read? The notice on the door plainly says '*No Cold callers*'. Whatever you're selling, I'm not interested. Good bye,' she said, moving to close the door.

'I'm Police Constable John Sparrow,' he said, showing her his warrant card.

'Oh, I'm sorry,' she said, 'I am surprised to see a Policeman at my door.' Her mind going into overdrive, her spirits rose briefly. Was he going tell her of Rupert's sudden demise? Should she prepare herself to play the distraught widow?

'Yes. How can I help?'

'I'm making enquiries about the RTC that occurred on the M5 just before Christmas?'

RTC? What do you mean, RTC?' she barked.

'Sorry, Road Traffic Collision.'

It was not the news she was hoping for. Had she been found out? Immediately she went on the defensive.

'I…don't think…'Sue said, hesitantly, suddenly feeling apprehensive, trying to second guess his line of questioning. 'Why do you ask?' she said, regaining her composure. 'Had somebody seen her in the Gravediggers car?' she wondered.

'We have reason to believe you might have been in the area that night.'

'Why do you think that?' she said, defensively

'A taxi driver remembers picking you up and driving you to this address.'

Realising there was no point in lying, Sue invited him in, conscious that her neighbours could overhear their conversation from the doorstep.

'Yes, that's correct.'

'May I ask what you were doing in the area?'

'There was an accident,' she said, trying hard to think of a response that wouldn't compromise a story that she might need to fabricate.

'Yes, it was a major accident. We had reports that a woman, bearing your description, was seen walking along the motorway after the accident. We were concerned that the person might have been injured. We just wanted to eliminate that concern.'

'Oh, is that all,' she said, relieved, unable to quickly think of an alternative reason for being there. 'Yes, it was all a bit of a shock. It was terrible; I just had to get away,' she lied, trying to 'milk' the situation.

'Yes it must have been dreadful,' he said genuinely.

'Oh it was. It was. I was very frightened.'

'Yes I can appreciate that. As I say, we need to identify everybody at the scene, especially as we have a car that we can't currently link to a driver. Can you tell me what you were doing on the motorway?'

'Well, it's all a bit hazy,' she said, trying to think of a reason that wouldn't link her with the Gravedigger's car.

'I err…was travelling to Bristol with…a… my husband, Rupert. The last thing I remember was we were talking about a funeral …and then I was getting into a taxi…I must have been thrown out…that's all I can remember,' she lied.

'Were you hurt at all? We couldn't find any record of you receiving medical treatment at any of the hospitals.'

'Oh, just a bit of whiplash, that's all. Nothing to worry about. I didn't want to bother the hospitals while they were so busy with real problems,' she said, melodramatically.

'Have you got it checked out?'

'No, it's only a stiff neck.'

'You need to get it checked,' he said, with genuine concern. 'You might have cracked a vertebra.'

'Thank you, I will. Umm…what is happening about the driver of the unclaimed car?'

'Well at the moment, we're trying to track them down by the VIN.'

'Sorry, VIN?'

'Vehicle Identification Number.'

'Oh!'

'All cars have a number attached to the chassis and this is recorded by the Driver and Vehicle Licensing Agency. What often happens, is the car gets sold on, but the new owner doesn't fill in the paper work to inform the DVLA of the change of ownership. So it's the devil's own job to find them. Never mind we'll get to the bottom of it I'm sure.'

'Yes,' she said, relieved that her run of good fortune was continuing.

'Oh by the way. Did you know you'd left some shoes outside? It looks like rain, so I've brought them into the porch for you.'

'Oh, thanks.'

'They look a bit muddy. Do you use them for gardening?'

'Well actually, I was wearing them the night of the crash. The heel is broken on one of them so I'm going to throw them away.'

'Oh I see. When's the best time to catch your husband?'

'My husband was injured. He's still in hospital.'

'Sorry to hear that. What hospital would that be?'

'Frenchay. But, why do you ask?'

'Just need to corroborate your story, that's all.'

'Oh. Don't you believe me?' Sue said, irritated that he was going to check on her story and afraid that her lies would be found out. 'I mean, is that really necessary? He's very poorly, suffered a really bad head injury,' she added, with false sympathy.

'Coroners and inquests I'm afraid, and as you say you were a bit confused. Don't worry, it's only routine.' He sought to reassure her. 'I'll have words with the hospital and we'll arrange to speak to him when he's recovered adequately. Thanks for your help.'

As the Policeman made his way up the path, Sue was already scheming to get Rupert to support her story. She was confident that she could persuade him to lie for her, especially as Joanne was in the same hospital and still in a coma. She would prove to be a valuable bargaining tool.

Meanwhile, Chief Collision Investigator Sergeant Fredericks duly arrived at the Vicarage and spoke to the

Vicar and Parish Clerk. They repeated their conviction that the large Polish man the Police were trying to trace, sounded like the Gravedigger Jan.

'Obviously we can't be sure,' he said, thankful that they'd gone to the press. 'But it certainly sounds like he matches the description of the Polish gentleman, who bought the car. It's too much of a coincidence for them not to be one and the same though. OK. I'll have words with my Murder squad colleagues and get some more details.'

'Why didn't you know about him anyway?'

'We're based in a different location to the Murder squad. We don't always get to see everything that's going on.'

'Is there anything else we can do, perhaps identify the car or belongings?'

'Thanks for the offer, but the car was caught up in the fireball that erupted after the crash. All we've got is an empty rusty shell.'

'So what will you do now?'

'We'll probably take a photograph of the deceased to the former Polo owner and see if he can positively identify him.'

'But if Jan was already…dead, how did his car get on the motorway?'

'Pure speculation at this stage, but perhaps his attacker was stealing the car and a fight ensued. Who knows? Thanks for the information.'

CHAPTER TWENTY SEVEN

4th January

Ben dumped his rucsac in the hall and hobbled up to the bathroom, his aching body reminding him that he had walked a long way.

He quickly showered and had put on clean clothes as Andy arrived to pick him up on time and they quickly set off for his appointment at the Police Station.

'How was the camping?'

'Yeah, OK thanks. A bit cold.'

'Well good on you. These things need to be tried, even in winter.'

'Yes.' Ben held back from telling Andy about why he was camping in the first place.

'Are you OK about the Police thing?'

'Yeah, a bit nervous,' Ben confessed.

'That's understandable. Now remember Ben, just tell them the truth. Exactly what you did and everything will be OK.'

'OK...umm.'

'Yes?'

'Umm...I'm not sure about something.'

'Go on.'

'Umm, you know that mobile phone that I called you from on the day that it all happened?'

'Yes. It was one that you picked up. Well nobody's going to accuse you of stealing it…unless…'

'Yes and I was going to tell the Police today and hand it in.'

'Good idea.'

'The trouble is…I think it belonged to the … Gravedigger… the guy that died.'

'What! Andy said, nearly hitting the kerb in surprise. 'How do you come to that conclusion? Did you take it off him?'

'No, I found it on the path like I said. I didn't even see his… you know, body.'

'What makes you think it's his phone?'

'There's a picture on it. I'm not sure if it isn't the person who attacked him. I swear it looks like they are holding the cross I made for Geoffery's grave.'

'Let me have a look,' Andy said, pulling into a layby.

'I can't, the battery's gone flat.'

'Damn. Well you really are in a pickle now.'

'Yes I know.'

Oh Ben! We go from one crisis to another, don't we?'

'I'm sorry.'

'Answer me honestly. This is important. Did you take the man's phone?'

'No, honest I didn't. It was just there on the path, covered in frost. I picked it up because I was desperate to tell you about the damage. I'm sorry.'

'If you tell them you have the phone, they will think you stole it from him and have something to hide.

'Why?'

'Because otherwise you'd have handed it in. We need something to prove somebody else was involved.'

'The photo on the phone, surely that might convince them?'

'It might do. But I need to see it.'

'Do you have a phone charger in the car?'

'What type of socket is it?'

'Here look.' Ben said, showing Andy the phone.

'That's a strange phone, never seen one like that before. No I haven't.'

'Do you think we could buy a charger lead and I can show you the picture?'

'Well we haven't got time to do that before we go to the Police, your appointment is in ten minutes.'

'Could we do it after?'

'What's the point when you won't have the phone? You'll have handed it in...'

'But I need to show you the photo first.' Ben implored.

'Hang on! What are you suggesting? That we don't tell them that you've got it?'

'Yes.'

'That would mean that we were withholding evidence. No we can't do that.'

'But they might arrest me.'

'Yes, that is a possibility.'

'No. I keep telling you, I haven't done anything wrong. Stop the car. Let me out.' Ben said, reaching for the door handle. The central locking meant that all doors were locked shut.

'Come on Ben,' Andy reasoned. 'Running away doesn't solve anything, as you should know by now. You have to face the music some time.'

'No I don't.' Ben said, getting upset.

'OK, OK. Against my better judgement we will say nothing about the phone. We'll hand it in tomorrow. We'll say we were tidying up Geoffery's grave and we found it.'

At the back of Andy's mind he was thinking his argument probably wouldn't hold water, for the forensic team would have found it during their fingertip search. The phone records would identify it had been used too. However it was the best he could think of on the spur of the moment.

Suddenly it dawned on him, that if the Police were actively looking for the phone, he would be implicated already because Ben had called him on it. He was feeling more and more concerned by the minute.

'Thanks Andy.'

'In the meantime, let's get the interview over with. God Ben, you do get yourself into some situations don't you?'

The interview went well. The Police Sergeant dealing with the vandalism of the grave listened to Andy explaining the friendship that existed between Ben and Geoffery. Andy told him about the cross that Ben had made out of some burnt timbers from the old Scout hut.

The Police Sergeant listened to Ben explaining his actions the morning he discovered the damage, and how he'd called Andy to get him to come to the graveyard. However, he omitted to say the phone he'd used was not his own. The Sergeant assumed that, like all young people, Ben owned his own phone and therefore didn't ask. Then Ben explained about the confrontation with the Dog walker and the reason he ran away.

Finally the Sergeant said, 'Look. In future don't run away when a Policeman asks to talk to you, because it makes people suspicious that you have something to hide.'

'OK,' Ben said, 'but what will happen to the person who actually did the damage?'

'Well we need to try and find them. The Scenes of Crime guy took lots of photographs of the damage. We'll just have to check them to see if there's anything we missed. For now you're off the hook.'

As Andy and Ben left the car park, the Mobile phone company liaison man rang and gave the Murder squad detective the numbers that Ben had rung.

'Do we know who they are?' The DC asked.

'No sorry. I can tell you that one is a landline and the other a mobile which has been called a couple of times. But it's not one of ours though. You'll need to speak to their supplier to get names. The alternative is you ring them and see who answers.'

'That might get them running before we can get to them, if they're involved in the theft.'

'I'll leave it with you then. Incidentally the phone was switched on and off before our guys could triangulate the signals, but it was in the Gloucester area somewhere. I've told them to try and catch it the next time and I'll be in touch when we got some more information. OK?'

'Yeah thanks.'

Sergeant Fredericks went back to his office and convened a meeting with his Murder Squad Colleagues.

'I understand you might have some information on an owner of a car we are trying to find.'

'Go on.'

'We're looking for a large Polish guy, described as being 6ft 6 and built like a brick…house.'

They quickly identified that he was one and the same and duly emailed a photo of the man to South Wales Police for them to check with the former owner of the car.

That done, Graham met with John to update each other on their various findings.

'So, what have we got?'

'The Polo belongs to the Pole. The Pole is dead, his car presumed stolen.'

'So who drove it?

'I've interviewed the Taxi driver and his fare, a lady called Sue Williams Screen, a right sour faced bitch. She was definitely the one walking away from the crash scene. I'm a bit suspicious of her explanation for leaving the scene.'

'Why?'

'Says she was thrown out of her husband's car, but he suffered serious injuries and she only has whiplash.'

'Can happen.'

'Yeah, but there was something…something I couldn't put my finger on.'

'Oh well at least she's on the radar.'

'We still don't know, for sure, who the Polo driver was though.'

Andy took Ben into Cheltenham town and bought a 'universal' car charger with multiple plug connectors, one of which fitted the mobile.

Andy plugged it into his car as soon as they got back, within a few moments the screen indicated it had some battery life and Ben switched it on to show Andy the photo.

Within a few seconds, forty miles away, an alert sounded in the Mobile company monitoring unit and the technicians flew into action. Using the available data they were quickly able to triangulate the mobile and pinpoint exactly where Ben and Andy were sitting in the car looking at the picture.

The liaison man was quickly on the case, ringing the Detective again to whom he previously spoken. The DC vainly tried to get a response car to go to the location, but, fortunately for Andy and Ben, there were no officers available in the area.

However, frustrated by being unable to act on the intelligence, he made sure that if the call came again he would get priority over other jobs that might come in.

'I see what you mean about that photo,' Andy said, studying it intensely. 'Whoever it is, they are pretty scary.'

'Look, there's the cross in the corner of the picture. See it?'

'Yes, I agree that it does look like your cross.'

'The Police didn't find it, did they?'

'Apparently, they didn't think it was significant to the case anyway.'

'I took a long time making that,' said Ben, woefully.

'I tell you what. I'm not due in to work til later, so let's go and see if we can find it.' Andy said, kind-heartedly, giving the phone back to Ben.

Ben switched the phone off as they drove back to Churchup Hill and after a short journey they parked opposite the Church.

'Come on,' said Andy,' let's do a bit of detective work ourselves. See if we can find out where this photograph was taken.'

'OK,' said Ben, following him slowly, his legs now stiffening from his marathon walk.

'First, let's retrace your steps and then we'll play 'hunt the cross.'

As they went through the gate into the Burial ground they could still see remnants of the blue and white plastic Police incident tape that had been tied around the gate, fluttering in the breeze.

'I came through that gate over there,' Ben said, pointing to the distant fence line.

'Right, let's start there.'

'I saw the… damage to his grave.'

'Yes and then what?'

'I thought, I've got to ring Andy, so I jumped on my bike and …umm went up this path here.'

'Where did you pick his phone up?'

'About here.'

'And the man was found just there,' Andy pointed, recalling his own involvement when the body was found. 'Assuming he was remonstrating with whoever was desecrating the grave, he must have been attacked somewhere along here.'

'If you say so,' Ben added, nervously.

'Let's have a look at that picture again.'

Ben switched the phone on again and within seconds the alarm sounded in the mobile monitoring room, within a few minutes the technicians had again triangulated the signal.

'They're right on top of one of our transmitters on Churchup Hill. Quick ring the liaison guy.'

'Let's look around and see if we can see that cross then,' Andy said, scanning in between headstones.

'Surely the Police would have found it when they were looking for clues?'

'They're only human like the rest of us. They could well have missed something.'

After searching around for fifteen minutes, they drew a blank. They were about to leave when Ben spotted something under a bench at the end of the burial ground next to the chain link security fence.

'There, look, it's under there,' he said, excitedly, running to the end of the path. Kneeling down by it, he was about to pick it up but an urgent warning from Andy stopped him.

'Don't touch it. Otherwise it'll have your fingerprints on it.'

'They're already there.' Ben volunteered casually.

'What do you mean? What are you saying?'

'I made it and stuck it in the ground, remember. Why, what did you think I meant?'

'Nothing,' said Andy, trying to cover up his wayward assumption.

Along the lane, they could hear a car travelling towards them at high speed.

CHAPTER TWENTY EIGHT

4th January

The Police car screeched to a halt beside Andy's Merc sending a shower of small stones into the gleaming white paintwork. Immediately the two Police officers bailed out and ran towards Andy and Ben who were standing near the entrance of the burial ground.

'Andy, what should we do?' said Ben, nervously watching the Police coming towards them. 'Should we run?'

Andy recognised them as the same two officers that came in response to the vandalism call from the dog walker.

'No Ben, we've done nothing wrong.'

'Oh, it's you two again! You obviously spend a lot of time up here?' said the Policeman, suspiciously.

'Yes. It's just over a couple of weeks since we saw you last, isn't it?' said the Policewoman, standing close to Ben.

Ben looked down at the ground unsure what to say.

'Yes, that was when you ran away from me wasn't it,' said the Policeman, looking sternly at Ben.

'Well that's all sorted out now,' Andy interjected, 'We've been to the Police Station this morning.'

'Yes, so I gather,' the Policewoman confirmed.

'We're glad you've arrived actually because we were going to call you.'

'Oh yes?'

'The Cross. We've found the cross.'

'Cross, what cross? The Policeman said, looking puzzled.

'The cross from the vandalised grave.'

'Yes it's the one I made for…for Geoffery.' Ben added.

'Ben made it to mark Geoffery's grave, before the headstone was installed. Andy expanded. 'We think it might have been used in the attack on the poor man that died here.'

'What! You mean the Gravedigger?'

'Yes.'

'How do you come to that conclusion Sherlock Holmes?' the Policeman asked, sceptically.

'We…we er…found a phone which appears to have a photograph of the Gravedigger being attacked,' Ben volunteered, starting to get the phone out of his pocket.

'Well isn't that a coincidence, we've come to investigate the use of a stolen phone, which we believe is here.'

Ben stopped retrieving the phone.

Meanwhile the Policewoman was dialling a number from her mobile.

'It's switched off, gone to voicemail,' she said, to her colleague.

Ben looked at Andy for guidance. Andy nodded. Ben knew that this was the time to come clean.

'It's me. I have the phone,' volunteered Ben, taking it out.

'Would you mind switching it on for me please?' the Policewoman directed.

Ben did as he was asked and the Policewoman dialled again. This time the phone rang.

'Can you answer it for me, please?' she directed.

Ben duly answered the phone and said, 'hello.'

'That's the one,' she said. 'I have to caution you that anything you say…'

'Is that necessary, we can explain,' Andy said, quickly.

'Ah, you must be Mr Spider?'

'Yes, that's right, but you already know that anyway.'

Just then his phone rang. He didn't recognise the number so was going to ignore it until the Policewoman said. 'Would you mind answering that, please Mr Spider.'

Andy did as he was bid. 'Hello.'

'That's the other one,' she informed her colleague.

'OK then folks. I think we need to take a trip down the Police Station to sort this out, don't you?'

'Should I cuff this one,' the Policeman said, walking towards Ben.

'No,' said Andy, looking at Ben. 'He won't run away, will you Ben?'

'No,' said Ben, looking sorry for himself. 'What about the Cross?'

'Show me,' the Policewoman said, pocketing her mobile.

Andy and Ben took the Police Officers to the bench.

'There look,' Ben said, kneeling down. 'Under there, look.'

'Looks like an ordinary piece of wood to me. Something that's fallen off the bench.'

'Why do you think it's your cross?' the Policewoman asked Ben, kneeling beside him.

'Cos I made it. I spent a lot of time doing it for my friend, Mr Foster.'

'Well if it is, the search missed it.' She said, reaching into one of the compartments in her belt bag for some rubber gloves.

'Do we need to get some backup up here with a camera before we touch it?' her colleague asked, reaching for the radio transmitter button.

'It's no big deal is it? What if it isn't the cross?'

'Could be the 'blunt instrument' they were looking for,' he continued.

'Let's see,' she said, reaching under the bench and lifting it carefully. Tilting it slightly she could see the name, carved in the softwood on the underside, *Geoffery Foster*.

'OK, let's get an evidence bag and put it in it,' she directed.

As she lifted it out, something on the corner edge of the horizontal of the cross caught their eye as it fluttered in the breeze.

'What's that, there?'

'It looks like red moss or…'

'Or blood and hair,'

'Let's get SOCO here, then. In the meantime, you two have some questions to answer down at the Police station. 'Can I have the mobile phone please?'

'Do you want me to show you the picture?' Ben asked as he handed it over, relieved that the phone was now no longer his responsibility.

'No I think we'll do that somewhere warmer.' She said, putting it in another evidence bag. 'We'd better tell control we have our target in custody.'

Ben and Andy were taken back to Cheltenham Police station for questioning, Andy insisted that his Merc shouldn't be left in the car park because it could be stolen or vandalised, so a delighted female Police Officer willingly volunteered to drive it back to Cheltenham for him.

'Nice car,' she said, throwing the keys back to him back at the station.

CHAPTER TWENTY NINE

4th January

A case conference was called to tie together the disparate events of 23rd and 24th December. The three Police teams involved consisted of the Traffic, Fast Response and the Murder Squad.

'Right, gents, my gaffer has suggested I take the lead role now we have identified that all these events are linked. We are investigating a motorway death and are following the RDIM – Road Death Investigation Manual procedures, whereas you guys in the Murder Squad believe your man died of hypothermia. Is everybody happy with that?' Sergeant Fredericks asked, looking around the room and receiving a nod of agreement from the other two teams.

'We've just literally had two pieces of the jigsaw provided for us. Hopefully that additional information will help us see the wood and the trees.' A murmur of approval went around the room.

'We've recovered the Gravediggers mobile, which contains an interesting image and we think we've found the 'blunt' instrument that was used to attack the guy. I've been able to add them into my presentation. So, let's review what we've got,' he said, switching on the projector and clicking on his laptop. A list of items appeared on the screen.

1. *'A burnt out Polo, driven by the 'invisible man';*
2. *A dead Gravedigger;*
3. *A vandalised grave,*
   'and the new bits'
4. *A kid that had the Gravediggers phone.*
5. *A wooden cross with traces of blood and hair*

'Theories anybody?'

'I agree that they're all linked. The chain starts with the grave being desecrated, the Gravedigger being clobbered, the car being stolen and crashing, then the kid picking up the phone which he used the following day.'

'OK. Who did what, then? The kid?'

'No, he couldn't have tackled the Gravedigger. He's not big enough.'

'We know the guy froze to death, probably due to the head trauma.'

'Approximate time of death?

'The pathologist says because of the low temperatures he can't be exact, but reckons late evening on 23rd.'

'The kid was at the wake of the bloke whose grave was messed up.'

'So could he have got back from the wake and done it?

'Possibly, but unlikely. Apparently he was pretty cut up about the funeral. The Scouter Leader bloke reckons he was very close to the old man.'

'OK. Do we know who had a grudge or are we talking about some local yobs that did it and worked over the Gravedigger?'

'Don't know. Could be either.'

'And the other new bit of information is the picture on the Phone.'

The photo appeared on the screen.

'Could be anybody. Eyes are a bit spooky, but it's all blurred.'

'See the cross in the picture? That's the other bit of the jigsaw.'

'Yes, it's just in focus.'

'I did a quick visual on the cross when they brought it in and it certainly looks like it was used to batter the guy. There were tufts of hair and blood on it. Look.'

The slide moved on and showed close ups of the cross. 'There are faint bloody fingerprints on it too as you can see.'

'So we'll work on the basis that the person in the photo is the attacker, Yeah?'

'Yes.'

'What about the messed up grave? Any clues there?'

'We got these photos of several footprints in the mud.' He paged through the slides.

'Those there around the edge of the grave look strange. What are they?'

'They look like imprints from the cleats of clip-on bike shoes. My son's got a pair, makes a right mess on my lawn.'

'That will be the kid then!'

'Let's assume for a moment that he left the footprints when he discovered the damage the following day.'

'What's that there look? There are lots of them all over the grave. Are they Walking stick marks?'

'No, I reckon it's a small heel print.'

'Woman's boot or shoe perhaps?'

'How big are the ladies on the forensic team?'

'Not very big. But they'd have your guts for garters if you suggested that they messed up the crime scene.'

'I expect they will have made some casts of the footprints as usual.'

'OK, so what about fingerprints?'

'That's with Forensics at the moment.'

'Any idea when we're likely to get some results?'

'They tell me they've got a backlog at the moment. Likely to be at least a couple of weeks.

'A couple of weeks! Can't we send it to another lab?'

'Already tried suggesting that. Budget cuts, no money for transfer charging to another force area.'

'Well, we'll just have to wait I guess. So, how did his car get on the M5? Who drove it there?'

'Whoever stole it?'

'Was it stolen though?

'What do you mean?'

'I'm trying to eliminate the Gravedigger.'

'Well time wise, it's possible for the Gravedigger to have driven it himself, been involved in the accident and got back to the burial ground and got done over.'

'Why would he go back there? The Vicar said he wasn't living up there.'

'So there would be no point. In any case, nobody reported seeing him there. No, I don't reckon he was the driver.'

'We're talking stolen then, yeah?'

'OK, assume that the person whoever did the Gravedigger, nicked the car.

'But who?'

'What about that woman who wandered off from the accident site?'

'Possible perhaps, but she's quite short.'

'Ah now, you might be on to something. Come to think of it, she had a muddy pair of shoes by her back door,' John Sparrow informed them.

'Oh come off it. She could have got that mud from anywhere, scrabbling up the embankment to escape the carnage for instance.'

'Be worth a check of the type of mud?'

'Yeah, go and get them and we'll put it to the lab… when they've got time.'

CHAPTER THIRTY

4th January

On arrival at Police HQ, Ben and Andy had been put into separate interview rooms.

Having just completed the case conference, and with the remit to bring all three elements of the investigations together, Sergeant Fredericks first interviewed Ben.

'Hello Ben. I'm Graham. Sorry to have kept you, but you have provided some useful information for us by finding that cross. Although hanging on to the phone was not helpful at all. I've come to talk to you about a few things related to our enquiries.

'Like what? I never killed the bloke.'

'Why would you say that?'

'Well cos I had the bloke's phone. I didn't know it was his when I picked it up. It was on the path, covered in frost. I spotted it when I was going to telephone Andy. I didn't see him. Didn't know anything about him…being dead until later that day.' Ben gushed, nervously.

'Oh! So how did you get to know about the bloke, as you put it?'

'The Policeman at the roadblock told us, when my friend James was driving me up to the Church.'

'Your friend James? Were you alone with him? Could he corroborate your story?'

'Yeah of course.'

'Right we'll have words with him then. So why would you ring Andy rather than anybody else?'

'Cos, he's my friend and…What are you getting at?' Ben said, suspiciously.

'Nothing, just trying to establish the facts. So you found the phone and you rang your…friend.'

'Yeah, well who else could I ring?'

'Just carry on with what happened,' the Policeman said, calmly.

'Andy said he'd come up and I went back to Geoffery's grave to start tidying it up. Then this fat old man walking his fat old dog came along and accused me of messing Geoffery's grave up.' Uncharacteristically, Ben's tough veneer cracked, his emotion strangling his vocal chords. 'I…I…'

'Take your time. Do you want some water?'

'No, it's OK,' Ben said, recovering. 'Geoffery was my friend. For the short time he was around, he was very kind and looked after me. He even gave me a key for the new Scout hut, so I could stay there, when I was kicked out of home.'

'Did he ever meet you there alone?'

'NO. Why would he?' Ben said, getting angry. 'You coppers have got filthy minds.'

'Son, we're only trying to protect you. There are some very nasty people out there.'

'Yes! But there are a lot of good people too. I know. I have some very good friends who are adults.'

'Have you ever heard of grooming?'

'Yeah, that's what they do to dogs and horses.'

'Don't get smart with me sunshine. You know exactly what I mean. I'm not a tame Scout Leader who you can bullshit.'

'Sorry,' Ben said, realising he was not helping his case by antagonising the Policeman.'

'Being so worldly,' the Policeman, continued sarcastically, 'you obviously know that some adults befriend young people to make them do things, horrible things.'

'You mean paedophiles, right?'

'As well. Yes.'

'Well I have two adult friends. It used to be three. One is a Scout Leader and one is Gay. Neither of them are Paedos, right?'

'I'm not saying they are. I'm just advising you to be careful.'

'Mate, I live on a council estate. You've got to be tough to survive. I do know about things.'

'It's OK to be streetwise, so long as you keep out of trouble. Talking of which, with-holding evidence is a serious offence. What have you got to say about that?'

'Like I said, I was going to hand the phone in…but forgot. Then I agreed with Andy, I'd give it in after the interview this morning.'

'But you didn't.'

'No, cause I wanted to show him the picture on it, and the battery had gone flat.

'Why was it important to show him the photo and not us?'

'Because I trust him, that's why. And you lot are always on my case.'

'Well judging by your record, we need to be. Wouldn't you agree?'

'No. Anyway we found the cross that I made for him, which was what I wanted to do, so I could put it back on Geoffery's grave.'

'Well obviously you won't be doing that now, because that's evidence.'

'When can I have it back? So I can.'

'Well, it hasn't been forensically tested yet. Then, there hopefully will be a court case, when we find the culprit… we tend to hang on to evidence for some time, in case there's an appeal.'

'So in other words, never!'

'Not for a long time, that's for sure.'

'I shall make him another then.'

'It's probably the best solution.'

'So what happens next?'

'We'll let you know if you will be charged with anything. But the events will go on your records.'

'Gee thanks. Can I go?'

'Yes. And remember what I said. Be careful and for Christ sake keep out of trouble.'

Ben left the interview room, relieved that he wasn't going to be sent to a young offenders institute.

CHAPTER THIRTY ONE

4th January

'I'm sorry to have kept you.' the Sergeant said to Andy, as he entered the other interview room. 'But the new evidence of the photo on the phone and the cross needed to be photographed etc.'

'I should think so too, I'm late for my afternoon shift.' Andy said, angrily.

'Well you've brought this on yourself to some extent by aiding and abetting young Ben. I've just interviewed your feisty little friend, Master Bird. I've told him to keep out of trouble. I'd appreciate your help with that.'

'Yes of course.'

'Thanks.'

'Are you going to charge him with anything?'

'No I don't think so.'

'That's a relief.'

'So, what's your relationship with the boy?'

'I'm his Scout Leader.'

'Can you tell me why you were with him today? It's a bit unusual isn't? Driving one of your Scouts around?'

'I brought him to the Police Station for an interview. What are you implying?'

'Nothing, unless you have something to hide.'

Andy felt himself getting angry and took a deep breath before he replied. 'Oh dear, I'm not sure how to answer. You have an overactive imagination.'

'Why do you say that?'

'My involvement with Ben is purely as a friend.'

The Policeman sat upright and looked Andy straight in the eyes. 'What sort of friend would that be Sir?'

'Somebody who is helping another human being, who has a shit life.'

'You'll pardon my scepticism…but why would you do that? What's in it for you?'

Andy felt his blood pressure rising but tried to stay calm. 'His mother is an alcoholic. He has no father, and he's been excluded from School several times. What should I do, ignore him? Let him get into bother, so he becomes one of your regulars?'

'I think he's already doing that quite well himself, in spite of your help. He's not the sweet and innocent boy that you claim.'

'No, he's got a record I know. But I hope we've given him a better chance than he would have had otherwise.'

'So you're his Scout Leader?'

'Yes, so?'

'I presume you've been screened through the Criminal Record Bureau process?'

'Of course! Are you accusing me of being a paedophile? because if you are, I want a solicitor.'

'I'm sure you're doing a wonderful job and we don't need to pursue that avenue of inquiry. However if you were exposed to the dregs of humanity that I have to deal with, then I think you'd be suspicious of everybody's motives. They all claim to be innocent, until we find evidence about some appalling crime they've committed and then they claim they had a bad childhood and it wasn't their fault.'

'And that's why I'm trying to prevent Ben going that way. I am winning, but he …he just seems to be in the wrong place at the wrong time and…'

'OK, talking about the wrong place at the wrong time. Let's get on with your involvement with the stolen phone.'

'It wasn't stolen…he'd picked it up…he didn't know who it belonged to.'

'You sure he didn't rob the poor bloke who had been killed?'

'He wouldn't steal it. No, of course not.'

'OK, but I gather you knew he didn't have a phone of his own. If you're his guardian Angel, why didn't you tell him to hand the phone in?'

'I…did. Things got a bit hectic and…well he forgot.'

'Until he was tracked down…and suddenly he remembered. Come on, I wasn't born yesterday.'

'He told me about the picture of the person who attacked the Gravedigger.'

'Alleged!'

'Yeah, alright alleged. He was going to hand it in when he was interviewed about the vandalism. But he wanted to show me the picture first. The battery was flat so we bought a charger in Cheltenham and he showed me the picture.'

'So why didn't you go back to the Police Station straight away instead of going to a hill alone with him?'

'He wanted to find the cross he'd carved for Geoffery.'

'How did having the phone help?'

'So we could try and see from where the photo was taken and look for the cross around that area.'

'Ok. Quite the super sleuths aren't we? But, pardon my sensitivities, finding evidence is what we do.'

'Well you didn't find it did you? It took two inexperienced people to do your job for you. We found the cross, and possibly gave you the lead to the person you're hunting.'

The Policeman felt 'wounded' by the suggestion of ineptitude, but quickly recovered his poise.

'Well Mr Holmes, while you're hot on the trail of villains, perhaps you can help us with the vandalised grave. Do you know anybody who would have held a grudge for Mr…'

'Foster, Geoffery Foster.'

'Yes Mr Foster?'

'There is one person I can think of who would have enjoyed dancing on his grave.'

'And who is that?'

'His nephew's wife, Sue Williams-Screen. She was falsely accused of trying to murder Geoffery…to be more specific Geoffery set her up.'

'Set her up?'

'Yes I'm sure you'll find all you need about the case on her records. However, she's a nasty piece of work.'

'Right. Thanks. We'll pursue that line of enquiry. Thank you. In the meantime there are two things you need to think about.'

'Go on.'

'You were complicit in withholding evidence…'

'Yes, I'm sorry. But it turned out to be helpful to your investigations.'

'Yes, I'll give you that. The other thing. Being alone with a child who is not your own is bound to raise suspicions. Be very careful. The newspapers have whipped the country up into hysteria about inappropriate behaviour…there is a witch hunt on…mind you don't become the bait.'

'Yes, thanks.'

CHAPTER THIRTY TWO

5th January

John Sparrow went back to Sue's house the following day, with the intention of collecting the muddy shoes he had seen at his previous visit.

'Mrs Williams – Screen, I wonder if I could trouble you for the shoes you were wearing on the night of the accident?'

'Why do you want them?' Sue asked, suspiciously. Were they on to her, she wondered?

'Evidence from the crash site, that's all,' he said, not wishing to alert her to the real purpose.

'I'm sorry, but after your last visit, I threw them away and the refuse disposal people have done their round.'

'I see,' he said, suspiciously, thinking he needed to check her explanation with the council's Refuse Disposal timetable. He cursed himself for letting potential evidence, literally slip through his fingers.

On his way back to the office, he had a hunch about the missing heel and went back to the scene of the M5 accident with the Highways Agency. The Agency closed off the inside lane and helped him search the accident site for it.

'You're hoping for a miracle aren't you? It could have gone up in the car or been cleared away by our guys, when they cleaned up after the accident and resurfaced the tarmac.' The Traffic Officer said, looking intensely at the charred ground. 'This is like looking for a bleeding needle in a haystack.'

After an hour of painstaking searching, they decided to give up. The Policeman was just getting into his car, when he spotted what he thought was the errant heel. It was not on the hard shoulder where they'd been looking, but near the central barrier in the third lane.

The Traffic Officer arranged for another crew to put on a 'rolling roadblock', which effectively stopped any traffic from coming along that section of the motorway. Eventually, the traffic stopped coming through. The Policeman ventured out onto the empty motorway and, to his delight saw that the small object he had spotted was indeed a broken heel from a ladies shoe.

'Yes,' he said, jubilantly. 'There you go, Mr Traffic Officer. 'There's the needle we were looking for. One muddy piece of heel.' That'll do nicely,' he beamed, putting it into an evidence bag.

CHAPTER THIRTY THREE

5th January

The collision investigation team were congratulating themselves on finding another piece of evidence in the jigsaw.

'Graham, I reckon the small heel prints on the grave will definitely match those of the broken heel I recovered off the M5.'

'Yeah, well done, a nice bit of detective work there John. However, we can't categorically say that it's hers though, because she's thrown away the boots.'

'But we know that she had a pair of boots with a broken heel, which she was wearing on the night of the accident.'

'OK. So she could have stolen the Polo after she'd clobbered the Pole?'

'Unlikely. She is a short arse, about 5 foot 2 and he was 6 foot 6 and built like a brick shithouse.'

'And another thing. She reckons she was a back seat passenger in her husband's car, which means…'

'Which means, that she couldn't have been driving the Polo, although I don't buy it myself.'

'Yeah, and the other curious thing is, why didn't she stay with her old man at the scene? He was badly hurt, for Chrissake.'

'Says she was confused, concussed. Didn't know what was happening.'

'What progress on forensics?'

'No joy. Still a backlog, thanks to the budget cuts.'

'So we still haven't got any results from the bloody fingerprints on the cross.

'No, or DNA matches against blood types to see if it they match the Gravediggers.'

'Damn! We have no factual evidence, only suspicions that she was not in her husband's car.'

'I'm waiting for the hospital people to get back to me and I'll go and see him.'

'I should chase them up if I were you. You know what these people are like.'

'What else have we got?'

'Let's just imagine, for a second, that she did assault the Gravedigger, though. OK, I appreciate it's highly unlikely, but...'

'If she did, the charge is likely to be manslaughter, as he died of hypothermia. Even if we got a successful prosecution, it's unlikely she'd get a significant sentence.'

'Why?'

'Because she could say she was defending herself and only hit him in self-defence.'

'Yeah, unfortunately.'

'She could have stolen his car – but we've got no proof of that either.'

'However, if she caused the M5 crash, we could charge her with causing death by dangerous driving.'

'Yeah, she might get a couple of years inside at least. But we can't put anything to bed until we get those damn forensics done.'

'I'll have words with the chief and see if he can put any pressure on.'

'In the meantime, see if you can get to see her husband and check her alibi.'

CHAPTER THIRTY FOUR

5th January

Rupert was sitting by the side of his bed in his private side ward thinking about the joy of becoming a Dad, when he heard footsteps. Assuming that it was his nurse coming to check on him, he didn't look up.

'Hello Rupert. I said I'd see you again, and as ever, I'm true to my word. Aren't you going to offer your wife a seat?' Sue asked.

Rupert felt a wave of fear and depression washing over him crushing his joyful thoughts.

As threatened, Sue had turned up again at the hospital, and had somehow gained access by talking her way past the hospital security people who were supposed to have stopped her.

He ignored her. He'd decided that was the best policy. That way he wouldn't end up saying the wrong thing and antagonising her.

'That's terribly rude Rupert, to ignore me. You'll regret that,' she whispered menacingly in his ear.

Sue looked around the room at the collection of 'Get Well' cards filling all the available shelf space.

'Very nice room. Hope this isn't costing US money. I'm terribly sorry, but I didn't bring you a card or a bunch of grapes,' she said, examining the cards. 'Nothing here from your girlfriend then? Oh, of course not. Silly me, she's still in a coma isn't she?'

Rupert sat impassively continuing to ignore her.

'If anybody asks you who was travelling in your car on the night of the accident, you're going to tell them I was with you and your lady friend.' She commanded, whilst she slowly paced around the room like a predatory animal, mesmerising its prey.

'What! You'd be the last person I'd have in my car,' he said, angrily, immediately chastising himself for rising to the bait and forgetting his intention to blank her.

'No Rupert. You misunderstand what I'm saying. I WAS in your car travelling down to Bristol on December 23rd.'

'Are you kidding me?'

'I see that tart of a girlfriend of yours is on a life support machine. Do you know she makes funny noises when you stand on her oxygen pipe?'

'What?'

'Oh, didn't I say? I popped into see her a few moments ago.'

'The nurses were supposed to stop you.'

'Why would they stop her 'distraught sister' from seeing her?'

'You're not her...'

'No, but they don't know that.'

'Bitch!'

'Now, now. Wouldn't it be ironic, if she survived the crash only to die in hospital?'

'You wouldn't.'

'Come now Rupert. You know me better than that. Don't goad me. You know I don't make idle threats.'

Rupert's new won courage, and his intention to stand up against Sue, withered instantly, now she was threatening to kill Joanne and their unborn child.

Sue would have found Joanne's pregnancy particularly repugnant, as she'd never wanted children, or anything that would impose any demands on her personal space.

'You see, the Police are asking questions. It would be so much easier for you to tell them I was a back seat passenger and must have been thrown out of the car. That's not too difficult even for you is it?' She glowered to emphasise her point.

'What have you been up to?'

'That's none of your business. Just do as you're told,' she screeched.

'When are the Police going to…'

'I've told them you're far too ill to be questioned, but they tell me the Coroner is pressurising them to complete their enquiries before the crash inquest is opened. It could be soon. They were going to talk to the hospital people about coming to see you.'

'What if I don't tell them you were with…'

The look was enough to persuade Rupert. Dissention wasn't an option. The action of her running her finger across her throat further convinced him. He had to lie to protect his new family.

Shortly after her ultimatum, Sister King came into the room. She was followed by a man.

'Oh,' she said. Mrs Screen!'

'Williams Screen.' Sue insisted.

'I thought I'd made it clear the last time. You were not welcome here.'

'You can't stop me seeing my husband. He needs me.'

The Sister looked at Rupert for confirmation. He looked at his hands to avoid her gaze.

'Mr Screen, I have a Policeman who'd like to speak with you, if you're feeling up to it?'

Sue looked relieved. She had timed her edict precisely right.

'No. I'm not feeling very well at the moment. I was just thinking of going back to bed,' Rupert said, trying to delay the moment when he would have to lie for his wife.

'Oh, I see you have your wife with you,' John Sparrow said suspiciously, stepping into the room. 'Hello Mrs Williams- Screen.

Perhaps, Mr Screen, I should have rung before I travelled all the way down from Cheltenham,' the Policeman said, hoping to influence Rupert's decision by emphasising his efforts and length of his journey.

'OK then,' Rupert said, reluctantly.

'Thanks. I won't keep you long. I was thinking on the way down here, that you were remarkably unlucky that you and your…partner.'

'Cousin,' Sue said, quickly. 'Joanne is Rupert's cousin.'

'As I was saying, it's remarkable how unlucky Mr Screen and his *cousin*,' he said, overemphasising the word - cousin, 'were so seriously injured when you, Mrs Williams Screen escaped without any injuries. Don't you think?'

'Yes, I guess my guardian angel was looking after me that night,' she said.

'Yes surprisingly lucky,' he said, sceptically.

'Now if you don't mind my husband needs to rest.' She said moving towards him with the intention of ushering him out.

The Policeman ignored her and watched the Sister help Rupert slowly get back into bed.

'Mr Screen, I was only going to ask you to confirm that your wife was with you in the car when it happened. Yes or No, and then I'll go.'

Sue was about to protest, when Rupert croaked unconvincingly, 'Yes.'

'OK, I'll be on my way. I hope you and your...*cousin* get back on your feet soon.'

'So do I,' Sue echoed, with false sympathy.

'Oh incidentally, Mrs Screen,' he said, again deliberately avoiding using her full name to aggravate her. 'It's a pity you threw those shoes away, because we found the broken heel on the motorway. You could have stuck it back on and nobody would have been any wiser. Never mind, it's too late now you've thrown them away, isn't it?'

Sue was perturbed at the mention of the heel.

'Why did you...why were you looking for it?' she asked, suspiciously.

'All part of evidence gathering into the cause of the crash,' he said, and turned on his heel, feeling smug that he'd had the last word.

The Sister followed him out and as they disappeared down the corridor Rupert sat up in bed and uncharacteristically quizzed her.

'So what part did you play in that crash? he said, bravely. Why would Gloucestershire Police travel down here to urgently see me in hospital?'

'Mind your own business,' she said, picking up her handbag. 'Hurry up and get well soon. We don't want you to miss the reading of the will do we?'

'Well you're not coming with me, that's for certain.' Rupert shouted, defiantly.

'Is that right?' she said, her hackles rising. 'I'll just pop and see 'my sister' to make sure she's still breathing, shall I?'

'You leave her alone. Do you hear me? Leave her alone,' he shouted, his last words tailing off as he started coughing, holding his ribs, in obvious pain.

'Careful now, otherwise I shall be going by myself. A rich widow.'

She turned and left as Rupert fought to control his breathing.

'Would he never be rid of her?' he wondered. 'Perhaps he needed another guardian Angel, now that Uncle Geoffery was no longer around.'

PART TWO

The Will

CHAPTER THIRTY FIVE

23rd January

Geoffery's meticulous planning meant that only a month after his funeral, Andy, three Godsons, family and friends boarded a chartered Hawker 800 jet at Gloucestershire Airport for the flight to the offices of Geoffery's Lawyers in Monaco.

The invitations to the will reading had been delivered by special messenger from the Law practice.

Andy had been at home when the messenger arrived and he quickly opened the letter. 'It's the invitation for the reading of the will,' he'd informed Helen.

'That'll be nice for you,' Helen had said, disinterested.

'Oh, it's in Monaco,' he said, reading down further. 'It says overnight accommodation has been arranged.'

'Huh!'

'You're invited too,' he'd added, quickly.

'Yeah and who's going to look after the kids. I don't want to go to a boring will reading anyway.'

'Yeah but it would be a nice break for you.'

'There's far too much to do here,' she said, picking up a pile of children's clothes and going upstairs.

'Please yourself,' he'd muttered. 'I'm going.

Sue had been alerted about the will reading inadvertently when the courier arrived at her house asking for Rupert. Anticipating that it might be something to do with the legacy, she told him Rupert was in hospital, to where she directed him.

She chased it up with another visit to the hospital and after subjecting Rupert to a bombastic interrogation, confirmed that he had been invited to the will reading.

Rupert told her that he didn't want to attend because Joanne was still in a coma and he was intending to stay with her. But Sue had not only convinced him to go, but she insisted in taking Joanne's place too.

James's invitation had been delivered to the clinic where he was continuing his 'drying out' regime. Unfortunately, his street days had resulted in serious liver damage for which he was also being treated, although ultimately a liver transplant would be inevitable.

Ben was excited at the prospect of the trip. Since the messenger had delivered the invitation, he had been 'hyper'.

The warning from the Policeman about being alone with Ben had made Andy nervous. It would only take one critical accusation and he knew the Safeguarding Unit at Scout HQs would suspend him and the troop would fold.

All his hardwork would have been in vain, in creating a safe haven for the council house kids.

But he couldn't desert Ben, especially now, while he was showing a surprisingly vulnerable side to his character.

So in spite of the warning, Andy picked Ben up from his Grandfather's house, and drove him, alone, to the airport. Andy was in the horns of a dilemma, forced into the situation of transporting Ben alone, because Helen and Beth were not going to Monaco.

Helen, because she didn't want to leave the children. In addition, their marital relations were still strained after she caught Andy with his arms around Nadine.

And Ben's mother, Beth, was back into a critical part of her treatment in the addiction clinic having badly crashed out of her rehab programme at Christmas.

Ben didn't pause for breath as he explained to Andy on the way to the airport that he'd never been abroad before, let alone on an airplane and a chartered one at that.

As they congregated in the small departure lounge, Andy was shocked to see that Rupert was accompanied by Sue.

He'd heard about the motorway accident and knew that Jo was still recovering in hospital, but for Sue to be there! She was obviously up to her old tricks of harassing Rupert. How he regretted being instrumental in giving her back her freedom. But Geoffery had set her up. It wasn't his fault.

She glowered at him as she spotted him looking at her. He quickly looked away, embarrassed at being found out.

James had mixed feelings about the trip. For in the days of his apparently endless wealth, he would fly with the same regularity as most people took a taxi. However, following his fall from grace, this would be the first time for many years, that he'd flown.

Tim had received the invitation whilst at his Mother's house, Like Ben, he and his mother Kay had never been on a plane before. There had been insufficient funds in the Springfield household to have holidays, let alone ones out of the country.

On the other hand Carrie had been all over the world in many different types of planes during her army career. Indeed, part of her build up to becoming a member of the SAS had been to develop all manner of parachuting techniques. High Altitude Low Opening – also known as HALO, was one she particularly enjoyed for the buzz of long free-fall. Flying, therefore, was second nature to her

Kay had been surprised to be invited to the will reading, but as one of Geoffery's former girlfriends, she had been secretly hoping to be included. Even if she wasn't written in to the will, the trip would be reward in itself.

The luxurious interior of the Hawker jet impressed Ben as he settled into a single white leather swivel seat which, like the eight others, were positioned either side of the narrow gangway.

He craned his neck to see out of the window hoping to be spotted in his new celebrity status. Across the other side of the runway he could see enthusiasts by the Aviator pub with their binoculars.

He had watched planes take off from the same spot himself, but never dreamt than one day he would be in one of them, especially a chartered jet.

He knew their radios would be tuned to the aircraft frequencies, listening into the brief voice traffic between plane and control tower.

The sound of the door closing made him turn away from his window gazing and he saw that an attractive uniformed flight attendant, who introduced herself as Evette, was doing the mandatory safety announcements.

After the briefing, she walked along the gangway giving out hard boiled sweets and checking that everybody was buckled into their seat belts.

The plane started moving along the labyrinth of taxiways and eventually turned on to the operational runway.

Ben felt butterflies in his stomach as they waited a few minutes at the end of the runway for clearance.

Suddenly the crescendo of engine noise increased, as the pilot pushed the throttles forward holding the jet on the brakes, until it reached a peak. Then he released the brakes and they were off, hurtling down the runway like a greyhound through starting gates. As the plane accelerated, Ben could hear underneath him the tyre noise as they sped along the bumpy runway.

It seemed that they must surely run out of runway, when suddenly he felt the kick in his back and his stomach 'drop' as the pilot 'rotated' the plane. The nose lifted and the tyre noise ceased, followed quickly by a clunk as the undercarriage retracted... and for the first time in his life Ben was flying and so were his spirits.

The sleek jet took off in a roar, quickly leaping into the sky over the roofs of Churchup. He saw the skate park disappearing under its wing, as it banked over to follow its declared flight path. Within minutes, it had punched a hole through the low cloud and emerged into the hidden sunshine.

Ben revelled in every aspect of the flight. Perhaps life was going to get better after all, memories of the upsetting Christmas and disastrous start to the New Year being replaced with the prospect of a new and exciting adventure.

Drinks and nibbles were served during the flight by Evette, who made sure that Ben had more than his fair share and even took him up to the cockpit, where he was impressed to see the pilot was wearing 'shades' in the bright sunshine.

The pilot explained to him about the autopilot flight plan and the vast array of buttons, screens and dials. He told him about various cloud formations, as the jet made its way across the hidden English countryside and over the coast.

As they left English shores, Ben had to return to his seat because of slight turbulence. Through holes in the cloud, he had tantalising glimpses of the white wake of ships crossing the Channel.

As they crossed over the French coast the cloud disappeared and he was treated to a panorama of patchwork fields, roads, mountains, lakes and rivers. A living geography map was opening up before his very excited eyes.

Carrie spent a lot of the flight talking soothingly to a frightened Kay, grabbing her hand when they hit turbulence. Kay was clearly very nervous, her earlier excitement now deflated.

Sue had sat quietly for the most part of the trip, self-conscious that she was in the 'lion's den' of Geoffery's cohorts. But she decided that the monetary outcome would be worth the short term discomfort of sitting with them during the flight.

She was also hoping to get a quick cash settlement with her share of Rupert's legacy, so that she could make herself disappear in Europe, out of the clutches of the British Police. It was obvious to her the trap was closing in.

However she couldn't stop from interrupting Carrie as she was trying to calm Kay's flight nerves. 'Don't worry, if the plane crashes, you won't know too much about it,' she said, callously.

Carrie ignored her and continued to reassure Kay, 'Of course flying's perfectly safe,' and told her about the hundreds of flights she had been on whilst in the forces.

'Yes she's right of course,' Sue interjected again, 'but I suppose the more flights you make, the more odds start stacking up against you, don't they? I mean that plane that caught fire in Manchester…'

'If yee don't mind like,' Carrie said, giving her a withering look' her Geordie accent surfacing now she was angry. 'This is a private crack. Keep yer nose oot. Reet?'

'Oh, sorry I'm sure.' Sue said, humiliated by the put down. 'I was only trying to help.' She mentally added Carrie to her hate list.

Rupert smiled to himself at her admonishment. It was the highlight of his day. Although Rupert's thoughts quickly returned to Joanne, lying in a hospital bed, without him by her side. What if she came around and he wasn't there? Would she think he'd deserted her? And the baby was it going to be alright while Joanne struggled with her own battle to get better?

He had been told that until she came out of the coma, they wouldn't know the severity of her back injuries or whether she would be paralysed or not. Whatever it took, he was determined to get her the best medical care his inheritance would buy.

Andy was wondering what he could do to appease Helen, perhaps he could track down some of the posh perfume that Nadine was wearing and make the peace. He hoped Nadine wouldn't be at the reading. The seed that Helen had planted of him being Nadine's 'bit of rough' might be too much for him to resist, if the opportunity presented itself.

Before long the note of the engines changed and the plane started descending. Evette did the rounds of her passengers, giving out hard boiled sweets again and checking that everybody was wearing their seat belt.

James gazed down on the familiar coastline. This was a descent he had made many times before, for this had been his playground. He had spent a lot of money and time at seemingly endless parties, here. The Cannes film festival, the F1 circus and the Casino in Monaco, to name just a few. It all seemed a lifetime away now though.
Here, he had an indulgent lifestyle. His money had bought him every pleasure imaginable. But, just like his rich friends, he had taken it all for granted.
A spectre of his former life flashed back into his consciousness. The pain of losing his lover Sebastian, firstly to another and subsequently his untimely death still haunted him.
The loss of Sebastian had been the catalyst for his downward spiral of depression. His ineptitude had lost

him his late millionaire father's legacy, his inheritance at the casino tables. It was the beginning of the end. As his trappings of wealth, the yachts, the cars, the lavish parties disappeared, so too did his so called friends.

The inevitable bankruptcy ultimately pitched him into abject poverty and onto the streets of London. On the streets, the bottle became his numbing salvation and eased the pain of his broken heart.

He had lost all self-respect until, thankfully, just a few months ago Andy and Ben had tracked him down and Geoffery rescued him from himself.

However, here he was back to where it all started, but with a fresh chance to restore his self-esteem. Geoffery's money would give him a new opportunity. He knew he mustn't blow it twice. There would be no other Guardian Angel to save him next time.

Ben was apprehensive, but excited, about the landing as the small jet, buffeted by turbulence, neared the runway at a sunny Nice Cote D'Azur airport.

Safely on the ground, the plane decelerated quickly as the Pilot applied reverse thrust. And after negotiating the taxiways for a few minutes, it halted. The doorway opened on to a temperate Mediterranean afternoon.

As Ben filed past the still seated Sue, he thought her face was somehow familiar, but he couldn't place it.

CHAPTER THIRTY SIX

23rd January

The Law Firm's representative, Monique, met them at the airport and chaperoned them through customs to a gleaming black, stretched Mercedes for the short journey over the mountains to Monaco.

Their route took them down the same serpentine road upon which Geoffery had nearly collided with the school bus only six months previously, whilst returning home with the devastating news of the terminal prognosis of his illness.

Ben was wide eyed at his surroundings, for as the rugged mountain panorama ended, the beautiful blue Mediterranean appeared, sparkling in the afternoon sunshine. Here he was, in a world beyond his wildest dreams, the adventure getting better and better all the time.

'Wow, this is brilliant,' he said, to nobody in particular.

Soon the sleek car pulled up in a fashionable area of Monte Carlo, outside an opulent three storey building, in the narrow Boulevard des Moulins.

The wide pavement was populated with a row of neatly trimmed trees in large square plant boxes, an elegant show of topiary, befitting the area.

Monique led the crocodile of expectant beneficiaries from the stretched limo into the elegant pastel painted building, its façade bedecked with columns and mock balconies.

Andy stopped and caught his breath, as he took in his surroundings. He was just as overwhelmed as Ben had been, for the day had become a blur of exciting activity, a brief flight in a luxurious chartered jet and now alighting into the relatively warm luxury of Monaco. It was a far cry from a busy day at the hospice and the gloom of the British winter that they'd left behind.

Framed above the roof tops, Andy could see the peak of Mont Agel peering down on the Principality, the late afternoon sun painting the rocky mountainside with an orange aura.

'Another one of Geoffery's sunsets. I wonder if he planned that too,' he mused.

Andy caught up with the others as they entered the building and was surprised at the transformation between the old exterior architecture and the ultramodern décor inside.

Opulence effused from the expensively carpeted reception area where a silver framed notice, declaring 'Excellence in Everything we do', hung behind the reception desk.

The others were in a group waiting by reception as Monique collected their building passes that doubled for door access swipe cards.

She hung the photo ID passes around her arm by the wide lanyard ribbon, emblazoned with the name of the Law firm, ICE, and handed them out to everyonr, except Sue.

'There appears to be a problem,' she said, looking perturbed. 'Excusez, where is Joanne please?'

'Joanne is in hospital,' Sue volunteered, while Rupert was clearing his throat to speak. 'I am Rupert's wife. I am here instead of her. Could you make out a pass for me?'

'But of course. I 'ope the lady gets well soon.'

'Yes! Quite,' said Sue, unconvincingly.

As they made their way to the lift, Andy grew more and more impressed about the professionalism of the Law firm as Monique explained about the practice.

'Here at ICE, we use much computing and do not use too much paperwork. Instead, all documents are scanned and held as electronic files, as are all legal reference books, although we do 'ave a small library for show. Customer papers are stored under the building in a special vault.

The desks are fitted with networked computers that can only be accessed by retina scan login, to access Customer files and latest version of EU legal documents.'

It was a world apart from Andy's own solicitor's office in Gloucester. Here most shelves were stacked with dusty legal volumes. Piles of case papers tied up with red ribbon littered most horizontal surfaces. He likened it to piles of legal excreta, just waiting to be poop scooped. Dusty casement windows completed the image of the Dickensian practice.

Monique led them to a modern conference room, in the centre of which was a large rectangular polished oak table. Around it's periphery were ten, black leather backed wooden chairs. In front of each chair, a notepad, pen and crystal glass tumbler.

Andy's resolution to be distant with Nadine all but disappeared, as she rushed over to greet him.

'Andee, Andee, mon cher.' she said, putting her arms around him and planting a kiss on his lips. 'It is so good to see you again. I 'ope you had a good flight. Welcome to my country. I will make sure you 'ave a good time,' she added, holding his hands and standing back to look into his eyes.

Andy was embarrassed at her gushing welcome. The others were forced to stop behind him by the embrace and wondered, if they too were likely to be given such a 'warm' greeting.

Sue, ever vigilant, noted the gushing greeting and pondered whether there was any mileage in using this display of intimacy in any way, to further her own ends.

In the corner of the room was a well-stocked drinks dispenser, from which they were invited to help themselves to tea and coffee.

A uniformed 'chef' assisted with their choices, flitting around to ensure that everything was kept meticulously clean and tidy. Used cups were collected almost as soon as they were put down.

Eventually, when everyone had made themselves 'comfortable', the law practice Manager asked everybody to be seated.

'Ladies and Gentlemen, welcome to Monaco. I am pleased to welcome you to our practice for the reading of the will of Monsieur Geoffery Foster.

First, I will tell you about your itinerary. After today's meeting you will be taken to your hotel to freshen up and then you will have a meal in the hotel's Michelin star restaurant. After this, you will be taken to the Casino to do as you wish- gamble, drink, watch and then you can wander around Monaco.

Tomorrow you will have breakfast and be taken on an exclusive sight- seeing tour up to the Royal Palace and then you will be flown by helicopter back to Nice for your flight home.

But first we have business for which you have travelled from your home.'

The Manager then sat down and operated a key on a small console which was on the table in front of him. A 72 inch video wall lit up behind him showing a sunset, gentle piano music played in the background.

The sunset slowly faded and Geoffery's face appeared, he was looking straight at the camera which gave the audience the impression that he was staring at them individually.

Ben had readied himself for the moment but still felt uneasy at seeing and hearing Geoffery again.

Andy recognised the background as the pergola that Geoffery had told him he'd built at the hospice when he was a young builder.

'Hello, it's me again. Hope you had a good party to send me off and not too many sore heads in the morning. Well this video goes hand in glove with my written will and is my last will and testament. I hope you've all been able to make the reading here in Monaco.'

Rupert felt the pinprick of tears as he thought of Joanne lying alone in Bristol.

'I've had time to think…don't worry this is pre-death. I haven't been able to find the after-death facilities yet.'

There were some uncomfortable chuckles from the listeners.

'It seems to me that my three Godsons are like the characters from the Wizard of OZ.

Geoffery's face was replaced by sepia tinted black and white images of the characters of the 1939 film.

Tim reminds me of the Tin Man. I appreciate that comment might not be too PC, as he has two prosthetic legs...but Tim you can try and sue me if you like.

'Stupid old git,' Tim muttered.

'Ssssh,' rebuked Carrie, looking at him and shaking her head.

Geoffery continued, *'I base my comments on my dealings with him and not on his physical condition. For I believe that Tim needs to look for a heart. He needs to be more sympathetic to other's needs, and less self-centred.'*

Kay, sitting the other side of Tim, agreed with Geoffery's assessment of her son, but kept her counsel

The video Geoffery continued, *'Rupert reminds me of the Lion looking for courage;'*

'Ha,' Sue said, under her breath. 'What! That pathetic piece of shit. And pigs might fly.'

The recording continued. *'He needs to be more assertive and stand up for himself, especially to that, hopefully, soon to be former wife of his -the wicked witch of the west, currently detained at her majesty's pleasure.'*

Everybody in the room looked round at her, her past now in the public domain again. She ignored their gaze and continued to send 'daggers' at Geoffery's screen image.

'Well that's where you got it wrong then isn't,' Sue hissed. 'You under estimated me, didn't you?...You mouldering heap of bones. Who is still alive? Who danced on your grave?'

'So it was her that vandalised Geoffery's grave.' Rupert noted. I wouldn't be surprised if she wasn't involved with the death of that bloke in the burial ground either,' he concluded, and shuddered at his hypothesis.

Rupert was overwhelmed by Sue's presence. She had pilfered his newly acquired resolve from him like a thief in the night. She had persuaded him that if he gave her half his inheritance she would leave him for good. He hung on to that hope, but in the back of his mind he knew it wouldn't be as simple as that to escape her cancerous presence.

The video continued and Geoffery added. *'Finally James, the Scarecrow; James is looking for a brain, except he has one, a very clever one that he hasn't used for a long time. He lost it after throwing his life away pining for his lost lover.'*

Ben looked at James as he gazed at the ceiling, obviously hurt by Geoffery's blunt observation and the mention of Sebastian, James's former partner.

'Right. The way this will work is that my Godsons will be taken into another room and will hold a mutually beneficial meeting chaired by Andy and make some important decisions.

The rest of you will have the pleasure of listening to your own individual sections from my will.

The video screen went blank as the law practice manager switched it off. The Godsons sat in stunned silence, looking at each other for some sign of comprehension to Geoffery's requirements.

As the manager showed Andy, James, Rupert and Tim into an adjoining room, Monique handed out tablet computers to the others, each tablet with an earpiece attached.

Each computer showed a picture of the intended recipient on the screen along with brief instructions on how to access the video file.

They all took the 'tablets' and moved to the four corners of the room at Monique's direction.

In spite of Sue's insistence that she should be given Joanne's, Monique stood her ground and refused to give it her.

Sue wandered over to the drinks dispenser and wondered what monetary benefits Rupert would let slip through his pathetic grasp without her guiding hand.

All the video clips started off with the same clip from Geoffery before having their own personalised message.

'My Godsons are going to have to work to get the money that I've bequeathed to them. You will need to support them as they strive to make things work.

It won't be easy for them, or you.

What! a groan I hear?' He paused dramatically as if anticipating the reaction.

'They'll appreciate it much better when they get it. How much they get depends on their efforts and the results they achieve.

It will not be easy, but, as we all know, there's no such thing as a free lunch. I have given them an opportunity to do something for the benefit of other people, including themselves. Their pay packet depends on their benevolence.'

CARRIE's personalised message;
'Carrie, you have a big challenge ahead of you to support Tim. I know that you have worked a miracle in transforming him into a semblance of a reasonable human being. Thanks for that, but I guess neither of us could have anticipated that Cupid would come calling. I know your love will carry you both through.

Your reward will be staying on my payroll if you continue to support Tim.'

KAY's personalised message;
'Kay, how I wish I could have my time over again. I now realise what I have missed by letting you slip out of my life all those years ago. But I took the path I did and well... the rest is history.

Having seen Tim at his worst, I think you have earned your legacy. I have therefore arranged for you to go on a world cruise. The trip will last for nearly four months during which time you will visit forty ports in six continents. Think of me occasionally at sunset. Have a great time.'

BEN's personalised message;
Ben, You don't need me to tell you that you have had a tough and confusing life. But I know that you have the makings of a great man inside you. There will be many challenges ahead, but always be true to yourself, always believe in yourself.

I hope that your new bikes will bring you lots of success in future mountain bike races. Enjoy

NADINE's personalised message:

'Nadine, Thank you once again for the time we shared together. I'm sorry it ended as it did. As I have said many times before, you have nothing to blame yourself for. I leave you a memento of our life together, a picture of the sunsets we shared on the pent house balcony.'

Had Joanne been there she would have heard the following:-

JOANNE's personalised message;

'Joanne, you are probably the best thing to have happened to Rupert in all his life. I know it will be difficult picking up somebody else's baggage, but I'm sure that with you by his side, he will find his courage and become a better man. Best of luck.

CHAPTER THIRTY SEVEN

23rd January

The practice Manager led the quartet into another smaller, but equally well-appointed, conference room and gave Andy a white envelope. After showing them the beverage arrangements he left, advising them to call him when they were ready.

The atmosphere in the room was tense. No-one spoke as Andy opened the sealed envelope. All eyes were focussed on his hands as he reached inside and pulled out a single sheet of paper.

Quickly he read the note to himself.

Tim broke the silence, impatient to hear Geoffery's apportionment of his fortune.

'This is the strangest will I've ever seen,' Andy said to his attentive audience.'

'Basically, there's no money on the table. He wants you to come up with some schemes to help other people and you all have to work together to achieve it.'

'What?' Tim said, incredulously, 'work together at what, for what? We barely even know each other.'

'When you've come up with the 'goods', then you get the money. He is using the 'over the rainbow' analogy.

He says we, including me, have to go on the way of the yellow brick road.'

'Yellow Brick road! What drugs were you giving him? He was obviously off his head when he wrote that. Isn't there something about, being of 'sound mind' when you write a will?'

'Look, I don't want to play his game. All I want is to get back to Jo. She needs me. He can keep his money,' Rupert said, disconsolately.

'What about the operation for your woman friend you were telling us about. Where did you say it was? In the States?'

'Yeah well, I'll have to pay for it some other way.'

'He sent me chasing up bloody mountains and now he wants me to go pissing off down a sodding 'yellow brick road', whatever that is.'

'It's a metaphor for a path of gold,' James added, quietly. 'Remember the story?'

'This is all a load of bollocks,' Tim said, standing. 'For a start we've got nothing in common.'

'Except for him,' James proffered.

'And his money. Which is the reason we're all here in the first place.' Andy added.

'So what happens next?' Tim demanded.

'It might be a good idea to introduce each other properly. I don't like being known as the 'Scarecrow',' James said, testily.

Andy noticed that James was starting to sweat and his face lost colour.

'Are you OK James?'

'It's just the withdrawal symptoms;- part of the detox. I've been getting a few pains in my stomach since I gave up the booze. I expect it's my liver trying to adjust to the lack of alcohol.'

At which point he doubled over in agony and let out an oath. 'Owww, that hurt,' he said, rubbing his stomach.

'Are you sure I can't get you something?' Andy asked, concerned.

'No, carry on. I'll be OK in a minute.' James insisted.

'Is there anything else in that letter?'

'Yes.' Andy read from the letter;

'*You each have strengths and weaknesses. You can help each other through life. Listen to one another. Decide how you can help your fellow man? I have brought you together. It's now up to you.*'

'It still doesn't answer my question. So when do we get the money?' Tim asked the question they were all wondering.

Geoffery might no longer be with them in body, but he was still manipulating their lives from beyond the grave.

Meanwhile, in the main conference room, the others sat in reverential silence, thinking about Geoffery and their individual messages.

Kay 'broke the ice', and deliberately shunning Sue asked everyone else, 'Would anyone like a nice cup of tea?'

Kay still believed that a 'nice cup of tea', was the British panacea for resolving all problems.

Being ignored further antagonised Sue, who was still seething from her earlier excommunication.'

'Non merci,' Nadine said, shaking her head, her mind full of emotional memories of her time together with Geoffery.

'Just as well,' Kay thought, 'or I might have been tempted to put some rat poison in it.'

'Not for me,' Sue said, determined to barge her way back into the circle, all the time, straining to listen to the conversation from next door.

'Carrie?'

'Yes please, I'll have a brew.'

'Ben?'

'Yes. Could I have an orange juice please?'

Relieved to be doing something, Kay busied herself making the drinks. The suspense in the room was palpable as they listened to the beverage making. After a few minutes, Kay again broke the silence putting the glass down in front of Ben. 'There you are young man,' she said.

'Thank you,' he acknowledged.

As he raised the glass to his lips he caught Sue's eye looking at him. His heart missed a beat. Surely these were the same hate filled eyes he had seen looking out from the photo on the Gravediggers mobile.

'What are you looking at?' Sue said, angrily.

'Nothing,' Ben said, tilting the glass to put a barrier between him and her piercing gaze. 'Was it her…?' He was frightened by the thought.

Carrie had heard enough from the irritating woman and lapsing in to her native Geordie, she said. 'Why, the moggie can gandie at a queen.'

'I don't know what you're on about. 'Sue said dismissively.

'It means a cat can look at the Queen.' Carrie explained. 'Nobody in their right mind would bother to look at you though.' She added angrily.

Sue ignored her comment. 'I don't know why he's got them in there by themselves. Rupert always needs me to help sort out anything complicated.' She said, to nobody in particular. 'Why all the mystery? Why can't he just give them the money? And there's an end to it.'

'Geoffery never does. Excusez,' Nadine corrected herself. 'Never did anything simply. E always made sure things were done correctly and people earned zere money.'

'Mmm,' Sue tutted.

'Excusez. I don't zink we have met. I don't remember zeeing you at the funeral.' Nadine said, studying Sue.

'I am Rupert's wife. No, unfortunately I was...er detained and couldn't get there in time.'

'Mais oui, so oo was the lady there with Rupert?' she asked naively.

Sue's hackles rose but and she ignored the remark. Carrie smirked at Nadine's probing question.

Having gone 'round and round' in their deliberations and unable to come to any clear way forward, Andy suggested that they tell the Law Practice Manager of their impasse. Summoning him back to the conference room as directed, he quickly returned.

On hearing of their inconclusive debate, he suggested that they needed to have time to consider their next steps to go home, and, if necessary, return to Monaco when they had some concrete plans to meet Geoffery's conditions. He reminded Andy that he would be the catalyst to ensure the three moved things forward.

He took them back into the conference room, where there was great expectation from the others.

But the mood soon changed as they filed into the room. Immediately they knew something was up, as they saw gloomy faces, not the expected happy faces of millionaires.

Sue was trying unsuccessfully to catch Rupert's eye, but from his dour face she knew he had failed yet again. Her plans for taking the money and disappearing into Europe, all but disappearing.

The Manager wished them all the best in their quest and said he looked forward to seeing them if they needed to return.

He called the reception desk and made arrangements for their transport to take them to the Hotel to freshen up ready for the gourmet meal.

Sue moved to stand next to Rupert as they left the room only to be frustrated by Carrie who deliberately blocked her way.

'Right missy, you'd better watch your step,' Sue thought, as she failed to barge her way past.

CHAPTER THIRTY EIGHT

23rd January

After a short journey from the law firm, the group arrived at the luxurious five star Hotel du Paris. Excitedly, Ben led the way up the short flight of steps into the vast air conditioned lobby.

'Wow, look at this place,' he enthused.' Pinch me; I think I've stepped into a fairy tale.'

The opulence of it all overwhelmed him. He stared wide eyed at the vast atrium with its high fluted ceilings supported by large decorative marble pillars, each one exquisitely adorned with intricate carvings. Flowing arches linked the room into the centrepiece of the circular ceiling, where a huge coloured glass dome filtered natural light into the chamber.

Suspended from the centre of the dome was a ten foot high crystal chandelier, underneath which, a colossal floral display of orchids effused elegance into the room.

The art deco style flower vase was precisely positioned on a highly polished antique mahogany table which was sited in the middle of a large hand knotted floral Chinese rug. It was an island of sophistication in a sea of marble.

'These polished marble floors are massive. I think you could play several games of football in here, all at the same time. They'd be great for sliding on too,' Ben said, his eyes gleaming with excitement.

'I think the hotel management might have something to say if you did,' James said, smiling at Ben's infectious euphoria.

Ben gazed around the vast vestibule at the casual configurations of sofas, chairs and glass topped tables, discreetly positioned around the periphery to form intimate lounge areas. Each area was brightly lit by the judicious positioning of mirrors and wall lights within the alcoves, further enhancing the natural light from the dome.

'Have they got a swimming pool?' Ben asked, looking around for a sign.

'Yes, several, indoors and outdoors.'

'Great! Oh damn,' he said, suddenly realising, 'I haven't brought my swimming trunks.'

'The Major-domo will provide a pair for you I'm sure.'

'The Major what? The Major Dumbo?"

No, the name is Major-domo. He's like the person in charge of all the staff down here.'

'How do you know?'

'I've stayed here many times before. But many years ago now though.'

'Look, there's even a statue of a bloke on a horse.' Ben said, looking up at the large marble statue.

'Zat is Louis XIV,' said Nadine, joining them. 'I 'ad forgotten you used to come 'ere too James.'

'But that was in a different lifetime. Yes, I did. Actually, I think we might have met here once before, at one of Geoffery's parties.'

'Probably before I moved in with 'im,' she said, leading them over to the oak panelled reception desk.

Andy was uneasy when he learnt that Nadine was also staying at the hotel rather than going home.

'If ze number in your party 'ad been smaller, I would 'ave hosted you in my villa, she'd said. But it is much simpler to use ze hotel. There is no need to travel for the entertainment,' she'd told him, her eye contact lingering uncomfortably longer than he felt it needed to for his comfort.

In spite of his loyalty to Helen, the absence of any resumed intimacy with her, following Molly's birth, was causing him some 'difficult' moments of frustrated temptation, especially now in the presence of a beautiful, very friendly and 'tactile' woman.

He shook his head to clear his licentious thoughts. She was after all just playing the good host. There was nothing seductive in her behaviour. He was reading the wrong signals.

Eventually, all the others were booked in and making their way to their rooms. Only Sue and Rupert remained.

'Right, we are nearly done. Finally I have a reservation for a double luxury room for Mademoiselle Joanne Carr and Monsieur Screen,' the receptionist said, expectantly looking at Sue and Rupert. 'Is that correct?'

'No, that's changed. Did nobody tell you?' said Sue, brusquely. 'Miss Carr is in hospital.'

'I am so sorry to hear.'

Rupert hadn't allowed himself to think this far ahead. Sharing a room with Sue again, was going to be a nightmare. The thought of being unchaperoned in the same space as her rendered him speechless. He feared for the consequences.

'I need a separate room,' Sue demanded.

'I am sorry Madam, but the hotel is full. Perhaps you could share a room with Monsieur Screen?'

'Oh this is too much. Are you sure you're full?'

'Yes Madame,' the receptionist said, rechecking her screen.

'Oh well if I must.'

'First I have to register you. Your name please.'

'Sue Williams Screen.'

The receptionist looked up at her and was just about to say something, but Sue's angry stare persuaded her otherwise. Instead she continued typing the change of occupancy.

Sue had not had the opportunity of speaking to Rupert in the short drive from the Law firm but, as they got into the exclusive sea view room, she wasted no time in launching into her interrogation.

'Well what happened? I gather from your miserable faces that you haven't been given the money.' Sue said, advancing towards him.

'No. he's…he's written in the will conditions that we've got to earn it.' Rupert said, backing away.

'Earn it! earn it! This is a will reading not an effing job interview. You don't earn money in a will. You get it given you. You receive it,' she erupted, sending a spray of spittle into his face.

Rupert felt the wall against his back. He was trapped. 'I'm sorry, but that's it…'

'Sorry! Sorry! I'll bloody give you sorry. You ought to know better than to try and pull the wool over my eyes,' she said, raising her hand to slap him across the face.

However, in her greedy desperation to establish when she could get her hands on the money, Sue had not closed the door of the room fully and Carrie, who was passing, overheard the grilling. Quietly she pushed the door open and alarmed at what she saw, stepped into the room.

'What the hell's going on?'

'Keep your nose out of this,' Sue said, ferociously, walking towards her.

'Ah couldn't help hearing what Rupert said, but Tim told me the same, they have to earn the legacy.' Carrie informed her.

'It's nothing to do with you. Now piss off and close the door behind you.'

Carrie's combative instinct came to the fore. 'An what are yee gunna do aboot it, if Ah don't?' she said, standing her ground.

'Don't tempt me,' Sue replied, facing up to her, Now get out of here before I…'

Carrie called her bluff. 'Before yee do what?

'I kick your plastic legs from under you…you…half woman.'

Before she knew what had hit her, Sue was flat on her back with Carrie on top. Momentarily surprised by the suddenness of Carrie's attack, Sue was shocked into inactivity for a second.

But Carrie had now gone into 'military mode', her right hand grasping the dress material on Sue's right shoulder and using it as an anchor pivot she forced her forearm across Sue's throat, restricting her airway.

'Why, now we're both the same. Neither of us needs our feet.' Carrie said, into Sue's face.

Sue was writhing underneath Carrie, desperately tugging at her arm, trying to relieve the pressure on her throat and attempting to shout. Frantically she twisted and bucked, struggling to throw her off. Carrie rode the bucking bronco underneath her, years of training ensuring that the choke lock stayed firm.

Rupert, a victim of domestic violence at Sue's hand for many years, could not cope with the viciousness before him. He was paralysed with fear, his whole being overwhelmed, unable to do anything but stare blankly, his mind seeking refuge in a far off place.

Tim was on his way back to his suite when he saw what was going on through the open door. He was horrified at seeing the two women thrashing around on the floor.

'Carrie! Carrie for chrissake. What the bloody hell are you doing?'

By now Carrie's mind was firmly in military mode. She was fighting for her life. She was transported to a hot dusty field in a foreign land. This was a life or death struggle. The choice was simple. It was either her or the insurgent beneath her.

'Let her go Carrie. Let her go.' Tim shouted, grabbing her shoulders.

By now Sue was starting to lose consciousness, her fighting getting weaker and weaker as the hold took effect.

Carrie released the throat compression and turned Sue over on her face, dragging her arms down behind her back and pinning them with one hand.

She moved her right hand to her waist searching for where her 'killing kit', pistol and knife, should have been. Unable to find it, she shouted. 'Don't just stand there man. Give me sum frigging plastic cuffs before she kicks off again.'

'Carrie, Carrie…It's me, Tim. For God's sake get off her,' he shouted anxiously.

At the sound of Tim's voice Carrie gradually stopped her restraint of Sue, finally letting go of her wrists.

Breathing heavily and still pumped up she was disorientated about her surroundings. She shook her head to refocus her thoughts. It took her a few minutes looking around to realise where she was. Tim watched as she mentally switched back from warrior to woman. Slowly she rolled off Sue and took Tim's proffered hand to help her stand.

'Did you start that?' he asked, concerned, looking at Sue's prostrate form. 'Is she…?'

'Why no, she's only winded. She'll be up on her feet shortly. The bitch has been asking for it all day. She pushed me too far this time.'

'She certainly got more than she bargained for, that's for sure,' Tim said, putting his arm around Carrie's shoulder. 'Christ, you alright mate?' he said, spotting Rupert cowering in the corner.

Rupert was like a rabbit caught in the headlights, eyes wide open, just staring. He heard a strange voice, a million miles away saying 'Yes.'

Holding her throat and gulping in lungfuls of air, Sue struggled to kneel up.

'What was this all about?' Tim quizzed, watching and wondering whether or not to help Sue up.

'He was telling her he had to earn the legacy,' Carrie informed him, 'but the greedy cow thought he was lying and was just going to land him one when Ah arrived.'

'Was she now? Come on mate,' Tim said, walking towards Rupert. 'You ain't staying in here with that money-grabbing bitch. We've got a suite. You can come in with us.'

In a trance, Rupert gathered his stuff together and followed Carrie out of the room. Tim walked beside him, putting his hand on Rupert's shoulder and steered him along the corridor.

In the meantime Sue had crawled towards the bed and was just trying to stand up as a hotel security man ran into the room.

'What's going on?' he said, urgently. 'We had a report of shouting and…'

'It's OK, 'Sue said, holding her throat. 'It's all over. Nothing to worry about.'

'Are you sure?'

'Yes, I told you. Now close the door as you leave.'

'As the door closed, Sue staggered to the mirror and looked at her bruised throat. 'You might have won this time bitch, but you'd better watch your back from now on. Nobody does that to me and gets away with it.'

Sue had felt fear for the first time in her life, and she didn't like it, one bit.

CHAPTER THIRTY NINE

23rd January

'Andy, you better get here quick. We got a problem.' Tim said, urgently. He had telephoned as soon as they got back to their suite with Rupert.

Within a few minutes Andy and the Godsons were seated in Tim and Carrie's suite.

'Where's Ben?'

'He's with my Mum in the hotel swimming pool,' Tim informed him.

'Good. No need to worry about him then,' Andy said, sitting back. 'So what's the problem?'

Rupert sat impassively as Tim relayed the episode that had taken place earlier, emphasising Carrie's subsequent intervention.

'The bitch is only here to steal Rupert's inheritance,' Tim added, dramatically.

'I knew there was something fishy about her accompanying you Rupert,' Andy revealed.

'She threatened to get Jo in hospital unless I brought her. I didn't want to, I'm sorry but what could I do?' Rupert explained, woefully. 'She said she would kill Jo and our baby.'

'Baby! You're going to be a Dad?'

Everyone looked at him in astonishment. Andy was first to break the stunned silence. 'Wow! Congratulations!'

Suddenly the room was transformed into a sea of smiles.

'The trouble is, that while Jo is in a coma they are concerned about the baby's development,' Rupert added glumly, putting a dampener on the good feel factor.

'I'm sure they'll be OK,' Andy said, encouragingly. 'There are so many developments taking place all the time and Frenchay is one of the best hospitals for her type of care.'

'Sue will be really angry now, after what happened.'

'Rupert, don't worry. It's going to be alright. Don't fret.' Carrie said, compassionately, rubbing his shoulders.'

'No it isn't! She always manages to wriggle off the hook. Look at Geoffery's attempted murder charge,' Rupert said, tearfully.

Andy shifted uncomfortably. 'Yes, well I'm sorry about that, but what else could I do? Geoffery was obviously acting for the best, to help you. Clearly he didn't know that there was a camera in his room.

When I discovered what had happened, I agonised over it for ages…but I couldn't see any other way around it. I had to take the recording to the Police.'

'Well recriminations aren't going to help Rupert,' James interjected. 'We need to be doing something to help him now.'

'If it helps, I heard her mutter during today's video that she was the one who danced on his grave.' Rupert volunteered.

'What?' Andy said, in astonishment. 'You heard her say that?'

'Yes, it was under her breath, but she said it alright.'

'Well I knew it wasn't Ben. I always had my suspicions that she was behind it. That's great news. We can now prove conclusively that Ben is innocent.'

'So she probably had something to do with the death of that bloke in the burial ground,' James mused.

'Oh my God!'

'Ay, she's certainly got the manic strength on her, to have done that,' Carrie said, rubbing her bruised arm.

'So what do we do?' Tim asked to nobody in particular.

'I think the Police might be on to her anyway,' Rupert volunteered.

'Why do you say that?'

'Because they came and saw me in hospital. They wanted to know what she was doing on the night of the crash.'

'What did you say?'

Rupert shifted uncomfortably. She…she…made me tell them she was in my car.'

'Was she?'

'No, of course not. I don't know why she wanted me to lie.'

'So why is she here with you now?'

'She was talking about taking her share of my legacy and disappearing off into Europe. That's why she was so angry earlier. I don't think she was planning on going back with us anyway.'

'By her share, what did she mean?'

'Knowing her, it probably would have been all of it.'

'The grabbing bitch,' Tim said, angrily. 'Don't worry, we'll look after you.'

Andy made a mental note at Tim's surprising intention to help Rupert.

CHAPTER FORTY

23rd January

The fight with Carrie had aggravated Sue's whiplash injuries, causing her considerable discomfort. She was in so much pain that she stayed in her room for the rest of the day and had room service bring her evening meal. Consequently she also missed the trip to the Casino.

Although she was very angry about missing out on the trip, she consoled herself, that when she had Rupert's money, she would come back again and do it, by herself, in style.

The period of forced inactivity however, gave her the opportunity to devise a scheme to get the other half of Rupert's legacy and plot a vitriolic revenge on Carrie.

Ben had never been to a restaurant before and was overwhelmed by the experience. The sheer elegance of the beautiful dining room continued to enhance his journey into this fairy tale world of unimaginable wealth.

Everything there, he found incredible, the wall frescoes, the starched linen, wine glasses of different shapes and sizes, the gold rimmed plates, stylish cutlery, and the padded chairs. He was amused to see that they even had a padded handbag chair for the ladies.

The food too was a culinary adventure for him, not much on a plate but amazingly and artistically presented.

Originally, he decided to have lobster, but soon changed his mind when he was invited to chose his own live one from the restaurant tanks.

However, determined to have fish from the Mediterranean, he chose a rock fish dish which he thoroughly enjoyed, but was amazed later to discover that it cost over a £100, just for his main course.

After the group had dined in the exquisite Michelin starred restaurant, Nadine led the party the short distance through a manicured square, with its gushing, elegantly lit water features, to the Casino.

Climbing the short flight of steps, they entered the lobby where people were patiently queuing to check in bags. The vigilant security guards, acknowledging Nadine by name, fast tracked them through into the Casino.

The complex was a labyrinth of gaming rooms, tastefully embellished with stained glass windows, sculptures, paintings and atmospheric lighting created by strategically placed bronze light fittings.

Populating most rooms, were suites of flashing slot machines. High stools carefully positioned in front of each encouraged the foolhardy gambler to stay longer than they'd intended to.

All around the room tourists were ceaselessly feeding money into the fruit machines; an occasional rattling of coins punctuated the silence as the odds briefly swung into the favour of a fortunate punter.

'Attention,' Nadine said, addressing the group like a tour guide, 'I suggest we split up 'ere and you can wander and do whatever you like.

Perhaps after you 'ave spent some money ere you would like to 'ave a wander around town. It is a lovely place, as you will see, and perfectly safe n'est ce pas? Zere is very little crime 'ere. Indeed, it is reported that zere are two Policemen to every resident, so we are all well looked after.'

Andy had persuaded Rupert that he should come out with the group although he was clearly still in shock after witnessing the Carrie and Sue brawl.

Rupert had sought solace in phoning to check on Joanne, and all he really wanted to do was to get back to her bedside and hold her hand, - a love struck suitor pining for her company.

Tim, Carrie and Kay took Rupert under their wing and they stayed together, joining the other tourists in 'fluttering' on the slot machines.

To his annoyance, Tim was talked out of gambling on the spin of the roulette wheel.

'Come on, I'm a millionaire, I can lose a few Euro,' he pleaded.

'You're not a millionaire yet,' Kay said, cautiously.

'No Tim, don't gamble it away before yee've even got it,' Carrie added.

In spite of feeling less than a hundred percent, James had joined the group at the Casino.

It hadn't changed much since his affluent days, when he'd won and lost fortunes here. It felt as if was only yesterday that he had frequented the place.

Ben stayed with James as they toured the complex. His wonderful adventure of how the other half live, provided him with a kaleidoscope of a world he believed only existed in films.

In spite of Andy's apprehension at being 'alone' with her, he followed Nadine into an area which was only open to 'vetted people; the high stakes exclusive club, where it was clear that Nadine was very well known.

Andy felt underdressed in the plush rooms in which they wandered. All the men wore white dinner jackets and bow ties. The women were all adorned in expensive, full length, low cut, evening gowns, similar to Nadine's.

Several of Nadine's bejewelled female acquaintances scrutinized Andy as they passed and made comments in French. Andy didn't understand, but it was clearly about him and her. Nadine laughed at their remarks, grabbling Andy's arm and pressing her perfumed body provocatively close to his, before leading him purposely away.

'This is where the real Casino is working,' she said, 'away from all the tourists. As you noticed, we were checked in by security guards before we could enter. That way the Casino Management control who can afford to play and lose here, without having any debtor problems.

I usually play Punto Banco. You'd know it as Baccarat I expect. Do you wish to gamble too?'

'No thanks. I don't gamble. Never had the money.'

'Well perhaps you will bring me luck at the table,' she said, holding his arm and steering him to a couple of vacate chairs.

'Um...if you don't mind I'd...I'd like to...um, have a wander around town.'

'Oh there is plenty of time to do that,' she said. 'The city doesn't sleep. The sights will still be there after we have played.'

Andy was feeling very awkward. He didn't want to upset his host, but on the other hand, he wanted to remove himself from the temptation of being so close to her.

The demons in his head were telling him that tonight could be a special night. The wine increasingly helped to persuade him to stay, as his stoical resolve crumbled.

'Hell,' he convinced himself, 'I'm never likely to experience a night like this ever again. Let's enjoy it while I can.' This was a 'one off' opportunity to visit the Casino with a beautiful woman on his arm. It was a lifetime away from a night shift at the hospice.

As the night progressed, and Nadine continued to gamble, Andy struggled to keep awake, his alcoholically enhanced ambitions disappearing in a wave of sheer fatigue. For he'd only caught a few hours' sleep after coming off a night shift at the hospice at 6 am before picking Ben up to catch the plane,

But Nadine had been on a winning streak and was reluctant to leave the Casino until the early hours.

Finally, after a brief tour around the city, they got back to the hotel at 4 am and Andy escorted Nadine to her room.

They stopped in the corridor outside. Andy was feeling very woozy. He had been drinking Red Bull cocktails all night to try to keep himself awake. But the alcohol was having the opposite effect.

'Andee, I 'ave a gift for you,' she said, holding his arm to steady him.

'A gift, for me? Whatever for?'

'For looking after me and ze girls, and for being there for my Geofferee.'

'I did nothing. It was my job and…'

'I zink you did more than just your job. Zank you,' and she kissed him gently on the lips. Andy fought the desire to envelop her in his arms and kiss her back.

'I must give it to you now,' she said, pulling away. 'Because I 'ave to go to a meeting early in the morning. Please come in and get it.'

Reluctantly Andy agreed. He was fighting the lustful desire that had been building all evening.

He didn't know whether she was giving him the 'come on' by inviting him into her room or whether there really was a gift. He was about to be tested, big time.

Sue had heard their voices in the corridor as they discussed the invitation.

'What's going on out there?' she said to herself, walking over to the door and peering through the door peephole.

She was just in time to see them heading into Nadine's room. 'Oh, now that is interesting! The nurse is going into her room. My, how the mighty have fallen. This is brilliant.'

Immediately she was thinking about how she could use his indiscretion to her advantage.

Nadine left Andy in the lounge area and went into her bedroom. Andy's imagination was on fire. Was she going to 'slip into something 'more comfortable?

He sat down on the sofa and waited. He decided he would take the opportunity if it presented itself.

CHAPTER FORTY ONE

24th January

Andy followed Nadine into the bedroom where subtle lighting painted it with a warm pink luminosity. Gentle classical music enhanced the mood and filled the silence.

She stopped suddenly and turned. 'Andee, mon cher,' she said, lifting her arms.

Andy walked into her embrace, her perfume seducing him, his breathing, heavy with desire, his heart beating madly, his head full of lust.

They cemented the embrace with a passionate kiss, Andy enfolding her, holding her tightly.

She responded, submitting herself to him as Andy's hands stroked her sensuous back through the silk dress. Her warmth, her exquisite perfume and her softness lighting a fire in his loins. His head exploded with desire.

Unable to control his ardour any longer, his fingers explored the top of her elegant dress and found the zip fastener. Slowly, gently, he guided it down, hoping she wouldn't notice and stop him revealing her exquisite body. Instead, to his delight she pushed her body further into his, encouraging him.

The fastener finally reached the end of its travel and his hands moved up, caressing the nakedness that he'd exposed.

He traced the line of her spine and brought his hands up to her petite shoulders. His fingers touched the soft gaping dress material and he gently lifted the edge and pulled it forward towards him. She responded by shrugging her shoulders to help with the removal process, releasing her embrace briefly, to slip one arm out at a time from the shoulder straps.

Finally the dress slipped from her body as she pulled back without reducing the intensity of their kiss. It cascaded over her breasts and puddled around her feet on the floor.

He pulled away and looked at her exquisite body, overwhelmed by her beauty. He scooped her up into his arms and carried her to the sofa. Gently laying her down, he feasted on her loveliness as he undressed himself. She watched as he cast off his clothes until he was naked. Then he lay down beside her.

CHAPTER FORTY TWO

24th January

James had been having a hard time of it, since coming off the booze. Fortunately, the temptations that had knocked Beth off the recovery plan had not come his way. although it was a hard and ongoing battle.

He hated all the anguish, the agonies and terrible symptoms of the withdrawal programme. The whole experience was galling, but he recognised that without it, he wouldn't have survived much longer. The pill regime they had prescribed for him was a necessary evil to control the worst of his symptoms, the heavy sweating, the racing heart, the muscle tremors.

However, when he'd come away from the influence of the clinic he'd managed to stay dry. He had somehow found the strength to be mentally strong over the cravings.

Consequently, he became fanatical about anything that would lead him back into 'temptation'. Having his drinks spiked by well-meaning people made him ultra cautious. So he always got his own soft drinks.

But he had not calculated for Sue's evil and vindictive nature. She had already arranged for a vodka 'spiked' jug of water to be put in his fridge.

Unable to smell anything, James had been inadvertently causing himself harm by drinking the water to ease his symptoms. The more he drank, the more painful the reaction.

He thought nothing of the reasons for the pain, as he knew that his liver was pretty well 'shot' anyway and he was expecting to suffer due to years of self-abuse. Consequently, his nights were normally punctuated by long periods of sleeplessness, and his days, by tired confusion.

The Clinic consultant had told him that, sooner or later, his ailing liver would need to be replaced. He had duly included this in his future plans, - his 'bucket list' as he jokingly called it.

He laughed, to himself, at the irony of his own categorisation. For he knew, if he didn't have it done, he would, without doubt, be 'kicking the bucket' anyway.

But an operation would only occur if that they could find a suitable living or dead donor with compatible matching blood and tissue types.

He found it amazing that some people were brave enough, to volunteer to have half their own healthy liver removed, to help save someone else's life.

It was during the sleepless night at the hotel, that he wondered what he should do to resume a normal life, and capitalise on the opportunity Geoffery had given him.

Clearly, his new world would be constrained within the limitations of his abused body, for he had a realistic understanding of what he'd done to himself. Living only for the next bottle had given him a legacy of ill health for an unpredictable future.

He thought about Geoffery's analogy that he was the Scarecrow in his OZ theme, looking for a brain.

He might have been closer than he thought, for at the moment his head felt like it was actually stuffed with straw.

He had been well educated and come away from the private school with some excellent qualifications, But never bothered to take up his University place.

Instead, the playboy life style, fuelled by his late Father's millions, had a greater allure. It also meant that he could pick and choose where he worked, or if he worked at all, the rest of his income coming from shrewd investments.

The trip back to his roots had again stirred up painful regrets, the Casino trip especially, for there had been a lot of faces that he recognised on their way into the exclusive 'members only' part.

He'd turned down Nadine's invitation for her to take him in there. The memories would be too painful, he decided.

But he doubted that they would recognise him anyway. For his physical appearance had changed enormously since leaving his Monaco bachelor pad and losing all the trappings of wealth.

Living on the streets had taken its toll. Gone was the smart, self-confident, athletic, man about town. In spite of his new clothes, now he looked like a tramp with swarthy skin, hollow cheeked and hair that had started falling out.

No. He had to move on, but where?

Ben was a nice kid and he just hoped all the pressure of the various traumas going on his life wouldn't send him off the rails too. What with the Police and his Mother and the threat of being taken into care, nobody could blame him if he did.

Perhaps that's where he should focus his efforts. The kid needed a break. Perhaps with Geoffery's money he could help him. Maybe send him to a good school…then again, thinking about it… he'd actually had a miserable school life himself.

Perhaps on the other hand, it would be better to support him in his cycling. Whatever, the kid deserved a lucky break. With that thought in his mind, he finally drifted off in to a pain free sleep.

CHAPTER FORTY THREE

24th January

Andy's body clock woke him up just before 5:30 am, the alcoholic excesses and lack of sleep, giving him a pounding headache. Bleary eyed he looked around and it took him a few minutes to realise where he was.

'Oh my god! What have I done? I'm in Nadine's room.'

Nadine heard him moving and got up. She put on a filmy white silk dressing gown. She had a small parcel in her hand.

Awkwardly he addressed her. Looking in to her face for any hint of derision at what had happened. 'Umm morning Nadine...um.'

'Andee you are awake, Oh good. I didn't want to disturb you.

'No...um. I was awake.'

We had a good time last night, no?'

'Umm...yes, from what I remember,' he said, feeling guilty.

'Anyway, 'ere is zee present,' she said, giving him the small box.' I 'ope you like it.'

'Well thank you. I don't know what to say. But thanks, I wasn't expecting it.'

'I don't wish to hurry you, but I 'ave to shower and get dressed as I said I 'ave a meeting to go to in Nice at 8am.'

Nadine opened the door to an empty corridor and Andy stepped outside, pocketing the gift.

Sue heard the door open as they stepped out of Nadine's room. She walked quickly to her door and looking through the peep hole saw them together in the corridor.

'Au revoir Andee, perhaps this is zee last time I will see you. Merci beaucoup.'

Hoping to catch them in a compromising situation as they said their goodbyes, Sue opened the door and crept into the corridor, mobile phone in hand. Quickly she selected 'record' in the photo option and clandestinely videoed the pair.

Andy, barely awake, didn't hear Sue creeping out of her room as he hugged Nadine's scantily clad body, her perfume still tantalising his senses. 'Nadine, thanks for last night. I really enjoyed it,' Andy said, blearily.

'My pleasure too Andee,' she said, returning the embrace, kissing him briefly.

Sue crept back into her room unobserved. 'I couldn't have wished for anything better even if I'd arranged that,' she said, smirking.

Andy heard the door close, but didn't see which one, and, tiredly made his way back to his room.

CHAPTER FORTY FOUR

24th January

Sue was now wide awake and feeling very pleased with herself, having caught Andy and Nadine in a clinch.

'Oh yes,' she said, kissing her mobile. 'You are going to pay for this, big time.'

However her euphoria was short lived as the pain in her neck reminded her that she had not packed enough painkillers in her travel bag.

Fed up with already spending a protracted time in her room, she decided to go down to reception and get some pills rather than ringing for room service. Glad to get out of the room for a brief spell, she made her way slowly down the corridor.

Ben had barely slept either. He was still buzzing, not wanting to waste any opportunity of this magic holiday.

As soon as he knew the swimming pool was open, he was down there, having great fun in his borrowed trunks.

After an hour in the pool, Ben was feeling hungry and having agreed to meet the others for breakfast at eight, he decided to take the lift back to his room.

As the lift the doors were closing, Sue stepped in.

Ben's heart skipped a beat and he immediately backed into the far corner of the lift.

Although still racking his brains to try to remember why she looked familiar, he couldn't avoid the temptation of staring at her.

Sue tried to ignore him. But could see, in the mirrored wall, that he was looking at her.

'What are you looking at?' she barked.

'Sorry,' said Ben, looking away. But within a few seconds, his eyes were drawn back to her reflection.

It was then that his worst fears were confirmed. She was definitely the 'owner' of the eyes in the photo, on the Gravediggers phone.

'I said stop looking at me, you little shit.'

'You're the one!' he whispered. Ben felt his heart sink, realising that he'd actually vocalised his thoughts.

'What do you mean?' she said, moving towards him.

'Nothing.'

'Don't nothing me! What were you on about?' she ranted.

'You don't frighten me lady,' Ben said, stretching himself up to his full height, and attempting to sound tough.

'Perhaps these will,' Sue said, grabbing a pair of scissors out of her handbag. 'Why do you keep staring at me?' she glared.

The demonic look was the one Ben had seen on the phone.

'You're the one in the photo on the phone, aren't you?' he demanded, bravely.

'Phone! What phone?'

Suddenly he realised what he'd done. By revealing his suspicions, he'd effectively 'put his head in the lions mouth'. Vainly he tried to come up with a feasible explanation.

'The err…photo…'

Sue's suspicions were now raised. But she couldn't believe that he would be talking about the missing mobile. It was too much of a coincidence. However she decided to interrogate the boy more.

'Don't bullshit me kid. I think you and I need a longer chat, don't you?'

Just then the lift stopped and the doors opened. There was nobody about so she grabbed his hair and put the scissors to his throat.

She led him back to her room and while she dug into her handbag for the card key, Ben was hoping to make good his escape, but she was too quick for him.

Plucking the card key out, she put it into the slot of the reader. A faint click and the green light confirmed it was unlocked and she walked in, still holding the scissors to Ben's throat.

She kicked the door shut behind her and marched Ben to a high backed chair by her dressing table.

'Sit down and don't move' she said, standing behind him, the cold scissors across his throat. 'Now what photo are you talking about?'

'You can't bully me, like you bully your husband,' he said, feeling brave.

'And what would you know about that, eh?' she said, slapping his head to emphasise her point.

'Ow!' he yelped. 'I heard the others talking about it.'

'Did you now? Well you can't believe everything people say. Now tell me about this photo?' she said, giving his hair another sharp tug.

'Ow, let go and I'll tell you.'

She eased the pressure slightly.

'It was on the phone.'

'On the phone! What phone?'

'I found a phone in the burial ground.'

'Burial ground!' Immediately she knew, but she wanted confirmation of her suspicions. 'What Burial ground?'

'The one on the top of Churchup hill.'

'Whereabouts, exactly?'

'It was on the path.'

'When did you find it?'

'Christmas Eve. The day after Geoffery's funeral.'

'What was on the photo?'

'Your face, blurred. You were holding the cross that I made for Geoffery. I recognised your eyes.'

'Where's the phone now?'

'It's with the Police. I gave it to them.'

'When?'

'What do you mean?'

'It's a simple enough question,' she said, tugging his hair again. 'When did you give the phone to the Police?'

'A few weeks ago.'

'Why only a few weeks ago? Why didn't you hand it to them straight away?'

'I forgot I had it. What with the Police accusing me of desecrating the grave and...'

'Desecrating the grave!' Sue repeated. She couldn't believe her ears. Dame fortune appeared to be smiling on her after all.

'Yes this bloke saw me ...there...'

'Did he now?'

'And the Police tried to say that I'd stolen the phone.'

Sue's mind was in overdrive. This was an unexpected bonus. Joyfully, she thought, I can use his own confession against him.

'Well you did do the damage, didn't you?' she said, cunningly.

'What do you mean, I did it? I sodding didn't'

'But I was there. I saw you do it.'

What! No you weren't, and I didn't do it. Don't lie,' he said, indignantly.

'Of course you did. When we get back to England, I shall have to tell the Police that you did the damage to the grave. Then, after YOU hit the poor man, you stole his phone. You'll remember, I was chasing after you, and that's why my photo is on it.'

'You're a liar. That's not what happened and you know it,' he said, furiously.

'I think you'll find that's exactly what happened. You appear to have forgotten.'

Ben was overwhelmed by her distorted explanation.

'Right now, here's what's going to happen. I want you to go to the suite where that army bitch is...'

'You mean Carrie?'

'Yes of course, don't interrupt...I want you to tell Rupert he's got to come here right away. Don't tell him I told you. Make up some story...say the hotel manager wants to speak to him about the incident yesterday.'

'Incident?'

'Just tell him. He will know what it means. Don't tell him I'm here.'

'What if I won't?'

Sue tightened the grip on his hair.' The Police will be interested to hear my story, I'm sure.'

Ben reluctantly did as he was told, finding that Rupert was in the room by himself as Tim, Carrie and Kay had gone swimming.

The hotel had made special arrangements for the amputees to have a private session, without other guests gawking at them, although Tim and Carrie had no problems with swimming with fully limbed people. They suspected the hotel were 'protecting' the sensitivities of the other guests.

Unable to think of a way of disobeying Sue, Ben did as he was told and brought Rupert back.

As they entered the room, Sue who had hidden behind the door, slammed it shut.

'Hello Rupert,' she said, evilly. 'Where are your friends now?'

'I'm sorry Rupert,' Ben said, desperately apologetic, 'she made me.'

'Don't worry Ben. I've known her ways long enough now to know what she's capable of.'

'Sit down both of you. We're going to have a nice chat.'

CHAPTER FORTY FIVE

24th January

When Carrie, Tim and Kay returned to their suite, following their swim, they were surprised that Rupert was not there, especially as they'd made arrangements to go down for breakfast together.

As Rupert still hadn't returned after they'd showered and got ready, they rang James to discover he hadn't seen him either. They tried calling Ben but got no reply. They also disturbed a very tired Andy, who had only just got to sleep, again.

Andy reluctantly agreed to come to their suite after hearing they couldn't contact Ben either.

After ringing down to reception and being informed that neither Rupert or Ben had breakfasted, they feared the worst.

'It's a big place, he could be anywhere.' Kay suggested.

'Ah've got a funny feeling that awful woman has something to do wee it.' Carrie said.

'Well, there's only one way to find out,' Tim said, realistically.

Kay stayed in the suite while the others went to Sue's room and knocked. 'Rupert are you in there?' Tim shouted, through the closed door.

'Ah, it's the SAS come to rescue you!' Sue said sarcastically to her 'prisoners' as she wandered over to the peep hole, little realising how close to the truth she was.

'Oh, it's nice to see you all,' she said, through the closed door. 'I think the Nurse is the only one I want to see. The rest of you, Sod Off. Otherwise I'll call the Manager and tell him you're harassing me.'

'No Andy, don't go in,' Carrie advised. 'She's a mean bitch. She's up to something.'

'I'm sure Ben would love to see his Scout Leader,' Sue goaded.

'Shit, she's got Ben too. I don't have a choice. I've got to go in,' Andy said, reluctantly.

'I agree with Carrie, don't go in alone,' Tim said, concerned.

'No, it's OK. I'll be alright,' Andy said, trying to convince himself. 'Ok, I'll come in. Open the door.'

'Tell the others to clear off. We don't want any heroics do we?'

The others reluctantly moved away from the door as she let Andy in and quickly closed it again.

Ignoring Sue, Andy walked straight over to a subdued Ben. 'You alright?'

'Yes.'

'Rupert?'

'Yes.'

'Oh, how charming or should I say, Andee how scharming,' Sue said in Franglais, mimicking Nadine.' Just got to your own bed, mon cher?'

Andy coloured up. His heart sank, as he realised it was her who had been in the corridor when he'd said goodbye to Nadine.

'Marvellous what you can do with mobile phones these days isn't it? Photos, videos, sound recording.

Andy decided to call her bluff. 'I don't know what you mean.'

'I caught you on film, kissing goodnight to your girlfriend Nadine.'

Andy closed his eyes to avoid Ben's look of horror.

'Oh, have I shocked your little dyb, dob boy by revealing your late night liaison with Nadine?' she said, catching Ben's look.

Ben was gutted. The man whom he admired for his principles had been doing what his mother had been doing - bed hopping. His hero had fallen from grace.

'Oh yes, useful these phones aren't they? It's quite ironic isn't it, that I caught your indiscretion on one and young Ben here, goes around finding, or should I say mugging people for their mobiles.'

Andy overcame his moment of shame and looked towards Ben at Sue's revelation.

'Ben!'

'I'm sorry Andy, it just came out!' Ben said, apologetically. 'She's definitely the one in the picture though.'

'He just couldn't keep his mouth shut. I told him that I saw him mess up that old man's grave and...'

'Don't talk rubbish,' Andy shouted, angrily.

'Tut, tut. It's rude to interrupt,' she said, wandering over to him. 'I'm sure the Police would be pleased to hear from a witness. Somebody who actually saw it.'

'What do you mean?'

'I saw him vandalising the grave.'

'You'll never get away with it.'

'No?' Do you want to try me? You should know better than to dare me to do anything. Isn't that right Rupert?'

Rupert looked at his hands and said nothing.

'What do you want?' Andy asked, afraid of her likely demands.

'I think I want a bit of respect to start with and a nice trouble free trip to the Palace and then we'll discuss releasing the legacy, shall we?'

'OK.' Andy said, completely flummoxed at the mention of the legacy.

'We'll go to the Palace without that bitch Carrie. She'll pay for what she did to me. Now I suggest you go and tell the others. Meanwhile, I'll look after these two…Andee.' She chuckled at her own mockery.

'Oh, just in case anyone wants to plan any rescue attempt, did I tell you I have a 'contract' out on his woman in hospital,' she said, pointing at Rupert. If I get arrested, it's curtains for her.'

'You haven't?' Rupert shouted, suddenly animated by the mention of Joanne.

'Do you want to try it out? You know it's amazingly cheap to hire a hitman these days,' she lied.

'You bitch,' Rupert said, rushing over to her and grabbing her.

'Steady on Rupert,' she said, dismissively pushing him away.' You might hurt yourself.'

Andy grabbed him and held him back.

'You'd better clear off, now,' she directed Andy. 'You, sit down again, she ordered Rupert, 'before I do something you'll regret.'

Rupert tearfully did as he was instructed.

Andy left the room and told the others what had happened, although he chose not to mention her threat about exposing his early morning visit to Nadine's room.

Sue was feeling good. Her luck had changed again at last. The irritations of Carrie's assault and delay in getting her hands on Rupert's legacy had weakened her manipulative abilities.

What with Andy's compromising situation captured on video, Rupert coming back under her thumb and finding out Ben had found the mobile phone, life was good.

She was back in charge. On top again.

CHAPTER FORTY SIX

24th January

The stretched limo took them from the hotel the short distance up to the Prince's Palace, which had been built on the rocky promontory overlooking the city.

The beautiful 12th century Palace, a former fortress, was a magnet for almost every tourist visiting the area, its fairy tale reputation still evoking wonder.

Nadine had made special arrangements for them to visit the Palace, normally only open to the public from April to October.

The Palace, the home of the aristocratic Grimaldi family, was a long and enduring family heritage.

Following the 'kidnap' of Ben and Rupert, the atmosphere in the group was tense, for Andy was now under her thumb as well!

Sue had forbidden Carrie to join them, but insisted that Tim and Kay went, so that Carrie would feel some 'angst' about being apart from them.

The group walked through the entrance of the Palace, past the two uniformed soldiers standing ramrod straight, their rifles shouldered and with bayonets fixed.

The Sentries colourfully bedecked in light blue, UK style policeman helmets, with gold shoulder braids on their black tunics. Each sleeve colourfully finished off in wide red cuffs, their hands encased in white gloves were held tight against smart light blue trousers decorated with wide red piping. Completing their ensemble, the guard's trouser legs ended over the top of immaculate white spats, worn over gleaming black boots.

Undaunted by the pettiness of Sue's dictat however, Carrie wasted no time in contacting her former army mates in Bristol.

She asked them to sound out the local villains to see if there was any truth in Sue's threat that she'd lined up a hitman.

Many of Carrie's former soldier colleagues had naturally migrated to the world of security when they left the service, and had 'ears to the ground' about many criminal activities.

While waiting the results of their investigations, Carrie asked them to arrange some low level security to ensure Jo had some element of protection.

Ben was 'gutted', his fairy-tale adventure in tatters. 'Yet again,' he thought, 'another case of adult double standards. Andy his hero, the man whom he'd held in great esteem, had let him down. He was no better than anyone else,' Ben concluded.' Then that mad woman Sue. She was just a vicious cow.'

Ben wandered subconsciously to the spectacular, 17th century Carrara marble staircase and slumped down. He didn't care that the artistically designed staircase had two circular unique 'double-revolution' sets of steps. Instead he stared vacantly at the Main Courtyard, his mind elsewhere. He cared not about the beautiful geometrical patterns created by an estimated three million white and coloured pebbles with which it was paved.

'Hi Ben, old chap, feeling a bit down at the moment?' James asked, joining him, quickly assessing the boy's body language.

'Yeah.'

'Well that's understandable, with that awful woman in our midst. Anything you want to talk about?' James asked, tactfully.

'No, not really.' But after a moment thinking about it, he said, 'Well yes, it's…it's Andy.'

'Andy?'

'Yeah, him and that woman, Nadine.'

'Oh, I see!'

'He's no better than the rest of you adults, is he?' Ben said, woefully. 'Sleeping with that Nadine.'

'Now just hold on. Where's that come from?'

'Rupert's wife took a video of them.'

'Don't get jumping to conclusions. You don't know the full facts yet.' James counselled.

'He didn't deny it though, did he? If she was lying, he would have said something, wouldn't he?'

'There might be a perfectly simple explanation why he didn't. Give him the benefit of the doubt until you know the full facts.'

'He was in her room.'

'According to that woman, yes. But have you spoken to Andy about it?'

'No, of course not. It's not my place to question what he gets up to.'

'Not your place! How long have you known Andy?'
'A few years.'
'So why the reluctance?'
'I guess I don't want to hear anymore lies. It's Helen, his wife, and the kids I feel sorry for, if he's been cheating on her. What if they divorce? Then the kids will grow up without a Dad…and I know how shitty that is.'
'Do you think he would lie to you?'
'I didn't used to think so, but, like all you adults, you claim not to tell lies but you just 'manipulate the truth'. That's the same as lying. Do you think us kids can't see through it? I should know more than most. My Mother has been doing it all my life.'
'And what do you think that horrible woman is doing? Isn't she doing exactly what you're saying. Lying through her teeth. She's no innocent. She has no moral scruples at all, that one.'
'Yeah, well I know she is lying about seeing me do all those things in the burial ground, cause I didn't do them… Yeah, I suppose,' he conceded.
'See? Sometimes you have to believe in your friends, even when people say horrible things about them.'
'Perhaps you're right.'
'I'll help to raise the subject with him, if you like?'
'Thanks.'
At that moment Andy came around the corner. 'This place is amazing isn't?' he said, trying to put a happy face on it. 'I've just been to the Throne Room. Its decoration is incredible and you should see the fireplace. It's from the Renaissance, I think.'
'Yes. In my former life, I've been to several social functions here,' James informed them.
'Really?' said Ben, impressed.

'Yes. They hold functions throughout the year, especially at Christmas, for the local Monegasques.'

'The what?'

'Monegasques. Sorry, natives of Monaco,' James explained. 'It really is a fantastic experience. I've even rubbed shoulders with Royalty.'

'Wow,' Ben said, open mouthed.

'Andy, Ben and I were just talking. He's a bit concerned about things.'

'Oh?'

'He's wondering about that woman's accusation… about you being in Nadine's room. I hope you don't mind us asking about it?'

Andy shuffled uncomfortably, clearly embarrassed that the topic was in the public domain.

'We appreciate it's nothing to do with us, but we're concerned about you. I was telling him about establishing facts before making judgements.'

Andy cleared his throat, clearly mortified. 'I'm not going to lie to you. Yes I was in Nadine's room. But,' he added quickly, 'believe me or believe me not, I had only gone in to get a gift that she bought me.

Unfortunately the combination of too much wine and little sleep…well I fell asleep on the sofa. Instead of waking me, Nadine left me there.

I wish she'd woken me and…. Well she didn't, and I guess the wicked witch saw me leaving later on. That's the truth. Honest,' he said, looking at each in turn.

'So you didn't…? You weren't…being unfaithful to your wife?' Ben said, looking intently at his eyes to judge the truth of his response.

'No Ben. Nothing happened, I promise. Unfortunately it sounds like Sue videoed me leaving the room. As I left,

I did kiss Nadine. It meant nothing. Just one of those goodbyes the French do, you know.'

'See Ben, I told you. If you get the full information you can make an informed judgement. Feel better now?'

'Well…Yes, I think so,' Ben said, thinking over Andy's explanation, wondering whether to believe him.

'The next thing to do, is to find out if she has actually taken a video, or if she's bluffing. If she has, we need to find it.' James said, purposefully.

'Why?'

'To stop her using it for her own purposes.'

'How do we find out?' Andy asked, perplexed.

'We 'borrow' her phone and look at it.' James said, patiently.

'Borrow? You mean steal?'

'No, we borrow it for a short time. Check it for compromising shots and give it back… after we've deleted anything which might be embarrassing for you.'

'You really don't need to get involved. It's my problem. I've got to sort it.'

'Andy, I…well, we all owe you. You've helped us. Now it's our turn to return the favour.'

'Are you sure?'

'Yes of course.'

'I don't know what to say. Thank you.'

'Let's hope we're successful.'

'When did you have in mind?'

'We need to do it sooner than later, before she downloads it onto a Laptop.'

'Easier said than done! How do we get our hands on it?'

'Rupert will have to help us.' James added.

'No chance. He's petrified of her.'

'It's the only way. At least we've got a chance now she's got him back in her… their room.'

'Just as well that the hotel has allowed us to keep our rooms until this evening's flight. I'll go and have words with Rupert,' Andy said, 'as it's to my benefit.'

'Good idea,' James agreed. 'See Ben, it's not all doom and gloom after all is it? Another of life's lessons. Tackle things head on; question things, don't just accept them.'

'Yeah, I see. But what about her telling the Police she saw me doing all those things?'

'Well, let's think about it as we walk round the Palace. You've got to seize the initiative. Do you know what I mean?'

'I think so,' Ben said, starting to feel happier.'

'Come on, let's see the rest of the wonderful marble Palace staircase.'

'I'll see if I can find Rupert,' Andy said, heading off in the opposite direction.

CHAPTER FORTY SEVEN

24th January

Within a few moments Andy came across Rupert who had joined Kay and Tim in the magnificent State Apartments, well known for its 16th Century frescoes, antique furnishings and decorative gildings.

'Hi, where's the wicked witch?'

'Don't know, gone to commune with Lucifer, I'd imagine.' Tim said, unhelpfully.

'Ok. Well at least we've got some space. Rupert, I wonder could I ask you a favour?' Andy asked awkwardly.

'What is it?'

'I need to get Sue's mobile.'

'Why?'

'I need to see if it's got some video of me on it.'

'Why would she video you?'

'She caught me saying goodbye to Nadine in the early hours of this morning.'

'Guilty conscience?' Tim interjected.

'No, I've done nothing to be ashamed of. My concern is that she already knows that I hold one of the 'theoretical' keys to releasing Geoffery's legacy; and she'll force my hand. Coerce me!'

'I got no problems with that,' Tim said, quickly. 'I'll join her, if she can persuade you to give us the money without going through this stupid scheme of his,' Tim added, too enthusiastically for Andy's liking. 'Let's have the money now.'

'You know, it doesn't work like that.'

'I suspected that might be the case.'

'There's a hint of blackmail in her threat too.'

'Bit overdramatic isn't it? It's only a minor indiscretion. The world isn't likely to suddenly got to war over it,' Kay added calmly.' What would happen if you called her bluff?'

'You're right of course, but I don't want to antagonise her. I could do without the grief if she shows it around.'

'Such as?'

'Such as work, Scouts and most importantly, the wife.'

'You made your bed mate.' Tim added, unhelpfully. 'I look forward to seeing it on YouTube.'

'That's just it. My bed was the sofa. Nothing happened, I swear. YouTube! Oh shit! I hadn't even thought about that.'

'Don't listen to him Andy. You know what he's like. A 'windup merchant',' Kay said, giving her son a withering look.

'It's not me you've got to convince,' continued Tim, ignoring his mother.

Rupert suddenly joined the conversation, 'Sorry, I don't think I can help you, I don't know where she keeps it.'

'In her handbag is the logical place, I would have thought,' added Kay.

'What if Rupert phones it and hangs up when she answers?'

'I haven't got my mobile with me, sorry,' said Rupert, miserably.

'What about one of us?'

'No, she's bound to smell a rat. She'll call back to see who called her.'

'What if I get Carrie to call her from the hotel?'

'No she'd guess it was her.'

'What about a callbox? Then it could be anybody.' Andy said, in desperation.

'Well…If that's all we can think of, I'll call Carrie now.'

Tim called Carrie and gave her the number Rupert had given him. Carrie went to a local pay booth and called them back shortly after to say her call had gone straight to voicemail.

'That hasn't helped. It could be switched off in her bag or…'

'Out of signal range…perhaps it's in the room safe,' Rupert volunteered.

'Room safe eh? Could Carrie get into your room?' Andy asked earnestly.

'Probably, but why do you ask?' Rupert queried.

'Can she crack a safe?' Andy said, expanding, his thoughts.

'Probably. That girl is always amazing me with her talents,' Tim said, proudly.

'If it's anything like ours, it's a four number combination which you can change everytime you lock it.' Kay said.

'Yes it is,' Rupert confirmed, 'she has a few favourite numbers that she might have used.'

'Let me have them and I'll get Carrie to give it a whirl.'

Rupert gave Tim several likely numbers, but Sue arrived before these could be texted to Carrie.

'So what are you 'children' looking so furtive about?' Sue's voice cut through them like a knife.

'Conspiring to overthrow me, or to thwart my plans? Well you'll have to get up early in the day, if you want to do that.

Rupert, it's time we headed back to the hotel,' she said, pushing him away from the group. 'But first, we'll see today's changing of the guard. It's nearly quarter to twelve. We've got ten minutes to get a good place in the square in front of the Palace,' she said, unnervingly and uncharacteristically excited.

'It's not like the changing of the guard at home. The Carabiniers du Prince wear white uniforms and English Police type helmets. We'll hear them coming because they're led by a drummer,' she continued.

'Bugger,' thought Andy, 'the best laid plans. There won't be any time for Carrie to get into their room and try the combinations, let alone find Sue's phone, and delete any compromising pictures.'

Rupert looked helplessly at Andy as he walked away from the group.

As Sue and Rupert walked out of sight, Andy said.' We've still got a chance. How long does the changing of the guard take?'

'Not long, quarter of an hour, something like that,' Kay suggested.

'Quarter of an hour and then there's the walk back.'

'Huh, that lazy cow wouldn't walk. She'd get a taxi. No, It's too risky.'

'What's the worst thing that can happen? Sue finds Carrie in her room.'

'Yeah and beats the shit out of poor Rupert in revenge. No, let's think of something else.'

'I reckon your best bet is Rupert, while she's off somewhere,' Kay suggested, thoughtfully.

'Yeah, perhaps you're right. We might as well join the crowd watching the changing of the guard too, in that case.'

CHAPTER FORTY EIGHT

24th January

Tim reassessed Andy's request and instead of joining the others watching the ceremonial changing of the guard, he called Carrie.

She agreed that a lightning raid on Sue's room was possible. They set a maximum time of twenty minutes for the mission based on fifteen minutes watching the changing of the guard and a five minute taxi ride.

Immediately after hanging up, Carrie grabbed a towel and a cordless hair dryer from the room and raced off to Sue's room. The corridor was empty; she was relieved to see, although she was aware of several surveillance cameras.

Winding the towel around her hair, she strode purposefully to the door and pointed the hair dryer, which she'd switch to the hottest setting, at the card entry slot.

After a few minutes, she turned the dryer on its side so it lay on the now hot reader. She then switched the dryer on and off rapidly four or five times, at the same time putting her foot against the base of the door and pushing it.

The electronics of the card reader went into fail safe as the induced current and heat from the hair dryer upset the delicate circuitry. The door opened.

Her SAS learnt skills had come to her aid once again. The covert entry course had been a good investment, although the army might not have had this particular operation in mind.

The reader electronics would start to work again as soon as it cooled down, so the room occupant would be unaware that anyone had gained access.

Quickly Carrie hurried in, closing the door behind her, and securing it with the manual internal lock. 'No surprises by unexpected visitors,' she recalled the instructor emphasising.

She went to the usual location of the room safe and was pleased to see it was in the cupboard where she was expecting to find it. Checking her watch, she saw that five minutes had already gone.

Carrie prided herself in being methodical. First she checked that the safe was actually locked. Many of her colleagues had failed the course because they'd missed the obvious - the safe wasn't locked in the first place.

She put the hair dryer down and got her mobile out. After their conversation, Tim had texted her the possible combinations that Rupert had given him.

Carrie punched the first combination into the electronic keypad. The LED indicator remained at red. Quickly she punched in the others. Still red. Still locked.

Using the knowledge from her training course, she started methodically going through other easy to remember patterns, when she heard voices in the corridor.

Someone was putting a card in the reader. She looked at her watch. It was only ten minutes. They had obviously come back early.

'Oh, this is very warm,' she heard Sue say. 'It's not usually warm is it?'

Rupert stood impassively by the side of her like a naughty school boy and said nothing.

'I'm talking to you,' she shouted. 'Feel that.'

Rupert did as he was bid. 'Yes it's a bit warm. Nothing to worry about, I shouldn't think. Sometimes the chips get hot.'

'Well it doesn't appear to be working,' she said, putting the card in and out of the reader quickly.

Meanwhile, Carrie had quickly scurried back to the door and stealthily undone the manual lock. She had already chosen a suitable hiding place when she entered the room, in case it was needed. All about thinking it through to avoid detection, the instructors had told her. 'Think of it as a sort of deadly game of hide and seek. They find you and you're history.'

Quickly she slipped behind the long drapes and listened to the now very ratty Sue berating Rupert.

'Let me have a go,' she heard Rupert say.

Carrie heard the click as the solenoid released and they entered.

'Well it wasn't working was it? You saw,' Sue prattled on, trying to repudiate herself from blame. 'I need some more painkillers. My neck is killing me.'

'I wish that were actually the case,' Rupert thought, but said nothing and instead walked to the large balcony window to gaze out on the Mediterranean, thinking about Joanne and their baby.

Meanwhile Carrie heard Sue entering the bathroom and locking the door.

'Rupert, don't say anything,' Carrie whispered.

Rupert jumped involuntarily from the sudden shock of hearing a voice.

'It's me Carrie,' she whispered.

'Thank God for that. I thought I was hearing things.'

'You're back early.'

'Yes, she was moaning about her neck.'

Carrie smiled, 'I'm pleased to hear that she's suffering.'

'Yeah, beware. She's after your blood.'

'Look, Ah've been trying to get into the safe. Those numbers you gave Tim didn't work.' Carrie continued.

'I've thought of another set she might use,' he whispered.

'Let's give it a whirl,' Carrie suggested, stepping out from behind the drapes.

They both went quietly to the safe and Rupert punched in the code he'd thought of. Success! Green light. He opened the safe and to their dismay there were only passports inside. No mobile.

'Damn. What about her handbag?' Carrie said, quickly. 'Where is it?'

'Over there.'

Quickly they made their way to the handbag, Rupert handed it to Carrie. This was forbidden territory for him to even look into Sue's bag, let alone go rummaging through it. Carrie quickly searched through the bag, turning over its contents carefully.

'Hurry,' he urged. 'You'd better leave before she comes out.'

As if on cue, they heard the toilet flush and the sink tap gushing water.

'No, it's not here,' Carrie said, disappointed. 'Where the hell could she have put it?'

Carrie ran across the room to the door and opened it ready to leave, followed closely by Rupert. She had just stepped into the corridor as Sue emerged from the bathroom.

'What are you doing lurking around here?' she barked, seeing Carrie in the corridor.

'Ah came to see if Rupert was OK,' Carrie replied, firmly. It was then that she spotted her hairdryer. 'Bad girl,' she thought, the instructors would have ripped her apart for making such a stupid basic mistake that could unravel all the previous stealth.

'Well, now you've seen him, you can clear off. By the way you would have loved the Princes Palace,' Sue said, bitchily.

'No problem, I've worked there many times before, when I was in the Services. Ah've been everywhere that Tourists aren't allowed to go,' Carrie said, boastfully.

Sue slammed the door. Carrie smiled at getting one over on her.

'But where the hell's that bloody phone?' Carrie wondered.

CHAPTER FORTY NINE

24th January

'What were you talking to that woman about,' Sue said, advancing on Rupert.

Rupert stood his ground. 'Nothing.'

'Don't take me for a fool,' she said, lifting her arm to smack him across the face. Rupert lifted his own to deflect the expected blow.

She stopped in mid swing, as her eye caught sight of her upturned handbag.

'What have you been doing ferreting in my handbag? I've told you before. You don't touch my things.'

Rupert moved back behind the sofa to get out of range.

Sue in the meantime went to her handbag and started examining the contents.

'Ah, I get it,' she said, glaring at him. 'You were looking for my mobile weren't you? Has that Andy put you up to it? He's desperate to get his hands on the video I took of him isn't he? Well you can tell him to think again,' she said, pulling the mobile out from her trouser pocket. 'This is my guarantee of becoming a millionaire sooner rather than later,' she said, waving it at him.

Sue then spotted the hairdryer. 'Where has that come from? I don't remember seeing that in here before.' She went over and examined it.

'Was that woman in here?' she asked, suspiciously.

'What woman?'

'You know what woman,' she said, advancing on him again. 'She was, wasn't she?'

Rupert wasn't quick enough backing away from her, for in spite of trying to catch her foot in mid kick, it still connected with his manhood.

He went down in agony, rolling over on his front, clutching himself. Sue had learnt as a precocious brat about the 'Achilles heel' on the male anatomy and had used it frequently to bully her way through life.

'You don't learn do you,' she shouted, kneeling on his prostrate form. 'I am beginning to think you like being hurt. Well, as you know, you've come to the right person,' and punched him hard in the back of the head. 'We'll try not to mark you. We don't want the others to suspect you enjoy being a masochist do we?' she said, angrily, repeating the blow. Vainly Rupert put his hands up to shield his head from her fists.

Meanwhile, still in the corridor near to Rupert's room, Carrie had called Tim to update him.

'Sorry Tim, tell Andy we failed. They came back early. Apparently her neck was playing up.'

'Damn. Are you alright? Did you get into her room though?' Tim said, anxiously

'Yes nearly got caught, but I did the safe with Rupert's help.'

'Rupert's help?'

'Yes, she had gone to the loo, so he was able to help me. Unfortunately the phone wasn't there or in her handbag. So it's either in the hotel safe or somewhere else.'

'Perhaps she had it on her?'

'What, in the loo?'

'Who knows! Anyway, we're on our way back now so we'll see you shortly OK?'

'Yeah, see you.' Carrie was already thinking about her next move as she heard Sue shouting followed by Rupert's groan.

'Christ, she's at it again. The poor sod. Well she ain't getting away with it again.

Carrie ran back to their room and hammered on the door. 'Open this frigging door you bitch,' she shouted.

'Eff off,' Sue said, momentarily stopping her assault on Rupert.

The distraction was enough for Rupert to throw her off his back and race to the door.

Sue recovered and chased after him, kicking his legs from under him. However, as he fell he was able to 'flick' the door handle allowing Carrie to force it open.

Pushing Rupert and the door aside, Carrie forced her way into the room.

Sue was ready for a fight as Carrie advanced towards her.

'Get out of my room,' she screamed.

'Quick, oot into the corridor,' Carrie instructed Rupert, lifting him by one elbow, whilst maintaining eye contact with Sue.

They stared at each other like gladiators, psyching each other out, ready to leap at each other's throats at any sign of weakness.

As Rupert quickly scrambled into the corridor, he shouted, 'she's got the phone in her pocket.'

'OK you. Give it to me and you won't get hurt.' Carrie ordered.

'Get stuffed. You don't frighten me,' Sue said, her quivering voice telling a different tale.

'Ah said, give me the phone,' Carrie demanded, advancing towards her, the adrenaline of a trained warrior coursing through her.

Sue backed away. For the second time in her life, she felt frightened, her spittle drying. Subconsciously she put her right hand to her pocket to protect the phone. Her hand movement telegraphed its location to Carrie.

'Ah said give it to me.'

Sue turned to run, but Carrie grabbed her shoulder as she did so and locked her arm round her neck. Sue screamed in pain as her damaged neck muscles protested at the assault.

Carrie forced her free hand into Sue's pocket and seized the mobile.

'Don't like it when somebody has a go at you, do you? If you even think about touching Rupert or anyone else again, next time Ah'll screw your effing head off your shoulders. Understand?' Carrie said, shaking her, to reinforce her threat.

Sue screamed again, as a lightning bolt of pain shot up her neck.

'Ah'm glad we agree.' With that she took her arm from around Sue's neck and kicked her in the back of the knee sending her sprawling.

Carrie backed out of the room and joined Rupert in the corridor, quickly trying to second guess what Sue would do next.

Would Sue report her to the Police? No. She'd be too frightened about being put behind bars for assaulting Rupert.

'Come on man, let's quit while we're ahead.' Together they jogged down the corridor and headed back to Carrie's suite, Rupert nervously looking over his shoulder. - Mission completed.

CHAPTER FIFTY

24th January

Carrie and Rupert went straight back to the suite. Carrie was pumped up ready for any escalation that Sue was likely to initiate.

Rupert was in despair. He was visibly trembling, hurt by Sue's attack on him and frightened as the ongoing recipient of her temper. In spite of being rescued by Carrie, he was upset by the violence of her intervention.

'I'm going to get myself a trumpet just like the Cavalry,' Carrie joked, trying to cheer him up, 'because I'm always coming to your rescue.'

'Thanks, but do you realise what you've done?' he said, miserably, barely able to get the words out.

'What do you mean?'

'She will kill Joanne now,' he said, starting to cry, '...and my little baby. We must tell the Police. Oh my god, this is awful. I don't know what to do. I don't know what to do.' He sobbed, burying his face in his hands.

'Don't worry, I've already got that sorted. Ah got some of my former army mates to keep an eye on her.'

'What do you mean?' he said, looking up. 'Keeping an eye on her?'

She avoided looking at him, his tear streaked face and puffy eyes eroding her toughness. She had to remain hard. This was no time for emotions.

'Covert protection. Nobody will get to her, don't worry.'

'Are you sure? Sue usually gets her own way, somehow.'

'Not when I'm around, she doesn't.'

Outside in the corridor they heard voices. Someone was trying unsuccessfully to open the door. Carrie had already taken the precaution of putting the internal lock on.

'Carrie. Carrie, are you in there? It's me.' Tim shouted. 'Carrie, open the door.'

'Are you alone?' she asked, anxiously.

'No, I've got Mum and Andy with me.'

'That's OK then. Just a minute.' Carrie opened the door and the trio entered.

'Why the locked door?' Tim quizzed.

'Ah've just had to rescue Rupert from the jaws of hell again. We thought she might be along here with the Hotel Manager or Security people.

'You OK Rupert?' Andy said, concerned, going over to him.

'Give me a minute,' he sobbed.

'Can I get you anything? I expect you'd like a nice cup of tea,' Kay said, upset at seeing Rupert crying. She bustled off into her bedroom, trying to busy herself.

'Thanks.'

'What happened?' Tim asked, concerned, holding Carrie's hand.

'After I spoke to you, I heard Rupert at the wrong end of a beating. I just had to go and help. Sorry.'

'That's OK, I'm glad you did.'

'Oh I nearly forgot. Good news. We got her phone, Andy.' Carrie said, retrieving the phone from her pocket and holding it out to him.

'The phone! Brilliant. I'd just about given up hope on that. Thank you so much. Have you looked at it yet?'

'No, we've only been back here a few minutes ourselves.'

'Well let's see what she's got on there, if she got anything at all, that is.'

'Yes, she videoed you. She told me,' Rupert chirped in.

Andy took the phone and taking a seat by the window, switched it on.

Meanwhile Kay had busied herself making tea from the kit she always carried when going away. 'You can't beat a nice, proper cup of tea from home.'

After a few minutes negotiating various screens, Andy found the video and played it on the phone.

It had captured the moment just after he'd exited Nadine's room. She was standing there in her silk dressing gown and he watched as he kissed her, almost too long, he thought, to be a 'quick peck.' The time stamp showed 0535 hrs.

'Found it?' Tim said, walking over, keen to see what all the fuss had been about.

'Yes, and now to delete it.' Andy said, with great relish, relieved at least that his minor indiscretion would never be seen.

'Oh come on, don't be a spoil sport. Let's have a look.' Tim persisted.

'Too late,' Andy said, relieved.

'Do you want to delete this video?' the screen prompted.

'Too right,' Andy said, touching the screen.

'You are about to delete the video. Do you wish to continue?'

'Yes.'

'Deleting.'

Andy was pleased to see the barometer running at the bottom of the screen as it was erased.

'Video deleted. Press OK to continue.

'Thank you Carrie, Rupert. You've probably saved my marriage. I'm sorry you got 'beat up' on my account Rupert,' he said, going over to him and putting a sympathetic hand on his shoulder. 'If there's anything I can do for you…well I owe you one. Thanks.'

Rupert just nodded.

'Nice phone, let me have a look Andy,' Tim said, putting his hand out.

'If you say so. I don't know anything about mobiles. Here,' he said, handing it over.

'Shouldn't think she's had it long, 'Tim said, examining it. 'It's 4G enabled. I gather it's got all the whistles and bells including cordless charging.'

'Cordless what?'

'Charge the phone using an inductor rather than a cable.'

'You're talking gobbledegook now.'

Tim's assessment continued. 'Even got a memory card for photos. Somewhere here,' he said, turning the phone over in his search. 'Oh dear.'

'What's up?' Andy asked, concerned.

'It's not here.' Tim said, looking at Andy.

'You might have deleted the video from the phone chip. But I wouldn't be at all surprised to discover that she recorded it to the memory card too.'

'Shit,' said Andy, uncharacteristically crude. 'I'm sorry Kay, I don't usually swear.'

'I've heard worse than that, haven't I Tim?'

Tim ignored the question.

'Damn,' said Andy, his hopes suddenly dashed. 'What if there was no card in the phone in the first place?'

'Just a second.' Tim flashed through several screens. 'Sorry but the save options in here definitely had *'to phone and memory card'* ticked. If I try to video anything now, it comes up with *'Unable to shoot, Card missing.'*

'Well, let's go and get it,' said Carrie still hyper from her earlier encounter.

'She won't let you in.'

'Well, I could grovel and tell her I'm returning her property. That way we could force our way in.'

'It's worth a try at least,' Tim agreed.

'No more violence, please,' Rupert pleaded. 'I can't take anymore.'

'You stay here. You'll be safe here. She won't touch you again, Ah promise,' Carrie said, confidently.

'I'm coming with you,' Tim said, standing by her side.'

'I'll come too. It's my mess that's got you into this.' Andy said.

Carrie, Tim and Andy left together.

Kay locked the door as they stepped into the corridor.

'Don't worry Rupert, everything will be OK,' Kay said encouragingly, not at all confident that her words would be borne out.

The trio made their way to Sue's room wondering how they were going to get in, but the door was already open.

Cautiously Carrie stepped in and looked around quickly. The room was empty. Sue had gone.

'She must have run for it directly we left. Her suitcase is gone too.'

'Damn, damn, damn,' said Andy, thumping the back of a chair in his frustration. He was not 'off the hook' after all.

'Don't worry, we'll get her at the airport.'

'What if she makes her own way home?'

'Shit. I hadn't thought of that.' Andy said, his world collapsing around him.

CHAPTER FIFTY ONE

24th January

Later, just as the sun was setting, the helicopter settled noisily on the hotel helipad. The group scrambled aboard into the luxurious cabin of the Agusta 109 and settled into the white leather bench seats. Tim, Carrie and Kay sat in the rear facing seats, while Ben, James and Andy sat in the forward facing ones. As expected, there was no sign of Sue.

As the doors closed, the pilot gestured for them to put on the headsets which were hanging on hooks above their heads.

Kay was thankful that the noise of the three rotating rotor blades was quietened by padded earpieces of the headset. Seeing everybody suitably attired, the pilot's electronically clipped voice broke the static.

'Welcome aboard. We will be flying along the coast to Nice and I will show you some of the wonderful views of Monte Carlo as we go.

Although the aircraft is capable of flying at up to 195 miles per hour, we will be going a lot slower to allow you to take in the scenery.

The flight would normally take about seven minutes. If you have any questions, your microphones are working, so please ask.

However I would ask you not to engage in any conversations between yourselves that might be distracting to me.

Please fasten your seatbelts.'

The noise from the rotors increased as the twin engine helicopter rose into the air, creating a small cloud of dust as it did so. Pitching forward, it soon gathered height and speed, quickly crossing over Monaco's opulent skyline and meandering network of roads, to arrive over the ancient deep-water harbour of Hercules Port; reported to have been a trading port used by the Greeks and Romans.

Beneath them, the bay was populated by scores of multimillion pound super yachts and boats moored in ordered lines along the quay; a decadent display of the wealth of the French Riviera, their white hulls and superstructures standing out against the darkening sea.

From their overhead vantage point, the port seemed like an enormous crab where the protective walls of the quays looked like giant claws that had scooped the yachts together ready to devour them.

The clunk of the wheels retracting made Kay jump and nervously she grabbed Carrie's hand. Carrie squeezed Kay's hand to reassure her; however, she too was feeling strangely tense.

For in spite of the fact that she had done countless helicopter flights during her service days, today was different.

She had always enjoyed the unique sensations of rotary wing flight, whether it was parachuting from them, dropping into a combat zone or making a fast exit whilst retreating from enemy fire.

But her airborne adventures had been cruelly cut short when she became a victim of a Taliban mine.

The rescuing Medivac flight had been her last helicopter trip until today. At the time, she didn't know much about it. She had sustained horrific injuries to both legs and was barely alive, drifting in and out of consciousness.

But deep down, she knew that the calm and efficient medics on board the Chinook would be her salvation, and so it proved. For without a shadow of doubt, they saved her life that day. Such was the severity of her injuries.

In spite of giving his passengers the promise of sightseeing en route, the short helicopter flight to Nice Airport and transfer to the chartered jet was all over and done within 30 minutes.

The chartered jet was quickly on its way and lifted off from the tarmac in a burst of noise

Ben looked out through window as the Mediterranean slipped away beneath them. The excitement of the weekend was over-shadowed by Sue's threat of going to the Police and lying about his involvement of the events on Churchup Hill.

His trepidation was further exacerbated by the fact that she had left earlier and was likely to be back in England before them.

'What if they were waiting at the airport to arrest me?' he thought, anxiously.

Andy, too, was apprehensive about their return. For the excitement and anticipation of a 'dream weekend' had turned out to be a dreadful nightmare.

He kicked himself for being so stupid to have been caught on film by Sue. Worse still, was getting the others embroiled in his problem, trying to get his hands on the recording.

He desperately needed to think of a strategy for telling Helen about the 'bedroom incident'. He couldn't wait until Sue dropped the bombshell. 'Oh God what a mess,' he muttered, under his breath.

If he admitted he'd gone to Nadine's room at all, she'd think the worse…especially after catching them in clinches at Geoffery's funeral and then again at the wake.

If he didn't say anything it would be worse when Sue did whatever she was going to do.

Normally so 'in control' of everything, he was beside himself for allowing a minor misjudgement to turn into a major problem. The thought of being exposed as an item of ridicule on the internet through 'YouTube' or 'Facebook', frightened him.

He had always thought of himself as a respected and responsible member of society…and now if the papers got hold of it. Oh God, he could imagine the headlines… *'Scout Leader in late night romp'*…It didn't bear thinking about.

Was it still too late to stop her? Could Rupert use his IT contacts to get it removed from the internet? Dare he even ask Rupert?

Why would Rupert even think of helping him? After all, it was Andy's actions of taking the hospice CCTV recording to the Police, which had got Sue released. Now she was back in his life and continuing her vicious reign over him.

To add to his angst, he was upset that Ben's perception of him had been undermined.

God it was a mess. His head was filled with questions but no answers.

Rupert was bruised emotionally and physically and he was at breaking point, fear clamped his aching head. He kept having flashbacks, reliving the fear he had experienced during the violent incidents which had occurred at the hotel.

His overwhelming desire was simply to get back to Jo's bedside. He'd never wanted to leave her in the first place. Her mere presence always gave him the strength to cope with the seemingly never ending angst that perpetuated his life.

The trip had been a complete and utter disaster for him. He had failed to get the anticipated money from his Uncle's will which would have allowed him to transfer Jo into a private hospital, where Sue wouldn't find them.

Even worse, as there was no money, his plan to engage the services of a consultant to closely manage Jo's recovery had foundered too.

What about the baby? His mind was a whirl of unanswered questions.

He knew for sure that Sue was now far more dangerous than when they arrived in Monaco. Sue would be 'white hot' with anger. Someone would pay dearly for upsetting her.

Carrie might have won a few battles and humiliated Sue, but she hadn't won the war. Instead she had 'sown the wind' but they would all 'reap Sue's whirlwind' of hatred, sooner or later.

Sue would be plotting some terrible revenge. He feared for its arrival. It was an inevitable consequence of standing up against the woman. He had seen her uncontrolled anger before and suffered the painful consequences many times.

Tim was enjoying posing as a millionaire. For in spite of the fact that he didn't have the money in his pocket yet and frustrated by the conditions of the will, he had no doubts that it would come soon.

His new life was proving to be a great adventure, especially with Carrie at his side. It was so far removed from his boring life of just a few months ago, that he had to keep pinching himself to ensure he wasn't dreaming.

Perhaps the old man had done something good for him after all, although he'd never admit it to anyone.

Kay was looking forward to getting her feet back on terra firma. She decided, she didn't like flying at all; the noisy helicopter and the turbulence in the jet. No, it was not for her.

Although she did have to admit that Monaco was 'nice' and allowed herself a moment of indulgent fantasy thinking about the lifestyle she could have enjoyed, had she stuck with Geoffery, all those years ago.

'Oh well, spilt milk and all that,' she said, realistically.

Although, she had to admit that Geoffery's unexpected return into her life had changed things for the better, especially with Tim.

For Tim's rude and arrogant nature had changed, thanks to Geoffery employing Carrie to 'toughen' him up.

Their blossoming romance was an unexpected bonus too. However, Kay was less comfortable with the masculine and violent side of Carrie's nature. She had to acknowledge that without her tough approach, Rupert would still be in the clutches of that evil woman.

Although still feeling less than hundred percent, James was at last feeling positive about his life again.

The veil that clouded any thoughts about a long term future was clearing. This 'step back in time' providing a glimpse of his old lifestyle, had been sobering.

He had been reminded of the decadent, arrogant, wasteful existence that he used to live. He decided that he would not go back to idling his life away on gambling and frivolous partying. He would instead do something positive with it. Geoffery had given him a chance and he was going to take it …but first he needed to sort out his health.

Meanwhile, Sue was on-board a train, heading towards Paris.

After Carrie had stolen her mobile, Sue had quickly left the hotel and got a Taxi to the rail station. Unsure of how she could get back home, she had been surprised to be able to immediately book a place on the twelve hour trip that took her from Monaco via Nice and Paris to London St Pancras.

Her plans to grab Rupert's money and run had been thwarted by that devious old man and the trip had turned out to be a painful waste of time, but she felt confident that shortly she'd be back in control.

It was dark by the time the chartered Jet flew in over the village rooftops back towards the Gloucestershire Airport.

Amongst the plethora of lights on the approach to land, Ben was able to identify a few streets and buildings as they prepared for touch down. His angst resurfaced as he spotted the lights, two red and one white, on top of the hill, where all his troubles had began. 'Would the Police be down there somewhere waiting for him?' he wondered.

PART THREE

The Legacy

CHAPTER FIFTY TWO

24th January

Ben alighted from the chartered Jet. Nervously looking across at the windows of the 'arrivals lounge' to see if the Police were looking out, he was relieved to see no staring faces.

As the crocodile of passengers walked towards the single story building that housed the 'arrivals reception, Ben kept to the side and back of James, to hide from anyone looking for him.

With great apprehension he followed the others into the building expecting any minute to be grabbed and bundled away, but nothing happened. There was only one uniformed man in the small room, which he took to be a Customs officer, but he showed no interest in him at all.

Perhaps this is a ruse, he decided. Perhaps the Police were waiting outside to grab him.

The group chatted for a few moments waiting for their luggage to arrive on the old fashioned roller conveyor before splitting up and saying their goodbyes.

Andy told the Godsons that he would be in touch shortly. As soon as he knew what he was supposed to do about releasing the money, he would call them. In the meantime, he suggested, they should start thinking about how they would 'earn' the money.

He apologised to Ben for not being able to take him 'home', but told him he was scheduled to work a night duty at the hospice and was dashing home to get changed. However, he explained that he had spoken to James who was quite happy to take him.

Andy wished Rupert all the best and said he hoped Joanne would be better soon.

They walked through the building without anyone approaching Ben, his relief increasing as they walked to James's car unhindered.

'Well that was interesting,' James said, as he steered the car up the airport exit road to join the narrow lane, heading towards Churchup.

Ben was now anticipating that the Police were going to be waiting at his Grandfather's house. It was inconceivable that Sue hadn't said anything to them.

'Penny for them,' James said.

'Sorry, what did you say?' Ben asked, vacantly.

'I said that was an interesting trip wasn't it?'

'Oh yes. Yes it was.' Ben replied, unconvincingly.

'What's the matter Ben, something on your mind?'

'No, nothing.'

'Come on. What is it?' James insisted

'Nothing, honest.' Ben said, shifting in his seat.

'Is it the trouble we had with Rupert's wife?'

'No...well sort of.'

'What is it?'

'She...she said she was going to tell the Police that I'd done all that stuff in the burial ground; you know vandalising Geoffery's grave and knocking over that bloke that died and stealing his phone. I thought the Police might be waiting for me when we touched down.'

'Oh, I see. Don't worry. We know the real truth don't we? The Police will know she's lying. Anyway, she's probably still travelling.'

Behind them, James could see two sets of car lights following them out of the airport. One set was Tim and Carrie who were taking Kay to her home and the other set was Rupert, who would be heading off down the M5 motorway, to visit Jo in Frenchay hospital.

Following the short journey from the airport, James pulled up outside Ben's Grandad's house.

'Well then, see, I told you. There was nothing to worry about. No Police cars, OK?'

Ben had already scanned the area, to see if there were any liveried cars parked anywhere around.

'Yeah OK. So I was worrying for nothing. But the suspense is going to be awful until she does tell them.'

'Well there's a couple of ways of tackling this. One, you wait. Perhaps she might never say anything.'

'Fat chance.'

'Two, you tell the Police yourself that she is going to make false allegations and leave them to sort it.'

'I don't like getting involved with the Police. They are biased against young people, especially as I've had a previous run in with them.'

'Well I suppose there is a third way.'

'What's that?'

'We persuade her to tell the truth.'

'Yeah, right ! Like that's going to happen,' Ben said, cynically.

Just then the front door opened and Ben was delighted to see his Mother coming down the drive. Suddenly Sue and the allegations were forgotten as he opened the car door and ran towards her.

'Mum, you're home!' he said, putting his arms around her.

'Wow, that's an unexpected, but lovely greeting. Hello son,' she said, returning the hug and giving him a kiss.

'Are you…is everything alright?' Ben asked, suspiciously.

'I've been given time off for good behaviour,' she said, beaming. 'Hello James, thanks for looking after my boy.'

'My pleasure. Treatment going well then Beth?' James said, smiling.

'Yes thanks. I feel like a million dollars at the moment. But you know all about the highs and lows, don't you?'

'Small steps, Beth, isn't that what they say?'

Ben got his bag out of the car and went into the house, pleased at least he was with people who loved him.

Coincidentally Sue was also back. She had arrived at London St Pancras and was checking the availability of trains from London Paddington to Bristol. Unfortunately, for her, due to engineering works, trains had been suspended and travel would be by coach instead. How typical, she thought. She could travel all the way through Europe efficiently only to be frustrated by Network Rail on the final leg of her journey.

However, she was now clear on how she was going to get her revenge on the others. They would all pay for disrespecting her, especially that Carrie for assaulting her and interfering with her punishment of Rupert.

And her pathetic husband Rupert, too, for not supporting her. He would regret disobeying her. His girlfriend needed another visit to remind him of his marital obligations. It would now cost him an increased share of his legacy. When he got it.

The data on the phone memory card, capturing Andy's indiscretion, was bound to help expedite an early payment from him. It was fortuitous that she had removed it from her phone before it was stolen by that army bitch. Andy would now pay personally as well. She was not above a bit of blackmail.

She chuckled to herself that the kid, Ben, had inadvertently supplied her with a 'get out of jail card' by admitting he had picked up the Gravediggers mobile.

Nevertheless, he too would suffer for crossing her. All she had to do was to drip feed the Police with a few details that would implicate him and lead them up a few blind alleys. By the time they found out the truth, she would have disappeared somewhere in Europe with Rupert's legacy. Perhaps things weren't so bad after all.

CHAPTER FIFTY THREE

24th January

Andy opened the door quietly knowing that the children would be in bed. Helen was in the kitchen ironing, 'You're cutting that a bit fine aren't you?' she said, hearing the door. 'I thought you might have gone straight to work.'

'No, I wanted to come and see you first before I went in.'

Well how was your trip?' she said, putting the iron down and coming into the hallway to greet him.

'Hello love,' he said, going to her and giving her a hug. 'Yeah, good.'

'Good! Only good? To go to Monaco on a private jet, stay at some posh hotel, and it's only good?'

'Well, you know. What about you?'

'I've been changing shitty nappies and looking after your children while you've been gallivanting off.'

'Geoffery has dropped me in it again,' he said, taking his coat off and hanging it over the bottom of the bannisters.

'What do you mean, dropped you in it?'

'He's put the responsibility on me of deciding when the money from his estate should be released to his Godsons.'

'What?'

'He's told them it's all down to me.'

'How can you decide when to give them the money? You're a nurse, not a flipping lawyer.'

'Your guess is as good as mine. The good thing is he's extended my contract until it's resolved.'

'So you're still getting paid then?'

'Yes.'

'Well that's alright then. I hope you don't have to see that dreadful woman, Sue, again.'

'This might be the opportunity of coming clean,' Andy thought, as Helen had raised the spectre of Sue, 'Well actually, she was there.'

'Never!'

'Yes I was surprised as anybody. But she was with Rupert. They were even staying in the same room, until...'

'Until?'

'Well, there was an incident and Tim and his girlfriend had to intervene and rescue him. He stayed in their suite after that.'

'What the hell was she doing there in the first place?'

'We reckon she was blackmailing Rupert.'

'You didn't get involved with her, did you?' She asked, concerned.

'Well, yeah. I...er...did.' Andy was just plucking up courage to admit to Helen about the bedroom incident as one of the children started crying upstairs.

'I don't know what's wrong with her. She's been like this all night,' Helen said, distracted from Andy's admission.

'She teething? Andy asked, concerned. 'Do you want me to go up and see to her?'

'Yes, please. I've been up and down to her all evening.'

'OK, I'll have a quick wash and put on my uniform while I'm up there.'

'I'll put your dirty washing in the machine. I was just going to do a load anyway. I just don't seem able to keep on top of it.'

Andy ran quietly upstairs as Helen flicked open the catches of his small suitcase. As she did so she caught a faint smell that made her hackles rise. She picked Andy's shirt up and sniffed it. The scent was unmistakable. It was that woman Nadine's perfume. She felt devastated, as if she'd been kicked in the stomach.

Andy tiptoed downstairs. 'She was crying in her sleep but she's OK now. I've decided to shower and change at work.' He stopped as he saw Helen holding his shirt. She stared at him, the words came in an angry torrent.

'You've been with that woman again, haven't you?' she said, angrily. 'I can smell her perfume on your shirt. I trusted you Andy, I trusted you,' she said, filling up.

'Well of course she was there,' he said, now wrong footed. 'She was his former lover. You'd expect her to be there,' he replied, tersely.

'Don't treat me like a fool Andy. I caught you, not once, but twice with your arms around her.'

'We've already had this discussion. There is nothing in it. How many more times?'

'How come her perfume is on your clothes then? You don't get that from, just being in the same room,' she said, sceptically.

'Well you know what these continentals are like. They're all kissy, kissy.'

'So you admit kissing her then?'

'It was a greeting, in front of everybody else. There was nothing to it. I promise,' he said, guiltily relegating the controversial 'goodnight kiss' to the back of his mind.

'I'm finding it harder and harder to believe you Andy.'

'Look, I've got to go to work. I'll tell you about it all when I get home tomorrow morning,' he said, exasperated that his plans to 'come clean' had been thwarted.

He gave her an unreturned hug, turned around and left.

After a few minutes staring at the closed door feeling upset, Helen mechanically emptied the rest of Andy's suitcase growing angrier as the woman's fragrance taunted her. The smell seemed to pervade all his clothes.

Upstairs, one of the children started to cry again and as she started tiredly to climb the stairs, she brushed against Andy's jacket hanging over the end of the banisters. She felt a small bulge in it. Thinking Andy had brought her a present, initially she resisted the temptation to look at it, but the desire to see what it was became overwhelming. She carefully took it out of his pocket, but her heart stopped as she read the neatly handwritten label. It was a woman's writing. '*Andy, thank you for everything, Love Nadine.*'

'Oh my god,' she said, slumping to her knees. She was devastated. Her trust had been well and truly thrown in her face. Andy had lied to her. He was 'two-timing' her.

She dissolved into tears, dropped the box and ran upstairs to Molly's room.

She looked at the sleeping baby, 'Oh Molly,' she said, holding the rail of the cot, 'what's going to happen to you? Daddy doesn't love us anymore.'

CHAPTER FIFTY FOUR

24th January

Rupert's trip from the airport to Frenchay hospital seemed endless. He used to do the return trip to Bristol daily and he reckoned he knew every pothole in the thirty mile strip of tarmac. Tonight, he recognised nothing.

The journey was taking forever. Perhaps, he thought, it was because he was anxious about what he'd find in the hospital that seemed to make the clock and odometer stop.

He shuddered, his stomach knotting, as he passed the site of their accident a month before. The crash had disrupted their life and left Joanne hospitalised.

Fortunately, at the time, he knew very little about it before he was rendered unconscious in the collision and subsequently evacuated by Air ambulance.

How he wished he could go back and do things differently. It was, after all, his insistence that they left the wake when they did, that put them on the motorway at that time. It had been the wrong time in the wrong place.

If only Andy hadn't told him about the hospice CCTV recording and Sue being released, then he wouldn't have panicked as he did.

He felt guilty about it. For although he didn't cause the accident, his hysterical reaction to being told that Sue was free, combined with the fact that he and Joanne had swopped places in the car, was the reason for Joanne being so badly hurt. It should have been him who was still in hospital, not Jo. Worst still, his actions had put the life of their unborn baby at risk.

To add to his depression, he feared for the real reason for Sue's insistence that she had been in the car with them. He was frightened that the Police would find out he had lied to provide her with an alibi.

Sadly, his new won courage deserted him, in spite of his intentions not to support her lies. But the threat to harm Joanne had been enough to unravel his resolve and bow to her demands.

Consequently, he was now complicit in whatever she was involved in – but what could he do?

The trip to Monaco had been a disaster and had just exacerbated his problems.

The violence during the weekend was dreadful. It upset him so much that he relived every fearful act over and over again. The terror in his mind had paralysed his thinking. He felt like a rabbit caught in the headlights. He allowed himself to become a victim, again.

First it was Sue's assault on him, then Carrie coming to his defence, as well as the fight trying to get the video footage. It had all been too much for him. God, would it always be like this? Why couldn't he grow a veneer to make himself less sensitive?

At the end of the day, the trip had all been a waste of time. No-one got any money. All they had succeeded in doing was getting Sue angry and he knew that he and Jo would be in her sights for punishment. He feared most for Joanne's safety. She was so vulnerable, for in spite of Carrie's talk about protecting her, it was unlikely to have been put in place.

Even now, Sue could be there at the hospital carrying out her threat. Perhaps he should have called the Police before they left Monaco.

What would he find when he got there? Were they both still alive? Had there been any complications? Would Sue be waiting for him and force him to take her into the ward?

He was shaking with fearful apprehension by the time he drove into the hospital car park, his palms sweaty on the wheel as he steered into a vacant parking place.

He dug in to his pocket for change and got himself a 'pay and display' parking ticket and ran quickly to the hospital.

Hurriedly, he made his way to the Neuro-Surgery ward, going along corridors he knew well. It had become a familiar routine for him.

He stopped at the nursing station which he always thought looked like a shop counter with its imitation teak veneered front panels hiding the desk and computers used by the nursing staff, who sat typing behind it.

The nursing Sister, Sister King, looked up at his approach. Could he read anything in her facial expression? Did he detect a sorrowful look? What would they tell him? His heart beat faster as he anticipated her report.

'Oh, hello Mr Screen. Did you have a nice trip?'

Was she just preparing him for bad news? he wondered, or was the question a genuine show of interest?

'Yes thanks,' he lied, his trembling voice betraying his nervousness.

'Monaco, wasn't it?'

'Yes…umm.' He was working up courage to ask about Joanne. Did he really want to know?

'Very nice too. Next time you go, I'll carry your suitcase for you,' she joked.

'How is, how are things…with Jo?'

'Well actually, we were just about to ring you.'

'Oh!' Rupert's heart sank, his mouth dried. They are going to tell me bad news, he thought. He wanted to run away, stick his fingers in his ears so he wouldn't hear what she was going to say. Perhaps she's died. He grabbed for the counter to steady himself, as he became light headed.

'You OK?' the Sister said, standing up ready to grab him. 'You've gone very pale. You're not going to faint on me are you?'

'Is she…is she OK? he stammered.

'Well come and see for yourself,' she said, coming to his side. 'Are you sure you're OK? Do you want some water?'

'No, no. I'm OK honest,' he lied. 'Just a bit tired from the weekend, that's all.'

'So you obviously had a lively weekend then? Good for you. You needed to get away from this for a while and re-charge your batteries,' she said, smiling, leading him towards Jo's side room.

'At least they haven't moved her,' he thought, thankfully.

Outside the room, sitting on a chair, reading a Kindle, was a short, thick set man with a 'number one' haircut, who looked like a bouncer.

'Hi Sister, is this Mr Screen?' he said, standing.

'Yes, it's OK John. He's Joanne's fiancée.'

Rupert was surprised to hear her explanation of his relationship with Joanne for, although he had always intended to propose to her, he had never actually got around to doing it.

'I gather you've employed your own security team to look after Miss Carr?' the Sister said, leading him into the room. 'How very exciting.'

'So Carrie's plans had worked after all.' He was pleased to see that his scepticism had been ill founded.

Rupert's attention was then fixed on the figure lying in the bed and the electronic traces on the monitor screen.

'Joanne, you have a visitor,' Sister King said, leaning down to talk closely in her ear.

Joanne stirred and opened her eyes. She slowly moved her head and blinking, she focussed on Rupert.

Tears leapt into Rupert's eyes. 'Joanne you're awake. Oh thank God.' He rushed over to her and gently lifted her hand, raising it to his lips. He kissed it tenderly all the while gazing into her eyes. 'Oh darling, I'm so glad you're awake. I've missed your smile.'

'Good news isn't it?' the Sister said, looking at the couple. 'Now. She's only been wakeful for a short time,' she counselled. 'So don't stay too long and exhaust her. There will be plenty of time to catch up later on.'

'And the baby?' Rupert asked, putting his hand on Joanne's stomach.

'Yes it's fine, too.'

Joanne smiled at him. Although not fully awake, she was conscious enough to understand that Rupert now knew about the baby. Their baby.

CHAPTER FIFTY FIVE

25th January

Tim stood on the bridge parapet gazing down at the river a hundred feet beneath him; his target, a large golden pool.

To his left he could see Rupert and James slowly slipping and sliding their way down the steep cliff path that led to the pool. Their slow progress sending loose rocks and stones tumbling down into the void. But he was going to get there first and stake his claim. The risk was worth it, he'd decided.

He edged himself gingerly forward, his palms sweaty as he raised his arms for the dive. This was the crème de la crème of all bungee jumps. He balanced on the edge and leant forward, gravity taking him.

As his body went from the vertical, he sprung gently forward into a perfect dive. Gracefully he plunged down towards the distant water, gathering speed, the wind taking his breath away. He plunged further and further down, going faster and faster as he plummeted down towards his goal. Suddenly he felt the tension increase on the bindings around his ankles as the bungee rope reached its full elasticated limit. But the stretch wasn't enough, the rope brought him up short and jarred his newly transplanted legs.

The recoil pulled him back up, away from the golden pool. There was a moment of inertia before the secondary fall took him back towards his target.

As gravity again took him down, he could see the golden footpath leading towards the pool getting closer and closer. He reached out to claim his prize, his fingertips tantalisingly close, but the elasticity of the rope dragged him away yet again.

As he plunged down for a third time his head went into the golden lake. His face submerged in liquid gold. He felt a sharp pain on the top of his head; he must have hit something submerged. He was having difficulty breathing. Something was very wrong. The euphoria of getting there first had turned to terror, as he struggled to fight his way out of the liquid. His dream had turned into a nightmare. He was going to drown in liquid gold.

He woke with a start, bathed in sweat. Someone was pulling his hair. His head was being yanked back so much so that it was hurting his neck. He felt something hard across his throat, digging into his Adam's apple, making it hard to breathe.

Initially he thought it was Carrie boisterously waking him for another passionate session, until a voice he didn't recognise screeched in his ear.

His fuggy thoughts tried to grasp for an explanation of the verbal onslaught. 'My God. It's that mad woman Sue, she's broken in,' he thought. She said she'd get even.

Although he didn't understand the words, they were delivered with such venom that he couldn't fail to comprehend the intensity of the speaker's hatred.

As the verbal assault continued, the loathing and animosity in the voice increased, as did the pressure on his throat. He reached out for something on the bedside cabinet to use as a weapon, but his desperate, floundering hands found nothing.

All the while he was wondering what had happened to Carrie. Was she OK or had that mad woman already killed her?

His assailant was lying behind him on the bed. He felt the pressure of legs being pushed hard into the small of his back. He moved his hand to pull the object away from his throat, so that he could breathe. His fingers touched metal. It was a knife, he thought.

His exploration was rewarded by increased pressure against his throat and his head being yanked even further back and a stream of indistinguishable words being shouted into his ear.

He was dry mouthed. He was seeing stars. And he was starting to lose consciousness, vivid flashes of light, swimming across his vision.

He was going to die unless he could do something quickly.

He stretched his arm out to the bedside cabinet again, in desperation to find something to fight back with, his muscles protesting as he extended his arm beyond their normal length.

As he was about to give up, finally his fingertips touched something. He couldn't grasp it. His frustrated attempts to grab the object pushed it further away, sliding further from his desperate fingers.

'Carrie must be dead already. Otherwise she'd sort it.'

He was starting to blackout, as his oxygen starved brain shut down.

Summoning every ounce of his remaining strength, he made a last lunge at the thing on the cabinet. His fingers at last made contact. The object stayed put, allowing him to get his fingers around it. He realised he had the table lamp.

He lifted it up and swung the lamp behind him, hoping that he would make contact with his assailants head.

He felt the lampshade crumple as it found its mark. The light bulb shattered shortly after as the lamp continued its backward trajectory. Fear had given him a maniacal strength that he never knew he possessed.

Momentarily his attacker eased the pressure on his throat. Tim swung his elbow backwards and felt the point hit the assailant in the ribs, causing a yelp of pain.

The hand pulling his hair let go for a second and Tim quickly turned to face his attacker. Quickly he balled his fist and was about to punch the face that swam into his vision, but it wasn't the husband batterer Sue after all. He was shocked to see that it was Carrie.

Carrie was still fighting. All the time screaming and shouting in a foreign language. Tim couldn't comprehend what was going on. She had now lost some of her maniacal strength making it easy for Tim to leap on top of her and pin her down, stopping her flaying arms from hitting him.

This was no passionate advance. They were not into S & M. The stark reality of it was… that Carrie had been trying to kill him.

She was hysterical. He had never seen a person in this state before and was frightened by what he saw.

He let go of one of her wrists and slapped her across the face. She immediately stopped struggling and started wailing. It was a frightening sound.

Tim couldn't comprehend what was going on. This tough woman was crying like a baby, her body wracked by uncontrolled sobbing. He switched on the lights over their bed and looked down on the contorted face of the woman he loved.

'Carrie, what the effing hell are you doing? You nearly killed me, you stupid bitch.'

He let go of her other wrist and tentatively explored his throat with his fingers to see if it was bleeding.

Fortunately the metal comb that she had been holding across his throat, like a knife blade, had not pierced the skin.

He looked at her crumpled, tear soaked face.

'What the hell were you doing? I thought you were that witch Sue come to murder us. You scared the shit out of me. I could have hurt you.' His words tumbling out. 'I thought you were already dead. That she had killed you. Carrie, what's going on?'

It took him five minutes to stop her sobbing. Her hair sticking to her hot blotchy face, tears cascading down her cheeks in torrents, soaking her nightie.

He couldn't get his head around seeing her like this. His tough, ex-soldier girlfriend had dissolved into a gibbering wreck.

'Ah'm sorry,' she sobbed, 'Ah'm so, so sorry. Ah thought they'd gone.'

'Gone! What do you mean gone?' he said, puzzled, hugging her to him. Her tears wet on his chest, as she buried her face into it.

'The nightmares. The awful nightmares.'

'Nightmares, what nightmares?'

'I thought Ah was out there again.'

'Out where for chrissake?

'Afghanistan. Ah thought you were…an… an insurgent in my tent. It was you or me. I was going to have to kill you,' she sobbed.

'Jesus,' he said, rubbing his hand across his throat.

'Battlefield survival. If has to be instinctive to survive. It just kicked in. Close combat. Fight to the death. You can smell their fear. It's you or them.'

'My God, you could have killed me then!'

'Ah thought you were the bastard that blew my legs off. The bomb maker, come to finish me off.'

'Oh Carrie you frightened the 'be Jesus' out of me,' he said, tightening his grip on her and kissing her hair. 'I've never seen you cry before. It's all so scary. Out of character for my soldier girl.'

'Ah've been having them since Geoffery's funeral. I saw that Union Jack on his coffin.'

'Union Jack?'

'Yeah on his coffin.'

'Carrie, there was no flag on his coffin. When you mentioned it earlier at the wake, I just thought you were pissed.'

'No flag?'

'No.'

'Oh! The funeral reminded me of my mate who…who didn't make it.

'You never told me about this before.'

'Ah felt guilty I survived and he didn't. He lost his life. Hell, Ah only lost my legs,' she said, welling up.

'Oh Carrie.'

'The Doctors told me that with PTSD… things… things that aren't there, can suddenly materialise. The brain makes images of what it thinks it ought to be seeing. During my own convalescence, I saw too many flag covered coffins.

Homecomings of our guys who didn't make it. Ah felt I'd let them down by not being there to help in the battles.'

'Carrie, Christ you'd already done enough.'

'You might think I'm losing the plot, but I saw infantrymen in Geoffery's grave before they lowered the coffin in.'

'You what?'

'Soldiers with guns. Full battle kit. His grave was just like one of many foxholes Ah dug out there. I just hope that it's not the start of another episode.'

'What do you mean?'

'When I was convalescing from you know,' she said, looking at her stumps. 'I was pretty bad with… with PSTD.'

'Do all you army guys come down with this problem?'

'We're not the only ones to get it. Some civvies get it as well,' she said, trying to explain the problem.

'Oh?'

'Yes, it's not only a Military Services problem. Fire and Rescue, Policemen, ordinary people get it too, if they're unfortunate to be involved in a nasty incident.'

'Is there a cure?' he said, hoping that it was a temporary condition.

'Apparently. But it's a long road.'

'Does that mean you're likely to try and kill me again then? he said, wondering if he could cope with further episodes.'

'Probably,'

'Oh shit. Just as I thought life was starting to get better.'

'Do you still want me around then?' she asked looking into his eyes for a truthful answer.

'Course. I…I like having you around.'

'Only like?'

'Yeah well...you know,' he said, awkwardly. He was too embarrassed to tell her his true feelings, that he loved her. 'Anyway, I'll help you sort it.

We've got money from the old man now. Well, soon, once we get this project off the ground,' he clarified, remembering the money was still conceivably a long way away.

'You mean that?'

'Yes. I owe you,' he said, kissing her face, tasting her salty tears.

Carrie responded, hugging him tightly.

'You were speaking in a foreign language too. I didn't recognize your voice.'

'Afghan,' she said.

'I didn't know you could speak Afghan...but I thought it sounded very sexy like in that film.'

'What film?'

'That film '*A Fish called Wanda*. You know, when John Cleese spoke Russian to Jamie Lee Curtis. It turned her on big time. Say something to me now.'

'I don't speak Russian.'

'No in Afghanese, or whatever they speak.'

'There's nearly 50 languages spoken in Afghanistan.'

'Yeah, but what language were you speaking?'

'Pashto.'

'Bless you.'

'This isn't an effing film you know. This isn't make believe. This is real.' Carrie said, angrily.

'Sorry,' Tim grovelled.

'That helicopter trip to Nice airport was the trigger I think. That's what started it off. Ah used to love helicopters too.'

'I wasn't going to tell you this, but you had an episode at Geoffery's funeral.'

'What sort?'

'A Chinook flew over and you ended up kneeling on the ground. I thought you were messing around.'

'You never said anything before.'

'No. It's because Andy suggested not to. He got your condition sussed right away though.'

'If it was a Chinook…it reminded me of being rescued…Oh, it's such a reassuring noise when it's coming in to rescue you. The heavy beat of the double rotors is very calming. It's like there's no panic, you know?'

'Even though you're under fire?'

'Yeah. It sounds like I automatically went into a protective stance…like we were trained to…to protect the helicopter in case there were insurgents waiting to ambush it.'

'Perhaps all we need to do is to keep you away from the sound of helicopters then.' Tim said, flippantly.

'If only it was that simple.'

'How's your head, where I hit you?'

'Sore,' she said, gingerly touching the abrasion on the side of her forehead.

'I've never seen you like this, in all the time we've been together. What's that about six months?'

'Ah haven't had an attack like this for over twelve months. Oh Tim Ah'm sorry I hurt you.'

'I hope it goes away again.'

'The Doctor's tell me it will always be there, but the flashbacks should lose their intensity – eventually.'

'I'll help you,' Tim said, kissing her gently, 'I'll help you,' unsure if he had the moral strength, to actually live up to his promise.

CHAPTER FIFTY SIX

25th January

Andy came home from his night shift and opened the door quietly to be confronted by Helen who was sitting at the bottom of the stairs, bleary eyed.

'A courier brought this for you, just after you'd gone last night,' Helen said, coldly thrusting an A4 envelope at him.

'What is it?'

'How should I know? Perhaps it's from that tart Nadine.'

'Why should she...?'

'You tell me, you've obviously got something going with her.'

'No I haven't. Now stop this. There is nothing going on.'

'Oh no! Then what about the present she gave you?'

'Present, what present?' Andy said, tiredly.

'You damn well know what present,' Helen shrieked.

'Look, I haven't a clue what you're talking about. I'm sorry but I haven't had any sleep for the last thirty six hours and I'm...'

Helen plunged her hand into Andy's coat pocket still hanging where he'd left it and pulled out the small gift box.

'This present,' she said, angrily throwing it at him. 'Now do you remember? You...you hateful bastard.'

'Oh that!' Andy's stomach knotted as he looked at the box, which now lay at his feet.

'How could you Andy, how could you?' she cried.

'I can explain...I haven't done anything...we...no it's not like that...'Andy struggled to vocalise his thoughts. Surely this would be the ideal time to come clean and confess about the bedroom incident.

'I trusted you Andy and you do this to me, to us...do you know what you've done to our lives?' she sobbed.

Andy walked towards her to comfort her.

'Don't. Don't touch me,' she screeched and ran upstairs sobbing.

Andy desperately wanted to go after her. Instead he watched her disappear into their bedroom and slam the door.

'Jesus, what a mess,' he said, shaking his head, annoyed that he'd forgotten Nadine's gift. Furthermore for being stupid enough to leave it where Helen could find it.

He looked at the envelope in his hand and spotted the Monaco Couriers name.

'This is all your fault Geoffery Foster. I had a happy life until you came along. SOD YOU.'

Andy threw the envelope on to the little oak table in the hallway and went upstairs and showered.

Desperately tired, all he really wanted to do was go to bed. However he didn't want to further upset Helen, who was still in their bedroom. Instead he went downstairs and made himself a cup of tea and a piece of toast, then opened the envelope.

Attached to the letter was a compliments slip from the firm of Lawyers whose offices they had just visited.

'What a waste of money. Why didn't they just give me the envelope while I was there?' he muttered.

Attached to the compliments slip was a letter from Geoffery. Andy recognised his barely legible spidery handwriting.

Dorothy & Tom Hospice
Hampton Leck
December

Dear Andy,
The reason that you're reading this letter is because I've 'kicked the bucket.'

Before I get into the detail concerning the instructions documented here, I'd like to record my thanks to you, for all your help over and above the 'call of duty'.

I knew I had made a wise choice recruiting you to help me sort out my Godsons. Apologies if your involvement has caused you any problems.

'Too right you have. That Nadine has become a bleeding millstone,' Andy said, to himself.

'You will have been told by now that I have given you the responsibility of releasing my legacy to my Godsons.

I'm sure you'll want to know why. The reason that I didn't just give them the money, is that I believe it wouldn't be in their long term interests. As you've seen, they are an interesting group of individuals, each with a significant amount of 'baggage' and by their nature, I feel that just giving them the money was not the best course of action.

For instance James would probably go back to his old lifestyle and blow it on parties, gambling and alcohol. He would probably be dead within six months.

Tim, unused to having a large bank account, would probably gamble it away and continue his self-centred life.

Rupert would probably lose it all to that bitch of a wife in a divorce settlement.

So you can see my dilemma. That's why I want you to manage what they do, before you authorise the release of the money to them individually.

I suggest that you release the money in several stages. Clearly they will need some start-up money in order to 'explore' what they can do to create something worthwhile and long lasting from their legacy.

You will recall my analogy to the Wizard of Oz characters. I feel quite pleased with the thought. The similarities between their individual characteristics, I believe, are quite striking.

Tim, no heart, is a selfish individual who doesn't put anyone else's feelings into his 'me' focussed life.

James, no brain, is actually a very bright person, but the booze has robbed him of his self-respect and 'killed off' his intellect. You might find him someone that you can use during this exercise.

Rupert, no courage. He has been subjugated by that bully of a wife but needs to have the confidence to stand his ground.

So on to your overriding criteria to releasing the money:-

Whatever they decide, it has to satisfy <u>you,</u> that they are planning to do something worthwhile and address those failings I have identified above.

I suggest you meet them individually in a few weeks' time, having already alerted them to what you will be telling them what you're looking for (I would have done this by prepared letter but unfortunately I know by my energy levels, time is running out).

However, I have produced other stage letters to assist you as best I can. You will receive these in response to your letters of progress to my Lawyers in Monaco.

I hope this additional involvement doesn't cause you any family problems and that the extension of the contract will provide you with an adequate reimbursement for your troubles.

Geoffery.

'Adequate reimbursement. Ha!' Andy said, cynically. 'My marriage is on the rocks because of you,' he ranted. 'I wish I'd never got involved. Now I understand the hospice rule of not getting personally involved with patients.

What the hell am I going to do to reassure Helen about Nadine? Oh God, what if Sue publishes that video? Then that's it. Marriage over, kids with no father, pilloried in the press. Oh hell. What a mess!'

Andy gave in to his tiredness and curled up on the settee, eventually drifting off to a disturbed sleep.

CHAPTER FIFTY SEVEN

25th January

'Oh, it's you! Kay said, opening her front door. 'Come in Tim. You don't have to knock. You might have moved in with Carrie, but this is still your home.'

'Can't find my key.'

'That's more like you! What's the matter, is Carrie OK?'

'No not really. I left her sleeping. It's her I've come to talk to you about.'

'Well she's made a bit of an exhibition of herself recently hasn't she?'

'Yes...and it got worse.'

'What do you mean?'

'Look at this,' Tim said, pulling the collar of his roll neck jumper down revealing a vivid three inch red line across his throat.

'What's that?' Kay said, concerned, examining the mark. 'Did you cut yourself shaving?'

'No...she...she had an episode in bed last night.'

'Episode! What sort of episode?'

'She...she tried to kill me.'

'Oh my God. Tried to kill you?' Kay said, in disbelief, putting her hand to her mouth.

'She thought she was killing an insurgent,' Tim continued.

'An insurgent! What do you mean?'

'Yes, she thought she was back in the army, fighting the Taliban.'

'Taliban! Oh Tim, what did you do?'

'I hit her, Tim said, uncomfortably. 'I had to hit her to get her to stop.'

'You hit a woman?' Kay said, shocked at his confession.

'She was trying to kill me, for chrissake. She's very strong.'

'Oh, my god! Was she dreaming? Is she on drugs?'

'No. It's this mental problem. She called it PTSD.'

'Post Traumatic Stress Disorder, I've read a lot about it in the papers recently.'

'I…can't put up with her like this. I want to move back here. I'll bring my stuff round later.'

'You mean leave her?'

'Yes.'

'But surely she needs you?'

'I couldn't stand it. Waiting for her to have another session. It would be a nightmare.'

'Do you love her son?' Kay asked, earnestly.

'Well…yes…I think so.'

'Then help her… Don't run away when she needs you. That bitch Nadine did that to Geoffery at his most vulnerable.'

'But…I mean we're not even…'Tim said, struggling to rationalise his thoughts.

'I know you're not married…but you must love her in the good and bad times; in sickness and in health.'

'But she's so…so irrational,' Tim said, trying to justify his intentions.

'She helped you sort yourself out, didn't she?'

'Yes, but that was different.'

'How was it different? You were miserable and so full of yourself that you had become a nightmare to live with. Tim, the change in you has been phenomenal. She helped you do that.'

'This is different though. This is a psychological problem. I can't help her, I'm no effing Psychiatrist.'

'No, but you can be her 'rock'. Her tower of strength.

'I'm not like that. You know me.'

'Yes, but when you love someone you change. You have to give and take,'

'What do you mean by that?'

'You have to compromise your own values, your personality to…to become an amalgam with the person you love,' Kay explained, patiently.

'Now you sound like a bleeding agony aunt. No chance,' he said, standing up and walking to the window.

'It's time for you to grow up son and stop being so self-centred.'

'I didn't come round here to listen to this crap.'

'Well it's about time you did listen to something other than your own selfish voice.' Kay added, angrily.

'I'm going.' Tim said, walking quickly to the door.

'That's right. Run away when there's something you don't want to hear.'

'Well…'

'Do you love her?'

'I've already told you. Yes…yes I suppose so.'

'Well, help her.'

'It's easy for you to say. But what do I do?'

'Be there for her. Help her find some professional help. Love her.' Kay said, sincerely.

'You make it sound so easy. You should have been there last night. I was shit scared that she was going to kill me.'

Kay walked over to him and looked into his eyes, she saw his pain. 'It must have been very frightening,' she said, holding his hand.

'She didn't know what she was doing. That was the worst thing. I couldn't get through to her.' Tim explained.

'Give her time and …'

'Patience?' Tim interrupted. 'Well you know I haven't got much of that.'

'It will come, believe me. I've never told you this before, but when you were a baby you were a nightmare, always crying.

You really got to me. Drove me up the wall. I thought at one time I was going to suffocate you to stop your constant crying. But I had a great midwife. She was a tough old bird and she said you've got to toughen it out or you'll end up in the 'loony bin'.'

'The what?'

'Oh, it's an old fashioned term for a mental hospital. Anyway, I used to put you at the bottom of the garden in your pram so I couldn't hear you crying.

At first I kept coming to see, if you were OK. First every two minutes, then five, ten and so on. It took me some time but slowly I built up an emotional toughness. Being a Mother isn't all a bed of roses, you know.' Kay said, reflectively.

'Come off it Mother. A crying baby isn't the same as my problem. This lady was trained to be a professional assassin. She could have killed me while I slept.'

'Perhaps not, but you have to adapt.'

'Adapt?'

'Like sleeping with half an ear open. Like I used to; to make sure you were still breathing in your cot.'

'Hello! Earth to Mother, this is somebody trying to kill me,' he said, patronisingly.

'Well you'll just have to sleep with your eyes open.'

'Oh thanks. That's a great help.'

'Look, there's bound to be lots of help out there for former soldiers. You shouldn't have to cope with this alone.'

'Such as?' he asked, now irritated by her persistent rhetoric.

'I read about one organisation called 'Combat Stress'. Why don't you call them?'

'Combat what?'

'Combat Stress. They have quite a good reputation dealing with service people, I gather.'

'Yeah. I hear what you say.'

'Tim!' Kay admonished, recognising his lack of intention.

'Well I suppose it's worth a try,' he agreed, reluctantly.

'At least it's a start.' Kay said, pleased that her persistence had finally paid off.

'I'd better get back to her. But if you don't see me again. You'll know the gamble failed.'

'Oh Tim, don't be so melodramatic. Goodbye son. I'm sure it'll be alright.'

As she closed the door, Kay felt uneasy, not convinced at all by her own assurances. 'I hope you'll be OK. Time will tell,' she said, resignedly.

CHAPTER FIFTY EIGHT

26th January

In spite of her bravado, Kay had been unnerved by Tim's revelation about Carrie's attack on him. The unprovoked nature of it and Tim's concerns had given her a sleepless night.

She decided to telephone Andy and ask for his advice, for clearly he was knowledgeable about the condition, as he had helped out during Carrie's episode at the funeral.

Helen answered the telephone after the third ring. 'Hello.'

'Hello, could I speak to Andy, please.'

Now suspicious of any woman calling him, Helen demanded, 'who are you?'

'Hello, Helen, I'm Tim's Mum, Kay. We met at the funeral. I expect you know all about Tim. He's the one Geoffery got climbing mountains with his girlfriend Carrie.'

'He's not here.' Helen said, bluntly.

'I wonder, if I could ask you, to get him to call me back?'

'I don't know where he is or when he is coming back.' Helen announced, flatly.

'Oh I'm sorry to hear that. I don't mean to pry. But is there a problem?'

'A problem? You'd probably know more about that that I.'

'Sorry, I don't understand what you mean,' Kay said, puzzled.

'Don't you? Or are you just saying that to protect him.'

'Protect him! Protect from what? Sorry, I'm obviously missing something,'

'You were in Monaco, I gather. Then you know what he was up to.'

'I'm sorry, I don't know what you mean. We went to Monaco for the reading of the will, that's all.'

'That's not the whole truth though is it?' Helen said, probing. 'What about the evening and the night time?'

'Well, yes we went to the Casino and had a tour around Monaco, but that was all.'

'And my husband was with you all the time?'

'Well no, of course not. Not all the time, no. He did spend some time with…' Kay stopped in mid-sentence suddenly realising what Helen was getting at.

'Go on. Sometime with whom?'

'Well, it was…'

'You don't have to protect him. I know what he's been up to. He's been getting into that woman's knickers, hasn't he?'

'Who do you mean?'

'That French woman. What's her name?'

'Nadine. Oh you mean that tart.'

'Yes. His clothes absolutely reek of her perfume. You don't get that by just exchanging a peck on the cheek. Which is the pathetic excuse that he's come up with.'

'Look I'm sure nothing happened. He's a good man and that woman will throw herself at anything in trousers. Sorry, I didn't mean to imply that Andy isn't an attractive man. But he's a gentleman, as far as I can see.'

'Oh, a gentleman is he? Well perhaps you can tell me why she's buying him gifts?'

'Did she? Well, I shouldn't read too much in to it though. Are you two OK?

'No, we have barely exchanged a civil word since he got back. I reckon your so called gentleman has been climbing into somebody else's bed and broken his marital vows. He has let his family down...the bastard.' Helen dissolved into tears.

At the other end of the phone, Kay was unsure what to do.

'Look dear... Helen. Do you want me to come over and we can chat about it face to face rather than like this.'

'No, you'll be wasting your time,' she sobbed. 'I know he's been tempted because...because, since I had Molly, we haven't...we haven't you know. Perhaps it's my fault he's strayed. I can't cope with this anymore.'

'Listen. Andy is a good man. He wouldn't do that to you.'

'Oh I'm so useless. This is the last straw.' Helen wailed.

'Helen, it's OK. Just catch your breath for a second...How old is the baby?'

'...Nearly six months.' She blurted.

'Have you been feeling a bit down recently?'

'Yes, I'm so tired, all the time. I just don't have any energy. But what's that got to do with my cheating husband?'

'Have you been to the Doctors recently?'
'No, why would I?'
'Perhaps you've got a bit of the 'baby blues'.'
'Baby what?'
'Baby blues. I think these days it's called Post Natal Depression.'
'But he's the one that needs treatment for cheating on us. Sometimes I think I'd like to castrate him for straying.'
'I think you've got it all wrong. Honestly, I'm not aware that he was overly-friendly with that French tart.'
'Well it sounds like you don't like her very much either.'
'No, I think she is a gold digging bitch,' Kay said, angrily. 'She left poor Geoffery when he was very ill. Then she turns up at his funeral all puffy eyed and…'
'That's when I caught Andy and her the first time.'
'Oh!'
'They were cuddling on top of the hill watching the sun go down. So say 'paying their last respects' to Geoffery.'
'I didn't know about that.'
'That's why we were late leaving the Church, for the wake.'
'Oh, was that the reason? But I'm sure you'll find it was her that dragged him there.'
'And then again. I caught them at the wake, I caught them cuddling.'
'Well she was very drunk, I don't know whether you noticed?'
'Oh yes, she and those girls she brought over as pallbearers had a right old shindig. I thought they were very disrespectful.

'She was up to her tricks after you'd left too. She was flirting with anything in trousers.'

'Yes, but that doesn't explain what happened over there.'

Kay was now starting to have doubts herself about Andy's virtue. Did she really believe that his overnight stay in Nadine's room was spent innocently sleeping on the couch?

What about the subsequent fuss over the corridor kiss captured on the mobile phone video footage? Should she tell Helen about her concerns or would that be the final straw? Clearly he hadn't confessed to her about it.

'Look, Helen. Let me come over and we'll have a cuppa and talk it over. I've had a few challenges with men myself and I'm sure we can talk this through.'

'I'm sorry I don't want to get you embroiled in my domestic affairs but I...I feel...so down.'

'I'll get a taxi and pop over. Remind me where you live.'

Reluctantly Helen gave Kay her address and within half an hour they'd had a cuppa, a good 'chinwag' and Kay was helping her with an accumulated mountain of washing and ironing.

'Thanks for your help. It's just all got on top of me. And now this thing with Andy, I just couldn't see any way around it.

He used to be so good helping me out, doing this sort of stuff too. But since Geoffery came into our life, he hasn't had the time...what with the Scout hut fire and chasing those Godsons....and now with this woman. Then he tells me Geoffery has made him responsible for deciding when the will money is released. I'm not going to have any help ever again.'

Helen filled up, but Kay was quickly with her and gave the distraught woman a hug.

'Ssssh,' she coaxed, smoothing her hair. 'Don't think about it. We'll sort this out. Don't worry, I'll help you.'

'Thanks,' she sobbed.

'Well from what you've been saying, it sounds like, whilst he was helping Geoffery, he deserted his family,' Kay summarised.

'Don't get me wrong. Geoffery was very generous and the money was particularly useful, especially as we'd had a run of expensive bad luck,' Helen added.

'But sometimes, money causes more problems than it cures,' Kay said, 'Look at that Sue. She's another gold digger.'

'Oh, she is such a horrible person.'

'Yes we had a few problems with her while we were over there. In the end there was an almighty bust up and she made her own way back from Monaco. I'd be happy never to see her again.'

Kay recalled the reason for the final row.It had been to do with the video of Andy's indiscretion. How the hell was he going to explain that away? Even if he convinced Helen that nothing happened, the signs weren't good that their marriage could survive the revelation.

CHAPTER FIFTY NINE

27th January

A few days after the eventful weekend in Monaco, a letter arrived at the hospice for Andy.

'It looks like it's from one of your many female admirers. It's perfumed,' the receptionist quipped light-heartedly, handing it over to him.

Andy, out of character, snatched the letter from her and was going to say something but thought better of it. Instead he stormed away from the reception area with a face like thunder.

Surprised at Andy's out of character reaction, the receptionist said to the Hospice Manager, beside her. 'Charming. If that's what going to Monaco for the weekend does, give me Weston – Super- Mare anytime.'

'He's been as miserable as sin since he's been back.' Ann Place confirmed. 'Perhaps he resented coming back to work here, after seeing how the other half live. If he carries on like that, I'm going to have to have a word with him.'

Andy studied the envelope. The printed label was addressed to Monsieur Andee Spider. 'God, what's Nadine writing to me for, especially here.' Andy's mind was working overtime. 'I thought I'd never hear from her again. I hope this isn't going to drag on. No, I'm going to have to tell her to stop this nonsense.'

Angrily he threw the letter unopened, into his locker and carried on with his duties. However, its mere presence made him unsettled all day. It wasn't until he went back to his locker at the end of his shift, that he picked it up again, wondering whether to open it or not.

If he didn't open it, then whatever she had written wouldn't upset him. On the other hand, he would be forever wondering what was in it.

Eventually, after staring at it for several minutes, he decided to face whatever she had written and he opened it gingerly.

Inside the envelope was not a letter. It was a picture, printed on matte paper from an inkjet printer.

The picture was overprinted with a large text box. The words '*LEGACY OR EXPOSURE? shouting at him*.

The picture was of two people; a man dressed in Jacket and trousers and a woman in a filmy dressing gown. They were kissing. The time stamp showed 0535.

Andy's world exploded. His worst nightmare had happened. This was the end of his marriage. His respectability. His self-esteem.

He slumped heavily against the cold metal locker, as the enormity of the picture and his actions hit him.

His mind went into melt down. He was unable to think. He stood and stared at the photo trembling in his hand.

Even though, he thought he'd mentally prepared to receive it. The anticipation was overshadowed by the devastating impact of seeing himself, caught in this compromising situation.

'It wasn't Nadine after all. This was evil Sue's doing. She had goaded him by addressing it to 'Monsieur'. The nightmare had begun.

He was mesmerised by the picture. The photo wasn't very clear. It was a frame frozen from a video. Their faces were slightly out of focus, but it was obvious who they were.

With Helen already distraught about her perception of his waywardness, how much longer could he keep this from her? Especially now that Kay had suddenly become Helen's confidant.

Perhaps he ought to come clean, but what impact would it have on Helen? She was already depressed before all this all kicked off. Surely this would send her over the top.

Bloody Nadine, you've got a lot to answer for…or was it Geoffery he should be cursing?

Whatever. The message was clear. He had to release the money from the will for Rupert at least, as soon as possible, or else!

Andy was now in the horns of a dilemma. He was constrained by the terms that Geoffery had laid down for releasing the money. Even if he could make a case for releasing it, just for Rupert, how the hell could he prove that Rupert had 'earned it', especially as he was spending all his waking hours sitting at Joanne's bedside.

What safeguards had Geoffery put into place with his lawyers to ensure Andy wasn't just playing lip-service to the terms of the will?'

It was a mess and he couldn't see a way out of it.

Meanwhile, Sue was smiling to herself as she imagined the impact, she hoped the picture would have on 'the bloody nurse'. She was enjoying her moment of control. However, a knock on the door stopped her preparation of yet another, 'encouraging' picture on her laptop.

'Who the hell is that now? Can't you read,' she said, angrily yanking the door open. 'No cold callers... What do you want? Oh it's you,' she added, recognising the Policeman. 'I'm busy.'

'So are we. Mrs Williams Screen, I'm arresting you on suspicion of causing the death of Jan Criscroski. You do not have to say anything. But it may harm your defence if you do not mention when questioned something which you later rely on in Court. Anything you do say may be given in evidence. Do you understand?'

'Oh don't be so stupid. I haven't killed anybody. You've got the wrong person,' she protested, her mind now rapidly thinking of how to lie her way out of this one.

John had wasted no time in going to Sue's house after receiving the news from a delighted Graham that the lab reports were finally in.

For as well as matching the heel casts with her broken heel that he'd retrieved off the motorway, the mud on the heel also matched the grave soil.

But the crucial piece of evidence was that the bloody fingerprints on the cross were definitely hers. Cross matched against fingerprints on file, taken when she was charged with Geoffery's attempted murder.

'I suggest you wait until we are at the Police station before you say anything else. In the meantime, I have a search warrant to look for evidence.'

'I want to speak to my Solicitor.'

'All in good time.'

'I just need to shut down my computer, if that's alright.'

'OK, but don't try any funny business.'

John Sparrow followed her into the room where she had been working. Quickly Sue clicked on the *close* cross in the Powerpoint programme she had been using to compile the next picture for Andy.

'*Do you want to Save?*' the programme asked. Sue quickly clicked the *NO* option. She didn't want any prying Policeman seeing her 'encouragement' pictures. She was about to pull the mobile phone memory card out of the Laptop port, but the Policeman prevented her.

'I think we'll leave that just where it is if you don't mind,' he said, picking up the laptop.

Upstairs she could hear the other Policemen starting their search.

'You watch what you're doing up there,' she shouted. 'I shall sue for any damages.'

CHAPTER SIXTY

27th January

The Police Team had been frustrated by the delay in getting the lab reports back. They had already pieced the evidence together and it all pointed at Sue. However, without the vital forensics, the supporting proof was not there.

Sue was taken to the Police station and, eventually, with her Solicitor at her side, the questioning began.

'Where were you on the evening of the December 23rd?'

'I had just been released from a trumped up charge of attempted murder and I made my way to the Church on the Hill to be with my Husband, who was burying his uncle.'

'But I gather you missed the funeral?'

'Yes, it was over by the time I arrived there.'

'So what did you do?'

'Well it was a lovely evening and I went for a little walk around the Nature Reserve on the hill.'

'In the dark?'

'It was not too dark. I could see where I was walking.'

'OK. At what point did you make your way back down the hill?

'Well I was just making my way, when I heard shouting.'

'What time was that?'

'I don't know, I didn't look at my watch.'

'OK, carry on.'

'There was a man shouting at a young boy for doing something.'

'What was it? Could you hear what was being said?'

'Well apparently, this young boy was damaging the newly filled in grave, kicking the flowers around, you know. The man was remonstrating with him.'

'I see. Could you describe the young boy?'

'Well it was quite dark by then, but...' Sue went on to accurately describe Ben.

'I see, and where were you while this was all going on?

'I was standing by the entrance gate to the main burial ground.'

'So how come your heel marks got on the grave?'

'Oh, yes. Well...umm, after the boy had hit the man, I rushed over to get hold of him and stop the assault... that's when it must have happened,' she lied, calmly.

'And your bloody fingerprints. How did they get on the wooden cross?'

'Oh. Let me see now. Yes I remember. The boy had kicked the cross over and I picked it up and put it back into the soil. An act of respect for the dead, you understand.'

The Policeman supressed his desire 'to be sick' at her pathetic attempt to show a reverential concern.

'Why were you bleeding?'

'I errr...don't really know. Perhaps the boy had a knife and cut me when I was trying to help the poor man.'

'Is there anything else you remember at all?'

'Yes. The boy stole something out of the man's pocket. I think it might have been his mobile phone.'

Sue mentally thanked Ben for his admission. Relaying the story about the mobile and the dog walker episode had, possibly, created the route to his own incarceration.

'OK. So the man had been assaulted and you tried to catch the perpetrator. How was the man when you left him?'

'Oh, he was shocked but alright. I sat with him on the bench for a little while to make sure…I gather he was the Gravedigger…and then I left.'

'How did you get back down from the hill?'

'I walked.'

'Which way did you go?'

'Down the road.'

'Did any cars pass you on the way down?'

'Yes, a black Polo.'

'I see. Did you see who was driving it?'

'No.'

'How did you get to be in the back of your husband's car when it crashed on the motorway?'

'I err…I walked to the…no I got a taxi to the hotel where the wake was being held.'

'Did anybody see you there?'

'No, I didn't go in. There had been some bad feeling between me and some of the people there and I didn't want to cause a scene. So I waited outside until he came out.'

'He was travelling with his girlfriend. Why would you go with them?'

'Well, I had accepted that our marriage was over and there was no point being resentful about things. So I…you know.'

'They were travelling to Bristol. Your home is in Cheltenham.'

'Yes…I errr…was going to see some friends of mine in Bristol and I'd scrounged a lift with Rupert.'

'Could your friends corroborate your story?'

'Well, as you know, Rupert has already done so…But my friends…errr… probably not, because they were over here from New Zealand, only for a short time. Now they've gone home.'

'Do you have their address?'

'I know this will sound contrived, but they were moving to a new house and I don't know their new address.'

'That's convenient,' the Policeman thought.

'So what do you know about the accident on the motorway?'

'Well it all happened so quickly and I don't really remember too much.'

'Why didn't you stop and help your husband?'

'As I say, I don't remember. I was concussed. I suffered terribly from whiplash…well I still am really.'

'Well officer, I think my client has answered all your questions satisfactorily. So I expect you'll de-arrest and release her?' the Solicitor demanded.

'No, I'm afraid not. Although her story sounds very convincing, there are other aspects, which we have not discussed that do not support her version of events.'

'This is an outrage,' Sue said, losing her temper. 'You locked me up recently for a 'so called' attempted murder, which I repudiated. The video evidence showed that I was set up. I shall be contacting my MP about this…this is harassment.'

'That's your right and privilege madam. But I shall be detaining you in custody for a bit longer.'

'Damn!' he thought 'she certainly got all the answers. Video…I wonder if the hotel has any video of the car park that night… That will prove if she's lying or not… and another Taxi ride too! I wonder if she can remember to taxi firm.'

CHAPTER SIXTY ONE

4th February

Andy arrived home from work and saw the letter on the carpet. It had a Monaco stamp on it.

Getting no response to his shouted announcement that he was home, he assumed that Helen was out somewhere with the children.

He made himself a cup of tea, sat down in the lounge and opened the letter.

'What's all this about now,' he wondered. 'Another one of Geoffery's missives sent by his Lawyers I see.'

Dorothy & Tom Hospice
Hampton Leck
December

Dear Andy,

You've probably been back from Monaco for a week or so now after the reading of the will. I guess you're feeling a bit confused and still rattled that I should put this additional burden on your shoulders.

As I write this letter, it's difficult for me to predict how things are likely to turn out.

Are they all being compliant with the idea of earning the money or are they causing you hassle?

Give them up to £10,000 start-up funds, but make sure it's being used sensibly. I know that self-centred Tim is likely to be gambling it away or wasting it on some selfish project...

'How wrong can you be Geoffery,' Andy said, to himself. 'Suddenly he's starting to care about other people.'

...and if that Sue wasn't in prison, I know she would be using every ounce of energy to get her hands on Rupert's money.

'Sorry Geoffery, you failed on that one too. You obviously didn't know about the CCTV camera in your room. But you're right about her money grabbing, thinking about the blackmail picture he'd received from her earlier and wondering if this might be a way of releasing money to her.

...difficult to imagine what James will be up to. Hopefully the clinic will have dried him out and put him on the straight and narrow.

'Well, so far he's being very strong. Fingers Crossed.'

In the meantime the following might help you decide when to release the money:-

- *Have they created and documented their own goals?*
- *Are their goals sufficiently challenging?*
- *Have they written a viable Business plan?*
- *Do their goals include helping each other and where necessary, other people?*
- *And later - Have they achieved their goals?*

When you are happy that they have achieved a good percentage of their aims, you can advise my Lawyers and the appropriate funds will be released.

'Good god, I guess if they've got a business degree they might be able to do that. I mean, what do I know about assessing people's documentation. What a nightmare.'

Note; there might be some circumstances where the above isn't relevant. I will allow you to use your own discretion in these cases. However, you need to know that my Law Team can be quite tough to persuade.

'Ah, now this might be a way of getting Sue or Rupert the money. Or should I be going to the Police and tell them about being blackmailed. Oh hell. I don't know,' he said, in frustration.

Apologies once again for adding this chore to your, already busy, life. But I know you're the right man for the job.

Good Luck and Best wishes
Geoffery.

As Andy put the letter down, the phone rang.

'Hi, Andy Spider.'

'Andy, it's me, Tim.'

'Hi Tim.'

'Andy I'm after some money. Any chance of getting an advance from the old man's will?'

'Why?'

'It's to pay for the protection team that Carrie arranged to safeguard Joanne down in Bristol. They've been working on promises up until now and some cash will keep them there.'

'Yes, I think I can arrange that.'

'Great.'

'That's spooky that you rang then, because I've just received a letter from Geoffery giving me some guidelines.

OK, I'll see what I can do. But why are you paying for it and not Rupert?'

'I think he's got his mind on other things at the moment, don't you?'

'Yes, perhaps, you're right.'

'Anyway I'm... we're... quite happy to fund it from my own account.'

Blimey, Andy thought, well you have changed. That Carrie has really turned you around.

'Anyway, I reckon Rupert will need all his own money to pay for the American spinal injuries specialist that he plans to engage.'

'OK, Tim, I'll contact the Lawyers and they'll transfer to money to the account you gave them.

'Just changing the subject, have you had any thoughts of a project to get the whole lot released?'

'Yeah, we were talking about it the other night. We might set up a Walking Company, aimed at people with disabilities. Obviously we're both physically in the right place to plan for something like that.'

'Good for you.'

'Well, as you know, Carrie really sorted me out... and we reckon it's something we could offer to other people. Carrie's idea is that we offer it to Meningitis sufferers, like myself; other amputees, especially service veterans and perhaps people suffering from PTSD. What do you reckon?'

'Sounds good to me. Well it certainly meets Geoffery's guidelines.'

'We were thinking of calling it 'Just do it Walking.'

'What do you reckon you need to start it up?'

'We haven't worked out the finances yet, but we believe the major outlays are- Internet Site, Publicity, Transport (Minibus); Staff and Specialist Equipment.'

'You've obviously done some thinking about it then, well done.'

'There is just one snag. Neither of us have any business experience. So we might need to buy in somebody.'

'It might be a long shot. But why don't you ask James? He used to be a bit of a business man I gather before he took to the bottle.'

'Yeah, good idea. I'll have words.'

'So, you're going to be busy?'

'If I'm honest we both need something to focus on. I don't know whether Mum has said anything, because she's been coming over to your place. But Carrie had a bad PTSD episode recently and we need some help.'

'Oh, I'm sorry to hear that. Where are you going to get help?

'Well initially we thought of you, but decided one of the veterans groups, probably Combat Stress, would be more suitable.'

Andy heaved a sigh of relief.

'We had a look at their website and it looks like they might be able to help.' Tim continued.

'Any progress?'

'Yeah, she's got an appointment next week.'

Andy had to admit he had been wrong in harshly judging Tim. Instead of sitting back waiting for the money, he was obviously motivated. He suspected Carrie's influence was the driving force.

'So we're going to give the walking company a go, after we've got Carrie on the road to recovery. At the moment she's my first priority.' Tim continued.

'Yes of course.'

'Her treatment will be a long job,' Andy counselled. 'Don't expect too much too soon.'

'No I won't. So long as she's getting the right treatment, I'm happy to wait and if necessary I'll pay for it too.'

In the background Andy could hear Kay talking.

'Just a second Andy, I'm at Mums at the moment. What did you say Mum?'

While they were in conversation, Kay had spotted an article in the local paper.

'I said…Joanne might not need the protection team anymore,' Kay said, looking up from the paper.

'What do you mean?'

'Listen to this.'

Kay read the article from the newspaper; '*Woman (39) arrested in Body in Graveyard Case.*'

Police today confirmed that a woman is in custody in relation to the death of the Gravedigger Jan Criscroski. Mr Criscroski's body was found in the burial ground of the Church on the Hill on Christmas Eve.

Police have not yet confirmed if they are linking it to the crash on the M5 in which Mr Criscroski's car was also involved.

'Well, how about that then? I wonder if it's that Sue. The paper hasn't given a name. Age is right though.' Kay said, conspiratorially.

'Why do you reckon it's her?'

'Remember Rupert told us that he'd heard her say she had been dancing on Geoffery's grave. She even told Ben she was up at the burial ground after we'd all left for the wake.

'Oh yeah. But that doesn't prove she killed the Gravedigger though.'

'Well they obviously had something else to tie her into his death. Perhaps Rupert got to the Police and turned her in.'

Tim relayed the information to Andy who was relieved to hear it.

'Fingers crossed,' he said. Well thanks for that great news, let's hope it's her.'

'Yeah too true. Let's hope they lock her up and throw away the key.'

Then doubts started entering Andy's thinking. At least, if she was in prison it would mean he shouldn't receive any more pictures.

But would she now create a smokescreen to deflect the truth of her own guilt and start making false accusations 'blackening his name'. What about her threat to Ben? He must contact him to make sure he was alright.

CHAPTER SIXTY TWO

11th February

Unfortunately, the hotel where the wake had taken place, was unable to find any car park CCTV surveillance footage to prove or disprove Sue's story that, on the night of the motorway crash, she had got into Rupert's car.

Rupert was now the only one who could disprove her alibi that she couldn't be the driver of the black Polo.

Meanwhile, although it had taken a few weeks, due to an unrelated child abuse investigation, the Police computer forensic team had spent some time analysing Sue's laptop.

The Computer forensic officer explained to Graham about the Video and Powerpoint slide he had found on the laptop.

'Well I don't know whether she's into extortion or not but there's this slide, that has the words 'Legacy or Exposure?' over the top of a screen shot from the video that I found in the memory card.'

'Let me have a look. Oh yes, a bit of corridor romance Eh! She into dogging do you reckon or is she just a nosey bitch?'

'Who knows!.'

'Somebody's been a naughty boy though. Look at the time. Do we know where this was taken?'

'No, but just in the shot there's a notice written in French. But it could be anywhere though.'

'Hang on, I recognise that guy. Isn't it that Nurse bloke, the Scout Leader that hangs around with that kid. Ben.'

'Ben?'

'The kid is the one that she's 'fingered' for belting the Gravedigger. I think we'd better have both of them in again, don't you?"

The Police contacted Andy about speaking to Ben and they arranged an appointment after he got home from school.

Ben had been in an anxious state for over two weeks, following their return from Monaco, waiting, any minute, to be arrested.

He was beside himself about Sue's threat, but finally the day had come. At least he hadn't been seized up off the street, as he'd feared.

Initially he refused to go, but Andy's gentle persuasion had, eventually, got him to agree.

'Look I know you've been dreading this moment, but it will be over soon. Sometimes the apprehension…' Andy said, trying to calm him.

'Is worse than the reality. I know, you've told me before,' Ben replied, disparagingly.

At the Police station they were shown into an interview room and anxiously awaited the session.

As the Senior Investigating Officer entered the room, Ben was concerned that it wouldn't go well, as he was the same Policeman he'd been 'lippy' to previously.

'Can I get you both a drink?' he said, smiling, putting his own cup of tea down.

'No…no thanks,' they both replied.

'Ok, let's get straight to it. We have received some contradictory evidence about your involvement in the events in the burial ground of the Church on the Hill on December 23rd. I would like to discuss these with you. Do you understand?'

'Yes, but honestly, she's lying,' Ben said, quickly.

'She?' the Policeman queried.

'Yes, it's that horrible woman, isn't? She said she would.'

'Did she now? What's the name of this horrible woman you're referring to?'

'Sue... what's her name Andy?' Ben looked at Andy for help.

'Williams-Screen,' Andy volunteered distastefully, almost spitting the name out.

'She said she'd tell you I was there. But I wasn't, I didn't do it.' Ben blurted.

'OK, but we'll be the judge of that. When did she say this to you?'

'In Monaco, when I told her I had picked up the phone in the burial ground. I recognised her from the picture. She was the one holding the cross.'

'Whoa, let's just slow done a bit. So you told her that you had picked up the mobile phone?'

'Yes.'

'And when did you pick it up?'

'On Christmas Eve, when I discovered somebody had messed up Geoffery's grave.'

'When did you use it first?'

'When I called Andy to tell him about the damage.'

The Policeman shuffled through some papers and checked, satisfied the mobile records confirmed Ben's story. 'Go on. Tell me about your meeting with her.'

'Well, after I told her that I recognised her in the photo.'

'Photo?'

'There was a photo on the phone that I spotted.

'Yes that's right,' the other said, checking the file again. 'And you told her you recognised her from it?'

'Yes it was her…her evil stare that convinced me.'

'Go on.'

'Well she grabbed me and got me in a room and threatened to cut my throat with some scissors'.

'Did you report it to the Monaco Police?'

'No, cause she was threatening she'd get me and anyway other stuff was going on.'

The Policeman made a note and invited Ben to continue. 'OK, go on.'

'Well, she forced me to go and get her husband, Rupert. She said if I told anybody she would say that I was at the burial ground after the funeral. That I'd messed the grave up, but she'd tried to stop me. She said she'd tell you that I hit the old man and stole his phone. It's not true, honest I didn't do it,' Ben pleaded, frantically.

'I can confirm his whereabouts.' Andy interjected. 'After the funeral he was at the wake all evening. He was having difficulties coping with the atmosphere at the wake.

'So you can vouch for him, all evening?'

'Yes.'

'When you discovered the damage to the grave on Christmas Eve, what were you wearing?'

'I was in my cycling kit. I was riding a bike that Geoffery bought me. I was going to show him how grateful I was. But the grave...' Ben filled up at the thought of what he'd found.

'OK son, take your time. Do you need a break?'

'No, it's OK, thanks,' Ben said, wiping the tears from his eyes.

'So you were wearing your cycling kit?'

'Yes.'

'What footwear did you have on?'

'My sidi shoes. You know; clip on ones.'

'Yes I know. Although the ground was frozen there were some faint footprints around the grave. You didn't stand on the grave?'

Ben was horrified at the suggestion. 'No of course not. That would have been an awful thing to do.'

'Yes of course. I think I'm satisfied with what you have told me. I don't expect that I will need to see you again. Is there anything you'd like to ask me?'

'Yes. Is she out?'

'What do you mean?'

'I understand she was arrested. Is she still locked up?'

'Why do you ask?'

'Because she said she'd come and get me and her husband, if we spoke to you about it?'

'Did she now? Threatening witnesses! The case gets better all the time. No don't worry, we won't be letting her out.'

'Well, thank you Ben, if you'd like to wait outside. 'I wonder if I could trouble you for a few moments Mr Spider. There are just a few loose ends we need to tie up. Ben, he won't be long.'

Ben looked at the Policeman suspiciously and then fearfully at Andy.

'Don't worry,' the Policeman reassured Ben. 'It's nothing concerning you.'

'Mr Spider, thanks for helping us with Ben.'

'What else can I help you with?' Andy asked, apprehensively.

'Have you been on holiday recently?'

'Holiday! No.'

'Not been to France?'

'France no, but I went to Monaco recently.'

'Do you mind if I ask why?'

'No, not at all. I am involved with the reading and execution of a will. A former patient of mine.'

'Former patient!'

'I can assure you there's nothing dodgy or sinister about it. I'm not a beneficiary.'

Andy relayed the circumstances of his involvement with Geoffery and the will.

'So, in Monaco, did you take your wife?'

'Umm, no. She had to stay home and look after the children. Look, I've got Scouts tonight and need to get back to finish the programme. Where's this questioning going?'

'I see…all in good time.'

'Did you take anybody else with you?'

'Well yes, the beneficiaries of the will and their relatives and friends…but I don't understand. What's this all about?'

'It's not our job to make judgements on people's moral fidelity, but were you having a fling while you were there. Away from the wife?'

'A what?'

'A tryst, an affair.'

Andy suddenly realised why the questioning. Sue had told the Police. His heart fell. He coloured up embarrassed. 'What do you mean?' he tried, bluffing it out.

'I think you know what I mean Mr Spider. In a corridor, a goodnight or should I say a good morning kiss.'

'Oh, that!'

'Yes that! Would you mind telling us of how a video and a picture of you and a young lady got on to a laptop computer?'

Andy was lost for words. In his worst nightmare he wasn't expecting to be quizzed by the Police about the corridor incident. The whole thing had escalated out of control.

'You know, of course, Mrs Williams – Screen?' the Policeman continued.

'Yes.' Andy tensed at the sound of her name.

'Was there some reason why she should have this material on her laptop?'

'She...I know it looks bad, but it's not like you imagine. It was quite innocent...'

'If I had a pound for everytime I heard that. Go on, please explain.'

'I was just saying goodnight to my hostess.'

'Hostess!'

'Oh God, not that sort of hostess. It was the former girlfriend of the guy whose will we went to hear. She lives in Monaco and had been showing me the sights.'

'I see at that time of the morning.'

'Well, yes, ...long story, short; I was drunk and I passed out in her room. And unfortunately it appears that the Williams - Screen woman must have heard us saying goodnight…and took a photo of us.'

'Yes, so I've seen.'

'She was trying to force me into releasing money from the will.'

Andy then explained his role in getting the money released from the estate and getting the Godsons their legacy.

'So what you're saying is she was trying to blackmail you then?'

'Well… Yes… I suppose, if you put it like that.'

'Well, well. There's no end to this ladies talents is there? Now we can add extortion to the charge sheet.'

Andy felt a sense of relief now that he had unloaded the story, albeit to the Police. There was still Helen to speak to about it.

'However,' the Policeman continued, 'in order to do that you will need to make a formal complaint.'

'Oh!' Andy said. 'Does that mean I will have to give evidence in court?'

'Yes, most likely. Is that a problem?'

'I'm not sure. I mean, I want her charged but…but…'

'But the publicity wouldn't be the ideal situation for somebody in your position,' the Policeman, mimicked. 'I know, I've heard it all before. Sadly that's why a lot of these people get away with it and bully their way through life.'

Andy thought of the irony of this situation. The Policeman had more or less repeated his own advice to Rupert about standing up to Sue and not letting her walk over him.

'Well it's down to you. Until you make a formal complaint, our hands are tied. Have a think about it.'

'I will, thanks.'

'Oh, there is one more thing we would like you to do?'

'Yes?'

'You obviously know the fear power of Mrs Williams-Screen. It appears that she has threatened her husband and forced him to give her an alibi about her involvement in the motorway crash.

We have very strong evidence that suggests she probably caused the crash whilst driving a stolen black Polo.'

'Black Polo, black Polo! Where did I see a black Polo? Andy said, stroking his chin, thinking. I've I got it. The night of the wake. Rupert and Jo left in a bit of a rush and a black Polo followed them out of the car park.

'Did you see the driver?'

'Sorry, no.'

'Ok, well that could have been the final nail in her coffin. Never mind. I need you to persuade her husband to tell the truth, to break her alibi, so we can charge her.

She has obviously terrorised him and got him where she wants him. It's especially amazing as his girlfriend was so badly hurt in the crash. You'd expect him to want to get even.

'Why me?'

'You appear to have some influence with him. I can't emphasise enough how important this is.'

'Yes, OK, I'll try.'

Andy left, his mind in a whirl. This was going from bad to worse.

CHAPTER SIXTY THREE

11th February

James, keen to find out what had happened with Ben at the Police station had called at Grandad Harold's house to speak to him.

'Well how did it go? Have the Police finished with you Ben?'

'Yes, I think so. They arrested that horrible woman and they're going to charge her with lots of things.'

'What about you having the phone?'

'They said they won't charge me for withholding evidence, or whatever it's called.'

'That's good. So what are you going to do now?'

'Don't know really, Mum's out from the clinic. But I don't know how long she will last without straying again.'

'Look, I know how hard it must be supporting her all the time. Why don't you find somebody else your age that you can talk to about it?'

'Yeah, I was thinking about doing that. There's a kid at our school who looks after his Mum cause she's got multiple sclerosis. Goes to a meeting every week. I think it's called Young Carers.'

'Sounds like a good idea.'

'I don't know. I mean, my Mum isn't ill all the time, like his.'

'No, but your life is significantly different from… from…'

'Say it, normal kids. Don't I know it?'

'Well then, give it a whirl. You can pack it up if it doesn't work.'

'Yeah, the trouble is…if the social workers get to hear of me…they'll put me in care…and I don't want that.'

'No, I think you're frightening yourself for nothing.'

'Yeah, I suppose. I'll think about it.'

'I've got a bit of thinking to do too. I might need your help.'

'What about?'

'It's all to do with complying with Geoffery's will. I was thinking about doing something for runaways. What do you think? I'd value your advice.'

'What, you mean like…like when I ran away to London?'

'Yes. Clearly, I can't stop kids running away, but at least I could help provide a safe place, a refuge, for them to stay in while they sort their life out.'

'Yeah, sounds like a great idea.'

'Perhaps you could give me some advice as to what would help. You know, like understanding their problems, giving them something useful to do while they are sorting themselves out.'

'Yeah of course.'

'…but that's for some time in the future. But first, Tim and Carrie want me to help them start up a Walking Company.'

'You what! A walking company! What teaching people to walk?'

'No. Well in a way, yes. It's an organisation that will take people into the hills and mountains to give them a bit of adventure on hiking trips. Showing them the tranquillity and beauty of nature'

'What sort of people?'

'I think they're gearing it up for people…people such as themselves… amputees.'

'Oh.'

'And people who have been affected by a big trauma. Like soldiers who have experienced horrible things.'

'You mean like getting blown up or being shot?'

'Yes, that sort of thing.'

'What about you though? I know you've got some… some problems with your guts.'

'Yes, I need to get that sorted too. Tim has offered to give me part of his liver; If we're compatible.

'Compatible! What like people are, when they get married?'

'No. Not that sort of compatible. Blood types and tissue matches. You know.'

'Yeah. I know. Just pulling your plonker.'

'I should have known. You scamp!'

'What's it like having a Dad, James?'

'I don't know. But I think it's best not to think about it. No point fretting over something you've never had or likely to have.'

'Yeah, but I hear my friends talking about what they do and…'

'You never miss what you've never had. That's the way I look at it.' James counselled.

'Course you never even had a Mum either, did you?'

'No I was orphaned by the time I was eight and I've grown up to be who I am.'

'I can still dream though,' Ben said, distantly.

'Yes, so long as you don't get disappointed that your dreams might be impossible ones.'

'Yeah, I suppose.'

'Enjoy the love that surrounds you now. Don't look for utopia. Hold your hopes in your heart. Don't look for something that might not exist.'

'Yeah, you're probably right.'

'Dream your dreams – they can be perfect; whereas real life might disappoint you. ...you might become disillusioned.'

'I guess I'll never know my Dad.'

'Whoever your Dad is, he's missing out big time by not being part of your life. But that's his loss and our gain.'

'You know what James, you'd make a great Dad.'

James was overwhelmed by the sudden compliment and with tears in his eyes he said, 'You'd make a great son too.'

CHAPTER SIXTY FOUR

12th February

Goaded on by Kay, a very nervous Helen made a call to Nadine's apartment in Monaco. After a few rings Nadine answered.

'Bonjour.'

'Ummm hello, is that Nadine?'

'Yes, who is calling?'

'I'm Helen, Andy's wife. We met at Geoffery Foster's funeral in England.'

'Mais oui. 'Ow nice to speak to you again.'

Helen wanted to shout and scream at the woman. Call her all the names under the sun. But she had agreed with Kay to remain calm and follow the questions they'd discussed earlier.

Helen came straight to the point. 'I need to know about the relationship between you and Andy.'

'Relationship! I do not understand what you mean. Relationship! 'E is, was, a friend of Geoffery's.'

'Yes, but what about you and Andy?'

'Me and Andee! Do you mean...how do you say...a liaison?'

'Yes.'

'Andy and I? I don't mean to say bad things…but 'e is not, what you say…not my 'cup of tea'.'

Helen felt her hackles rising. Her cheeks flushed with anger. In spite of her angst with Andy, this woman was denigrating her husband and she needed, irrationally, to defend him from the derisory comment. Kay, listening next to Helen, put a calming hand on hers and gestured for her to remain cool.

'I 'ave an 'andsome man in my life already,' Nadine continued. 'E is my prince scharming. I am very much in love with 'im.'

Helen was apprehensive about asking the next question and cleared her throat to sound casual.

'What about Andy and you in your room?'

'Oh, I zee. Now I understand why you call me. It is perfectly…um… innocent. I bought 'im a little gift to zank 'im for being so kind to me at Geoffery's funeral. Zat is my way. It meant nothing.'

'But I gather he was in your room all night.'

'Well it was not all night. We got back from the casino at about four and 'e left before six.'

'Yes but he was still alone with you. In your room for nearly two hours!'

'Yes, for sure. He 'ad too much wine and was asleep in my lounge on the settee. I was in my bedroom. Zere was nothing.'

'So you didn't?'

'Didn't! I do not understand. Didn't what?

'Sleep with…'

'Sleep with 'im? No…It was not like that. When I returned with ze gift 'e was asleep.'

'But why the gift, if there was nothing?'

'As I said, I was repaying iz kindness that he showed to me and the girls when we were in England. I also wanted to thank 'im for looking after Geoffery, that is all. I was being a good host showing him all the local sights, nothing more.'

'But I caught you and him after the funeral…in an embrace.'

'It was a sad time for me. I loved Geoffery very much. But when the treatment started, I couldn't cope. I know I am weak …but I was frightened by the terrible effects of the chemo. Geoffery understood and let me go. Andy recognised my pain, my guilt. E was comforting me that was all.'

'If you say so,' Helen said, relieved. 'Thank you for being so…so open.'

'I am zorry if this had caused you any…umm pain. I 'ope you will still love 'im. E is a good man. You are a very lucky lady.'

After they had exchanged goodbyes, Helen turned to Kay. 'What do you think? Do I believe her? Or is she lying through her teeth?'

'What do you want to believe?' Kay asked thoughtfully, studying Helen's face.

'I want to believe that nothing happened…but my head and my heart disagree.'

'Has he ever given you any reason to doubt his fidelity before?'

'No.'

'Then I should give him the benefit of the doubt and love him as you did before.'

'I'll try.'

'I know Andy's not 'er 'cup of tea', but let's have one anyway, shall we?' Kay said, mocking Nadine's comment.

CHAPTER SIXTY FIVE

12th February

Above Joanne's bed an alarm sounded.

Rupert was returning from the vending machine with a bar of chocolate for her when he heard the electronic screeching. As he got closer he could see that it was emanating from her room.

John, the on duty security man was standing looking into the room, concerned.

For in spite of Sue's incarceration, Rupert had insisted the security team stayed in place as Sue was only on remand and her lawyers were fighting to get her released on bail.

'What's happening, John?' Rupert quizzed.

'Don't know mate. The alarm went off and there was flood of people rushing in. It looks serious.

'Oh my god,' Rupert said, dropping the chocolate bar and pushing the door open.

'What's going on?' he asked no-one in particular.

There were several people around Joanne's bed all looking very concerned.

'The baby is showing signs of distress,' the sister informed him, not taking her eyes off the monitor. 'We have put in an urgent call for an obstetrician to attend. I anticipate that he will conduct an emergency caesarean section.'

'Surely it's too soon. The baby is still too young.'

'We can't afford to wait.'

'But why a caesarean?'

'There is a risk of causing Joanne further spinal damage by inducing her. We're just preparing her now. If you like you can be present at the birth when we take her to the theatre.'

Rupert fought the fear that was swelling in his heart. 'I'm not sure I'm brave enough,' he said, looking into Joanne's eyes, who was amazingly calm amidst all the frantic activity going on around her.

'I'm sure you are,' the Sister, added encouragingly, 'Joanne would like you to be there too, wouldn't you?'

Joanne, who was still recovering from her head injuries, gave the thumbs up sign and smiled at Rupert.

'There you go. Just think how wonderful it will be,' the Sister enthused, 'to be there at your child's birth. What do you say?'

'OK, but what if I pass out?'

'Don't worry, you won't. You'll be OK, believe me,' she said, confidently. 'Now let's get her to theatre,' she said, opening the door and steering the bed out into the corridor. Rupert fell in step, holding Joanne's hand.

Joanne was given a general anaesthetic and an obstetrician delivered the baby, a boy, quickly by caesarean section. The baby was very pre-term, only 24 weeks, and was immediately placed into an incubator brought over from the Special Care baby unit in the nearby Southmead hospital.

Rupert couldn't believe what a momentous occasion this was in his life. Amidst all the gloom, this little boy had brought him incalculable joy. As he stared into the incubator, the reality of it hit him. This little red wrinkled infant was his son. He was a Dad and he wanted everybody to know.

The sister explained that the baby needed specialist treatment and he was being rushed to the Neonatal Intensive Care Unit in a different hospital.

'Will he be alright?' Rupert asked, concerned, as they wheeled him out.

'He's in the hands of a great team of Specialists. I think he's going to be a tough fighter, just like his Dad.'

'Yes,' he said positively. 'Just like his Dad.' And it was if he'd been injected with liquid courage. He felt emotionally stronger. The paternal instinct to protect his off-spring, his son, his heir, was primal. The event had fired off a hormone response in Rupert that prepared him to do battle with some unknown marauder to defend his tribe. Sue was in for a big surprise, should he ever see her again.

CHAPTER SIXTY SIX

12th February

Following her caesarean operation, Joanne had been moved to the surgical recovery suite her condition being carefully monitored because of her other injuries.

Rupert, in the meantime, had returned euphorically to Joanne's room to await her return, receiving hearty congratulations from John and the nursing staff on the way.

He felt contented. The act of becoming a Dad had made him feel wonderfully happy. But why? Nothing had changed. He was still in the same predicament as before, but suddenly the world had taken on a rosy glow.

The gloom and depression had lifted. The mask of self-pity vanished. Was this the start of a new beginning? He recalled the words from Starlight Express played at Geoffery's funeral. *'Just believe in yourself, The sea will part before you, Stop the rain, turn the tide.'* Perhaps Geoffery was still helping him after all.

Hearing footsteps, he assumed John had returned but it was Andy who came through the door.

'Andy, what brings you here? Have you heard my news? I'm a Dad,' Rupert said, excitedly without waiting for a reply.

'Oh, many congratulations,' Andy said, going over to him and pumping his hand. 'Well done. ..well done,' he beamed. 'Are they both OK?'

'Jo had to have a caesarean and the baby was premature so is in intensive care.'

'Premature, what was his weight?'

'I think they said two pound two ounces.'

'Oh I'm sorry to hear that.'

'No, don't be. I'm assured that they'll be OK. The staff around here are brilliant.'

'Have you thought of a name yet?'

'I think we're going to call him Jeffery, with a 'J' not a 'G'; after my Uncle.'

'Good...good.' Andy said, becoming distant. 'Umm...this probably isn't the right time then...but the reason that I'm here. The Police want to interview you again.'

'Oh God! Not again.'

'I said I'd come down and help them…and you. They're waiting outside.'

'The Police…why do they have to spoil things? That's the last thing I want at this time.'

'Yes, I appreciate that, but they have to charge Sue within the next few hours or they'll have to release her.

You have to tell them the truth about her not being in the car with you,' Andy implored.

'I can't… She will get out of prison sometime and she will hunt us down, I know it.' Rupert said, fearfully. The first test of his new resolve had failed at the first hurdle. He had reverted to type. 'And my son deserves a better start than me constantly looking over my shoulder.'

'At some stage in your life, you have to make a stand. Otherwise you will always live in fear. When one episode is over, you will just start fearing the arrival of the next incident. That's no way to live your life.'

'I know, I know…but If only it was that simple!'

'Nobody said it was going to be easy. Nothing worth having in life is…'

'I can't…it's too risky.'

'One thing I can guarantee, is that unless you make a stand, you will always be in the same situation. She will continue to haunt you.'

Rupert paced around the room trying to resolve the conflict in his head. After a few minutes deliberation he 'tapped' into his new resolve and agreed to see the Police. Andy led them in.

'Thanks for seeing us. You've already met my colleague John Sparrow, I'm Sergeant Graham Fredericks,' the Policeman said. 'Congratulations on becoming a Dad.'

'Thanks.' Rupert said, his excitement, now subdued.

'I'm dreadfully sorry to bother you at a time like this. But we are at a critical point in our investigations and your earlier statement about your wife being a passenger in your car is stopping us moving forward.'

'Oh.'

'It's all down to you Mr Screen. As you know, your wife is saying that she was a passenger in your car and therefore couldn't have been the driver of the Polo, who caused the dreadful accident. Obviously I don't need to remind you of the seriousness of the accident, which put you and Joanne into hospital,' he said, trying to evoke some desire for revenge.

'I ask you again. Is that correct? Was Mrs Williams-Screen in the car with you?'

Rupert looked at the floor, his mind full of uncertainty.

'If you confirm she was with you and you are subsequently found to have been lying, you will be charged with perjury. Do you understand?'

'Yes.'

'I also have to advise you that perjury carries a prison sentence. I'll give you a few minutes to think about it.'

'No, no, I don't need time,' Rupert replied, firmly. 'I need to be thinking about my family. My little boy needs me to be strong. He is so small. I need to be there for him, especially while his Mother is poorly'

'Yes, I'm sorry.'

'She was definitely ….'

'Damn,' the Policeman cursed inside, 'she's off the hook again.'

'Definitely…NOT in the car with us. She forced me to lie. She threatened us all. I'm sorry.' Rupert said, all in a rush; relieved at last he had found the guts to disobey her.

'At last! We've got her. Thank you.' The Policeman heaved a sigh of relief.

'What about…my earlier statement?' Rupert asked, glumly.

'We know what she's like. Don't worry, we won't be pressing charges against you. But we'll add threatening witnesses to the charge sheet. Right, let's get her charged. Causing death by dangerous driving, together with the manslaughter charge will see her banged up for a long time.'

'See?' Andy said, putting his arm round Rupert's shoulders…'the Lion has found some courage after all. Now you're on the yellow brick road, at last.'

CHAPTER SIXTY SEVEN

12th February

After persuading Rupert to tell the truth and destroy Sue's alibi, Andy drove straight home.

During the journey up the motorway, he reflected on the changes that had occurred in Geoffery's Godsons.

Perhaps Geoffery's legacy was more subtle than he'd imagined. Maybe it wasn't just about the money. Possibly, it was all about transforming the Godsons characters for the better.

His comparison with OZ characters was surprisingly spot on, he thought.

Good old Rupert; the lion looking for courage. Well he'd certainly found some at last. He has clearly discovered a hidden pool of emotional resilience and tapped into it, thereby breaking the shackles of fear with which Sue's violence had bound him. Perhaps, the crash along with his loving relationship with Joanne and the life changing event of becoming a father had been the catalyst. Hopefully with the ogre of a wife behind bars again, he will be able to escape her fearful influence for ever.

Then of course there's the amazing change in Tim; the tin man looking for a heart. The formerly self-centred individual has revealed a different side to his character. He has a 'heart' after all…what with taking Rupert under his wing to protect him from his cruel wife; paying for Joanne's protection team and, apparently, even offering to donate some of his liver to James. I guess Carrie's, PTSD problem must have helped put his life in to a different perspective.

James the quiet one; the Scarecrow looking for a brain. I'm not sure you got that one right though, Geoffery. At least he's still off the booze but has a mountain to climb as far as his health is concerned. Having said that, perhaps bartering with Tim for a 'slice' of his liver in exchange for his business expertise was an inspired plan. Getting Tim's planned walking company off the ground would be an excellent joint venture.

As to himself, he decided that he must also 'stand up and be counted'. It was time to tell Helen about the Monaco room and corridor incidents and accept the consequences.

Meanwhile, Sergeant Fredericks had made his way to the prison, where Sue was being detained, and arranged to interview her again. She was brought up from the cells and led into the interview room.

'Sit there please,' the warder instructed, pointing at a chair the far side of a large, graffiti scratched wooden table.

Shortly after, Sergeant Fredericks entered, acknowledging the warden. He strode over to the table.

'Mrs Williams-Screen, I've come to talk to you about your role in the multivehicle collision on December 23rd.'

'And it's about time too!' she said, contemptuously. 'I shall be writing to my MP about this false imprisonment. Let me out this instant.' She stood up and started walking towards the door.

'I suggest you sit down again,' Sergeant Fredericks directed firmly.

Standing her ground, she glared at him.

Unfazed by her arrogance, the Sergeant sat down himself and took his notebook from his pocket. 'We've just been to see your husband.'

'And he has obviously told you that I was in his car the night of the accident. So what are you waiting for? Release me immediately.'

'I'm afraid not. I believe you won't be seeing the outside of Her Majesty's prisons for a long while.'

'What do you mean?' she demanded, moving back toward the interview table.

'Your husband has told us that you were NOT in his car on the night of the accident.'

'Well he's obviously forgotten,' she said, flummoxed by the news. 'You realise he was injured. He had brain damage. It's obviously given him memory loss.'

'Furthermore, he told us that you threatened to kill his young lady if he told us the truth,' the Sergeant continued, ignoring her interruption.

Sue could see the 'noose closing in' on her and she was desperately trying to think of another reason to discredit the revelation. 'Well that's a pack of lies. His mind is clearly damaged. My lawyers will rip his evidence apart.

'We have another witness who saw you in the Black Polo which followed your husband's car out of the Hotel Car park on the night of the 23rd,' he lied, exaggerating Andy's observation.

'Well, he's...mistaken. It wasn't me. He's...a...lying....This is yet another conspiracy,' Sue ranted, her face contorted with rage. She stood up and leant across the table, glaring at the Policeman, banging her fist aggressively on it to emphasise her point.

The warder was on his way to restrain her, but the Sergeant signalled him back.

'Do you want to add assaulting a Police Officer to the already long charge sheet? If so, carry on,' he goaded, preparing himself to take avoiding action, if she tried to hit him. 'Because I'd like to see you try. You're obviously a cowardly bully and a nasty piece of work. Prison is the right place for you and your kind.'

Sue's tough veneer started to crack. The prospect of spending years behind bars was frightening her.

'OK, I was there. But somebody else caused it. It wasn't me!'

'Just like you didn't cause the death of the Gravedigger,' the Policeman said sarcastically. 'Or intimidate witnesses, or kidnap people or blackmail somebody. Sorry, but your halo has slipped. The Crown Prosecution Service has confirmed that you will be charged. Take her down officer.'

'I demand to see my Lawyer. I shall instruct him to get me bailed as soon as possible. I'll make sure that you lose your job over this. You'll regret ever messing with me,' she threatened, her face white with anger.' We'll take you and the Police force to the cleaners.'

'You'll have to do better than that. I've been threatened by tougher people than you. Still, you'll have plenty of time to think about it, when you're locked away. OK officer,' he said, gesturing to the warden.

The warden gently touched her arm to invite her to leave, but Sue's anger was such that, without thinking, she swung at him. He quickly blocked the punch and with impressive speed, before she knew what had hit her, she was face down on the table with her arm high up her back.

'Oww, you're hurting me. Let me go, this instant,' she shrieked.

'Stop struggling and I'll let you up,' the warden demanded.

After a few minutes, Sue did as she was told, fear now replacing her anger. She couldn't think of anything else to say to mitigate the charges. She had to accept the inevitable; she was unlikely to wriggle out of the situation easily.

I'm sorry,' she grovelled, as she was led away. 'I didn't mean it,' she pleaded. I didn't mean it.'

'Tell that to the poor sods whose lives you've ruined.' The Sergeant said, quietly.

CHAPTER SIXTY EIGHT

12th February

Finally, reaching home, Andy parked the Merc and went through the front door with great anticipation, ready to confess all and await the consequences. As he strode purposefully through the hall to find Helen, he was annoyed to see Kay in the lounge.

'Damn and blast it,' he thought. He had rehearsed in his mind what he was going to say and where he was going to say it, but Kay's presence threatened to derail his plans.

'Oh hello Kay, nice to see you,' he lied. 'I've got some great news, Rupert's a Dad. Joanne had to have a Caesar and the baby, a boy, was born earlier today. It's in the Special Care unit because it's very premature.'

'Oh how lovely,' she said, beaming. 'How are they both?'

'OK from what I gather.'

'How's Rupert taking it?'

'Oh, he's over the moon.'

He found Helen in the kitchen making tea for herself and Kay.

Helen turned and acknowledged his presence, but didn't move away from her task.

He steeled himself for the confession, his stomach churning, unsure now how to start.

'Helen, I… I've got something to confess.'

'Yes?'

'I have not been particularly open with you about what happened in Monaco.'

'Oh?' she said, anticipating what was coming.

'I…umm.'

'Yes?' she teased.

'I had a little too much wine…and I…mmm.'

'Go on,' she said, enjoying watching him squirm.

'I passed out in…in…Nadine's room.'

'You did what?' she said enjoying the moment.

'I passed out…in Nadine's hotel room.'

'Yes, I know. So why didn't you tell me this before?' she said, sternly.

'What! You knew?' Andy said, taken aback by her response.

'Were you going to tell me about being videoed too?' Helen added.

Much to Andy's consternation, she left the kitchen and carried the tea tray into the lounge. He followed instinctively behind her.

'How come you knew about me being in Nadine's room and being caught on camera?' he asked, perplexed.

'You've heard the expression, 'beware your sins will find you out?'

'Yes, of course.'

'Well, clearly you weren't going to tell me, but somebody else thought I ought to know.'

Helen put the tray on a small coffee table and sat down on the settee. Andy sat next to her.

Andy, looked across at Kay, who smiled back.

'So you know, I wasn't having an affair. It was just as I said, all along.'

'So I'm led to believe.'

'So are we… talking to each other again?'

'I suppose so.'

'I'm so sorry. I didn't plan any of this,' he said, putting his hand on hers. 'It just… happened.'

'Your 'caring nature' got you into trouble, that's what it was,' she said, generously.

'Yes, I suppose.'

'Oh, by the way, I've booked us a meal out at the Queens Head.'

'A meal! What about the kids?'

'No they're not coming.'

'I know that, but who's babysitting?'

'I am,' Kay said, smiling.

'You'd better get ready; the table's booked for seven thirty.'

Andy felt like a ten ton weight had been lifted off his shoulders, perhaps his erotic dream that he'd had on Nadine's sofa had been about the wrong person. He hoped he would find out later that night.

Also available by GHP

Godsons – Counting Sunsets

(The prequel to this novel)

Paul Gait

Like most Godfathers Geoffery Foster had little to do with his Godchildren after their christenings. But he is determined to rectify that omission before he dies.

Together with his hospice nurse, Andy Spider, Geoffery embarks on a quest to find and improve his three Godsons lives.

But their mission isn't easy as they soon uncover the problems of childhood Meningitis amputee Tim, the alcoholic 'drop out' James and the abused husband Rupert.

Coupled with a mysterious fire, a teenage runaway, the guilt of an intimate session with somebody else's new bride and a high stake gamble with Geoffery's life in the hands of a woman spurned.

Readers Comments

It's a page turner

Couldn't put it down until I'd finished it

Took the phone off the hook and read it from cover to cover. A good read.

A sensitive subject delicately handled.

It's not about death and dying, it's about hope and inspiration.

Can't wait to see what happens to the characters next.

Lightning Source UK Ltd.
Milton Keynes UK
UKOW04f0705041013

218455UK00001B/3/P